Ponce de León:
A Modern Sequel

Thomas H Murray

BASTET PUBLISHING

TABLE OF CONTENTS

INTRODUCTORY NOTES

This is a work of fiction. Names, characters, businesses, places, events, and incidents are either the products of the author's imagination or used in a fictitious manner. Any resemblance to actual events and persons, living or dead, is purely coincidental.

Though by no means a specialist in renaissance Iberian history, the author has done extensive research on the life and times of Juan Ponce de León, including visiting his hometown of Santervás de Campos in Spain. However, this novel is historical fiction, and nothing should be taken as historical fact.

The truth of the matter is we know relatively little about the man. For example, his year of birth is commonly accepted as either 1460 or 1474, a fourteen-year difference. Whenever there is a conflict like this, I have generally relied on the information from the museum in his hometown and common sense.

Rather than give a metric conversion every time for my non-US readers, I have put a conversion table below:

1 statute mile = 1.6 kilometers
1 nautical mile = 1.15 statute miles
1 foot = 0.305 meters
1 pound = 0.45 kilograms = 450 grams
1 ounce = 28 grams

PRELUDE

Thick Florida winter fog enshrouded the ocean side house. Wisps of gloom leaked through an open window into a dark bedroom. A single flickering candle cast dancing shadows on the walls of the men gathered in a semi-circle around a bed. A priest in a simple robe tied together by a rope was on his knees by the upper left of the bed, bearing a large wooden crucifix. On the other side was another kneeling man, gently holding the pale, weak hand of the dying old woman lying before them.

Besides waves crashing against the rocks, the only other sound was a shallow rattle coming from deep within the woman. She was looking with dim eyes at the grieving man, her lifelong husband. Love still bound the two, but life was slipping rapidly away from one. She struggled a bit, but then found her voice.

"Juan, please tell me the truth. If not for the love of God, then for the love of me you always said you have. I know I will not see morning, so whatever secret you have will die with me. Why is it that nearly every Sunday, you visited a forgotten cemetery an hour away to lay flowers on strange women's tombs? Many have been dead for hundreds of years. Yes, I had a detective follow you. I had a jealous mind."

The only reaction from the man holding her hand was tears streaming down his face.

"Well, my dearest, it's..." His voice broke.

"Why is it that the older I became, the younger you remained? I know you dyed your hair gray to match mine, but I could see that even as I entered my eightieth year, my husband's body was no more than forty. Please, my dear Juan, please tell me just who are you? What are you?"

Juan was sobbing with his forehead resting on her hand. After a few moments, he raised his eyes and replied, "Sandy, the dearest love of my life, I am…".

The priest had reached over and placed his hand on Juan's shoulder and shook his head "No".

Juan faltered and then went silent.

It did not matter what he would have said. Sandra's hand relaxed, her breathing stopped, but her vacant stare still held her beloved husband's eyes. The anguished cries of a grown man had their effect on the other two dozen men crowding around the bed. They had to look away to the floor to the walls anywhere but to share the sorrow of one of their own. They all believed that men were not supposed to cry but witnessing the death of a loved one was an exception that made their own eyes tear.

The priest finished his last rites, closed her eyes, and covered her face with the blanket. He walked over to Juan and pulled his hand from the lifeless one, letting it drop. He helped Juan to his feet and started walking him to the door. Juan waved him away and collapsed in a chair in the corner where he would pass the rest of the night, mourning her death and remembering their life together for thirty-seven years. That is how the day's first light would find him seven hours later.

CHAPTER ONE

A Funeral

The mood was as somber as the dense fog blotting out the sun, as melancholy as the dark Spanish moss hanging like ghosts from the ancient oak trees. Dressed in black, a group of men mourning with downcast eyes gathered at the same familiar wooden church they always did for the funeral of the wife of one of their own. High above the crashing waves, a forest hid the gray Spanish colonial-style church. It rested on the foundations of the original chapel from Spain's earliest attempts to create a viable colony in northeast Florida 450 years before.

Their dear friend, Padre Pedro, presided over the funeral service using the original last rites of the Roman Catholic Church from five centuries before, done in High Church Latin. Incense and the heat of a hundred candles weighed upon the air. The open casket revealed the once beautiful wife of their dear El Capitán. Well made up, she appeared to be merely taking a peaceful nap before a formal soirée later that evening.

El Capitán was sitting in the front pew, shoulders slouched and tears streaming down his cheeks. He did not hear any of the familiar droning Latin, familiar from so many funerals he had attended. Memories crowded his mind, images of his beloved Sandra, recollections of his past deceased wives. How many had there been? His mind was in too much turmoil to count. Could he take any more?

His best friend and First Mate, Antón de Alaminos, patted him on his shoulder, startling Juan back into the moment. It was time. Eight men donned their top hats and approached the casket. One of them closed the lid before they raised it to their shoulders. Padre Pedro solemnly led them to the open front door. El Capitán slowly followed, with his eyes fixed on the casket as it made its way to the old cemetery beside the church. The other attendees followed behind the grieving widower. The sky commiserated, and rain poured down.

The peaceful, silent cemetery, dotted with jumbled stone crosses, elaborate sepulchers, and macabre statues, belied the serenity of the place. Mossy stone plaques with only names and dates had replaced the old, rotted, wooden crosses hundreds of years old. Everything was a weather-worn gray with ageless lichen slowly turning even the stone into dust.

The heavy iron door of the largest marble sepulcher was wide open. The heavily laden pall bearers, escorted by many open black umbrellas, slowly entered the dimly lit interior behind the priest. They passed the five stone caskets of El Capitán's children and first wife. Carefully, they continued down the stone stairs to the next level, which also had five caskets. It took them almost thirty minutes to carefully descend the stairs until they reached the seventh level.

This floor was excavated out of the bedrock over forty years ago. There was one last empty space carved out of the rock walls for its future inhabitant. The pall bearers stopped before the waiting emptiness and gingerly placed the casket securely within. Juan kneeled beside the casket with his arms wrapped around it, quietly sobbing. After twenty minutes of Latin beseeching for the peaceful rest of her soul delivered to the loving arms of her Creator, the ritual ended.

Juan rose, and a great groan of sorrow escaped his chest. He decided to bury his pain yet again and be strong for his mates. He followed behind everyone as they filed up the stairs and out into the rainy, wet winter air. Hidden by thick ivy above the crypt's entrance were carved the words: Ponce de Léon.

Everybody was standing in small groups under umbrellas, their gentle murmurs barely heard. Padre Pedro led the despondent group back to the parking area. He reminded everyone of the reception at Antón's home back in Saint Augustine.

Antón opened the back door of his car for Juan, who dragged himself into the seat. He hurried over to the other side to sit beside his morose friend. Antón instructed his driver to start the slow procession home. The police rumbled to life their motorcycles and escorted the procession, making sure all the red lights were green along the way. The procession all had their headlights on. Any car they passed, pulled over respectively to the side of the road.

The hour drive took two hours. Antón knew that at times like these, silence was the rule with El Capitán. So, he joined his old friend and stared out the window at the foggy rainy day. It was perfect weather for the mood of the day. A cheerful, sunny day would have been a taunting insult.

Antón worried about the state of his friend's mind. He was becoming worse with every funeral. Yet he knew that there was nothing he could do or say to help. Juan preferred in times like these to lose himself in the darkness of his heart, waiting calmly for the storm to pass, which, until now, it always had. Juan's friends all knew they would need to wait patiently until the tempest calmed and their dear friend would return to them.

They turned onto the 206 towards Crescent Beach. Juan became quite agitated, squirming in his seat. When the procession turned south on Highway A1A, Antón had to put his arm on Juan's shoulder to try to calm him. Juan's house appeared, compelling him to open the door of the moving car. The reception was to be at Antón house about five miles further down, past Fort Matanzas.

"Let me out! I need to go home. She's there waiting for me. I know it."

"Capitán! No! She is not there. We are going to my place. All of your friends will be there." Antón yanked Juan's arm away from the door. Antón's chauffeur locked Juan's door from his control panel.

Juan lunged at Antón, eyes full of anger. Antón pushed him hard against the seat with his forearm pressing Juan's throat. "She's gone, Capitán! She's gone!"

Juan gripped Antón's shoulders and went limp. "Why? Why did she leave me? Why again? Why couldn't she have stayed?" His voice croaked with tears flowing, disappearing into his beard.

Antón sat back in his seat in silence. He had no answer other than the obvious. He could only look at his friend with sadness and sympathy. Juan stared out the window, slouched with unseeing eyes.

The procession turned into Antón's large horseshoe driveway. Cars filled the driveway and even parked along the side of the A1A. Antón told Juan to stay in the car until he could calm himself. He got out and invited everyone into his majestic home on the beach. He returned to sit by his friend in his time of sorrow.

After twenty minutes, Juan patted Antón on the arm and said it had passed. He walked over to the pool house to wash his face and regain his composure before joining the others. Antón accompanied him. Soon, Juan emerged and marched confidently toward Antón's home. Antón followed slightly behind, alert to any sudden relapses of grief.

The shrubbery within the horseshoe driveway hid most of the house from the road. The entrance was flanked by a long columned veranda that made up the entire front. Above was another matching columned veranda that stretched along the second floor. The mansion was the color of adobe, matching the sand of the beach behind that stretched as far as the eye could see in both directions. Palm trees filled the property, shading it from the southern sun.

Being First Mate, Antón had the second-largest house of their band of twenty-nine friends. Padre Pedro's house was only slightly smaller. El Capitán had three mansions connected by covered wooden walkways. Their twenty-nine homes formed a line south from Crescent Beach for about five miles.

Many years before, they used to live together on Vilano Beach, much closer to the town center of Saint Augustine. But then the city wanted to rezone and develop the area more along commercial lines. The city offered them in exchange the southern part of Anastasia Island from Crescent Beach to its southern tip, almost ten miles of uninterrupted beach on one side and the Matanzas River on the other.

It contained the old Spanish Matanzas Fort, built in 1740 on the site of the massacre of 245 Huguenots by the Spanish nearly 200 years before. No one wanted to live there, so the city thought it was getting the better part of the deal with the exchange. But Juan and his crew knew all about the event and had no fear of vengeful spirits. They were happy to oblige after the county promised they would never need to pay any property taxes. Vilano Beach was becoming too busy, anyway.

The double old oak doors were open when they entered. They crossed the foyer and entered the vast living room. Decades before, Antón decided he wanted to modernize his home's interior. He exchanged the previous heavy Spanish Colonial style for a more contemporary Art Deco style. He tore down walls and created a living room of 1,000 square feet. The bold geometric Art Deco shapes were evident everywhere in furniture, wall decorations, statues, lamps, wallpaper, etc.

Crossing through this remarkable collection, they joined everyone else gathered in small quiet groups on the back porch, open to the cool sea breeze. The winter Atlantic crashed on the beach, drowning out the voices of one group from the other. Waiters stood about with trays of wine and hors d'oeuvres. They gathered around Juan, the guest of honor. He shook his head, in no mood for eating. He never drank alcohol in times of stress and mental anguish.

Everyone stopped talking and bowed to Juan as he passed them. He sat on the back steps leading down to the boardwalk that connected the house to the beach. He stared at the waves, trying to find a philosophic path out of his funk. Antón sat next to him in silence.

Finally, Juan broke the silence. "How many, Antón? How many has it been?"

"How many of what, Capitán?"

"How many wives has it been? How many women have I loved, only to see them decay and die in my arms?"

"Well, I think you know the answer. We passed them all in your family crypt."

"Twenty-six, Antón. Twenty-six. And four children, too. A father should never see his children buried. Many years ago, I had the bottom floor carved out with five more empty spaces. How can I continue filling up the spaces? I remember the excavator telling me we couldn't continue any farther down, as we would soon hit the water table. I will have to build another sepulcher and start filling that one, too." He fell back into silence.

"Capitán, you know very well what we have been telling you all along. Stop marrying them. Do what modern people do and have short-term relations. We are overwhelmed with flocks of young northern women coming south to find some fun for their vacations. When they've had their fill, they return home, never to be heard from again."

"And Antón, you know very well what my answer has always been, and Padre Pedro would agree with me. I do not believe that fornication is the answer."

"Padre Pedro? Are you joking? You've noticed as well as the rest of us who visits him every Friday night. You even have the phone number he uses. He gave it to you. I have even others you could use."

"Yes, yes, I know all that. But I can't help but fall in love with them. I want a mate, not a plaything. Someone to share the joys and sorrows of life. Someone I can show the world to and reveal my inner heart. Someone who can inspire me."

"But it always ends with a broken heart and sorrow. You realize that every time you start a new relationship. Our answer is simply do not allow yourself to fall into the same trap. You know what the definition of…"

"Yes, I know the definition of an idiot: someone doing the same thing over and over, expecting different results."

"No, no, Capitán. I was not suggesting you are…"

"Maybe not, but I agree it appears that way. I think it's time for a long walk alone on the beach."

Antón followed Juan to the end of the boardwalk and onto the fine white sand. Juan turned left in the direction of his home. But Antón gently turned him in the opposite direction.

"Remember, Capitán. You are staying with me for the next few days. It is no time to be alone in your house just yet."

Juan nodded absent mindedly and slowly trod towards the southern end of the island, wondering how to find a way out of his mental turmoil.

CHAPTER TWO

First Arrival

In 1493, aged thirty-three, Juan Ponce de León arrived at La Navidad in present day Haiti on Columbus's second voyage to the Americas as a 'gentlemen volunteer'. Already a military veteran of wars fought for Castille against the Moors, he was a welcomed addition to the other 1200 farmers, priests, and soldiers that constituted Spain's first step to colonize the 'New World'.

They found La Navidad, established with the thirty-nine crew members of the grounded Santa Maria only one year before, demolished. Columbus accosted Guacanagarix, the chief of the neighboring Taíno village, who originally consented to the presence of the little enclave. He protested his innocence. A simple investigation uncovered the corroborating evidence.

After Columbus left them, they quickly fell to quarreling with themselves. They sent raiding parties to steal women from a neighboring unfriendly tribe who operated simple gold mines in the area. The Spaniards exacerbated the situation by raiding the gold mines, carrying back the gold to their outpost. Their chief, Caonabo, lured twenty-nine of them to a larger gold mine further inland. There Caonabo's men ambushed and killed the greedy Spanish interlopers.

Caonabo then attacked La Navidad itself. Despite Guacanagarix and his warriors coming to the aid of the outpost, they were defeated. Caonabo killed the remaining Spanish and burned La Navidad to the ground, where it has since disappeared into the marshland of Haiti's northern coast. Guacanagarix remained a friend of Spain for the rest of his life.

A year later, Ponce de León had the chance to prove himself to Columbus, who sent him to capture Caonabo. Ponce de León, with 200 men, twenty horses, twenty war hounds, and Guacanagarix's help, successfully defeated Caonabo's tribe. They brought the warrior chief back in chains, where he died in captivity. Columbus rewarded Ponce de León well with gold and promoted him as a commandant in the colonial army.

Before these events, Columbus's second voyage continued further east along the northern coast and in late 1493 founded a settlement, Santa Isabela, in the present-day Dominican Republic. Evidence of gold further south of the island made Columbus establish a town there, now Santo Domingo, the present capital of the Dominican Republic. He sent his younger brother, Bartholomew, with Ponce de León and a few hundred Spaniards to build a second colony there. Columbus returned to Spain after discovering Cuba and Jamaica for the Spanish crown to prepare for his third voyage.

As for La Isabela, disease not only decimated the nearby native Taínos but also the Spanish colonists. Two hurricanes, originally a Taíno word, completed the task. The first one ever experienced by Europeans threatened the colony in 1495. The Taínos fled to the caves in the hills above, while the colonists stayed to watch the spectacle. The storm destroyed most of the town, sank the ships, and killed many of the spectators. A second hurricane sealed the village's fate. Columbus later cut his losses and abandoned it.

While Columbus was back in Spain, preparing for his third voyage, the mayor he left behind, Francisco Roldán, revolted and took a large part of the Spanish colonists into the interior. He and his faction did not care to be ruled by foreigners, referring to Columbus, his brothers, and eventually sons, who were all Italians from Genoa.

Columbus tasked Ponce de León, as second in command, to locate and bring to justice the renegades. They eventually found Francisco Roldán and his men in the Jaragua region of present-day southwest Haiti. Roldán was prepared in a well-provisioned fort. He knew that Columbus's forces would have no cannon and they would have to either storm the fort or starve them out. In addition, he had made an alliance with the local Taíno chief, whose warriors constantly harassed the besiegers.

After a year of losses and costs with no results, Columbus negotiated a peace. He gave Roldán back his office of mayor. Those of his followers who wanted to return to Spain could do so, and those who chose to stay were given a house and land. The whole affair was attributed to "false testimony of a few (unnamed) evil men."

Though well rewarded for his efforts, Ponce de León was disgusted at the leniency. He would have conducted the campaign differently. Until he was a governor of his own colony, he had to accept silently his orders. Even so, the experience placed him in high esteem with Columbus's colonial government.

Ponce de León settled into colonial life in Santo Domingo, the main colonial base for Spain. He was awarded a large estate on the outskirts of town with cattle and horses. Confirmed as second in command of all colonial military forces, Ponce de León became the primary contact with the Taíno tribes. By all accounts, he treated them firmly but fairly.

He tried to mitigate the conditions of enslavement of the native peoples by the colonists. Unfortunately, Columbus set up a feudal system as the easiest method of governing. Columbus sold large tracts of land with the rights to the people living there, especially the gold mines and later sugar plantations. In return for paying annual taxes on top of the purchase price, the owners could run their fiefs as they wished. Up to 80% of the natives died from terrible conditions, disease, and being over-worked. This disaster led directly to Columbus' decision to import African slaves into the Americas.

These were all decisions beyond the scope of Ponce de León's position. He concentrated on his immediate responsibilities, always alert to any opportunity for advancement. He knew that genuine success would come from outside of Hispaniola as governor of one of the new colonies. He had to bide his time.

Meanwhile, the remaining Taíno who survived the European diseases had passively settled into their strange reality. Ponce de León watched as fresh colonists arrived and the town bustled with energy. He noted with interest other explorers preparing their ships for departure from the port to find new lands to bring under King Ferdinand's flag and cross.

Despite his early success, Ponce de León was restless, both mentally and physically. A wife would satisfy at least one of his desires. He considered returning to Spain to bring back a wife from a well-connected family. After all, he had position and growing wealth. He was descended from noble stock. His ancestor of 200 years before was the illegitimate daughter of King Alfonso IX of León, hence the 'de León' of his name.

Returning to Spain would require overcoming many obstacles. The most important would be how to find a good match and negotiate a marriage. There were matchmakers who could help, but how could he do that from across the ocean? Besides, he would have to arrange a leave of absence of two years or more. In reality, he would need to resign and lose all he gained since his arrival. He would return merely as a farmer rancher. He was too ambitious and restless for that.

The only other choice was to find a wife locally. There were very few Spanish women in the colony at 1500. Most men took native women to be their wives. Ponce de León pondered a third option of living celibate, but quickly banished that from his mind. His blood was too passionate to consider that.

Pedro, one of his lieutenants from a few years before, retired from active duty and opened a tavern. Ponce de León had dinner there nearly every night. During this time, he became friendly with the barkeep, a young Taíno woman. She was a young girl and the only survivor of her village, being somehow immune to the smallpox that wiped out her people. Pedro took her in as a servant and later as the barkeep of his newly opened tavern.

Xixi, as they called her, learned to speak Spanish well. She easily accepted what life had thrown her way. Pedro's Taíno wife kept him on a short leash, a fate he willingly accepted. Meanwhile, Xixi was blossoming into a beautiful maiden. She ignored the attention from the lonely colonist men who frequented Pedro's Tavern.

Xixi understood on an intellectual level what the men wanted. She was already at the age she would have been the mate of a man in her old village. The ways of Spain were vastly different. She did not know how to proceed with her own growing desire to have a man and a family. In response, she retreated into herself and concentrated on her work.

That was until Ponce de León arrived. She was impressed by the respectful nobility of the man, who stood out from the others by his education and demeanor of a natural leader. It also helped that he was easy on her eyes.

As for Ponce de León, he took notice of Xixi, too. She was sixteen and full of energy. A quick smile lit up her face like a dawn's first light. She was tall for her people, with lush dark hair falling to her maidenly hips. After bringing him his glass of wine, she would sit with him and engage him in conversation until Pedro would growl at her.

After many months, Ponce de León started warming to her, responding to her flirtations. Finally, one night, with passion rising in his heart, he whispered to her that he would be standing across the street when the tavern closed. If she would meet him there, that would be wonderful. If not, there would be no offense. She giggled and disappeared to the back.

He waited nervously at the spot and time, fearing that she would not appear. After waiting some twenty minutes, he decided he had made a fool of himself and turned to go home. And there she was, hiding in the shadows, secretly watching him. He smiled and took the few steps to her. She leaped into his arms and whispered for him to take her back with him. Thus started their relationship. He would meet her discreetly after her work and walk her the twenty minutes to his home, silent but full of desire.

Despite being careful, Pedro suspected what was happening. He good-naturedly accepted it, knowing that she found herself a special man destined for great things. Several months after they consummated their relationship, Nicolás de Ovando, the new Governor General of the colonies, arrived. By 1502, it was clear that the Columbus administration was in trouble. King Ferdinand commanded de Ovando to bring order to the chaos, starting with putting down several Taíno rebellions, first in the colony's northwest and later in the Higüey region immediately east of Santo Domingo.

Ponce de León knew he would be called away for maybe a few years. Would she wait for him? She complicated everything when she informed him that she was pregnant with their child. During the months de Ovando was preparing for the campaign against the Taíno rebellions, Ponce de León recognized he had to act and fast.

First, he had her baptized. As a baptized Catholic, she had legal rights that the natives otherwise did not have. He gave her the Christian name of Leonora. It was not the most imaginative, but it served its purpose perfectly. Then, with this important step taken care of, he married her shortly after. Leonora gathered her few belongings and moved into his home with her growing belly. She was Mrs. Leonora Ponce de León, the respected wife of one of the most important men in the Spanish colonies. She had status and, most importantly, her man.

Three months after he put his domestic life in order, de Ovando completed his preparations for the campaign. Together with a few close associates, de Ovando led the expedition himself, with

Ponce de León as an important lieutenant. Just as he feared, the offensive to subjugate the Taíno of western Hispaniola lasted nearly two years.

In 1505, de Ovando ordered Ponce de León to lead the fight against the rebelling Taíno in the Higüey region directly to the east of Santo Domingo. His strict orders to do so with extreme prejudice reflected the thinking of the time that mercy to one's enemies was a sign of weakness that would only encourage them to rise again. Ponce de León followed orders and crushed the rebellion.

They were brutal wars fought with hundreds of Spanish soldiers and calvary as well as thousands of Taíno warriors from allied tribes. De Ovando committed many massacres and all manner of other atrocities, considered excessively cruel even by the standards of the time.

When word reached Queen Isabela, she was horrified. On her deathbed, she made her husband King Ferdinand promise to remove de Ovando and make him answer for his cruelty. The King did as he promised. He eventually removed de Ovando as governor and forced him to return to Spain in 1509. The King replaced him with Columbus's son, Diego. De Ovando was allowed to keep whatever wealth he could carry back from the colony. He died two years later with a very tarnished reputation, tarnished not by his actions but for falling from royal favor.

Before he was removed, de Ovando made Ponce de León the frontier governor of the newly conquered region with instructions to enlarge the colony with newly founded towns. In addition, de Ovando gave him large land holdings and gold mines. Ponce de León founded the provincial capital for Higüey at Salvaleón. There he moved his growing family.

The year was 1506. Life was calm on the island as the Taíno were completely crushed and subjugated. Ponce de León's wealth grew with ranches, plantations, and now gold mines. During intermittent conjugal visits home between various campaigns,

Leanora gave him four children: three daughters (Juana, Isabela, and Maria) and one son (Luis).

Leanora had a good head for business and managed their estates well. Ponce de León provided her with a large staff of her fellow Higüey tribesmen. While his restless heart was always thinking of the next ambitious plan, at home, he always gave her his undivided attention. He loved his children dearly. They would crawl all over him like kittens as he laid in his four-post bed until late in the morning.

The passion he had for his wife had only grown since the first night when she came to him as he waited outside Pedro's Tavern. In the late afternoon, they would go to their private beach and swim in the warm waters of the Caribbean. She had learned how to be a proper, modest Catholic wife in public. However, in private, she returned to her uninhibited native ways, much to the delight of her husband.

In the dusk, she would run first into the soft waves, just like she did as a child. She would leave a trail of her clothes behind her until she was as nude as the day she was born. They would frolic like children in the warm shallow water. As the frolicking became more serious, they would make love in the sunset. Afterwards, they would saunter the short distance back to the manor house, where a sumptuous dinner was waiting. Later they would sit on the veranda sipping rich sherry from Spain and watch the moon journey across the sky of thousands of stars.

CHAPTER THREE

The Fountain

Six months after the funeral, his old friends noticed Juan seemed to have bounced back to his normal self. He immersed himself in his usual activities of managing his large real estate holdings, his several businesses, including a sea freight service connecting all the Caribbean islands, and discrete ways to help Santervás de Campos of Valladolid, the small, poor, farming village in Spain where he had been born.

He made an anonymous donation to renovate the dilapidated and unsafe Romanesque village church. Another discrete donation founded a museum about him in his village of barely seventy full-time residents, which only displayed the commonly accepted details of his life. He made sure that it included his native wife, Leanora.

Soon it was time for their special annual banquet at the stone castle they built in the middle of the Florida Everglades. This solemnly serious event prevented much thought of anything else during the week before. Juan was always very agitated and would spend the days before wandering endlessly up and down the beaches, only stopping to stare out at sea for hours at a time.

When the day came, they took every precaution to arrive secretly to their hidden destination. The normally three-hour trip took over six, as they meandered their way there, making sure no one followed them. After all their precautions, they turned on to an unmarked heavily overgrown path, unworthy of even being called a dirt road.

They continued on the path for about ten miles past towering live oak, silver maple, cypress, mahogany trees with Spanish moss hanging from the branches like sheets drying on a clothesline. Close by on either side were mangrove swamps filled with alligators, poisonous snakes, and swarms of mosquitoes. The path ended at a gorge formed by a large rock formation nearly three stories tall. A thick stone wall completely hidden by ivy blocked the narrow entrance.

Stopping before the blocked path, one of them got out and approached an ancient cypress tree. There he removed a part of the bark, revealing a complex locking mechanism that required keys and combinations in the exact order. A few moments later, he returned to the wall and pushed it open like a gate. Their vehicles entered. He closed the wall behind them, removing them from the eyes of the world.

The vehicles parked near the entrance to a stone façade with another hidden, intricate locking system to open the front door. One of their mates started the electric generator that powered the lights. The rock ceiling above them blocked any natural light. They were in a hollowed-out cave where they had built very comfortable lodgings within an impregnable redoubt. Each of them gathered their things and spread out to their personal quarters for their few days' stay.

They had built their haven from the world in the style of a 500-year-old hunting lodge in the Sierra Nevada Mountain range of southeastern Spain, except the walls did not have the preserved heads of various hunted local fauna mounted on them. Juan never could see the point of that barbaric custom of hunters. He believed that their home of life should not be stained by vestiges of death. But it otherwise was the same in every other detail, including the heavy wooden furniture and the wrought-iron chandeliers with dripping candles above.

This band of brothers unloaded the victuals they brought with them, including a suckling boar, which would be the main dish of their dinner. The next day, two of them prepared the fire and the spit for the boar that they would slowly rotate the rest of the afternoon. Others busied themselves replacing and lighting the many candles, setting the table, and preparing everything else for the annual feast.

While everyone else was busy, Juan, First Mate Antón, and the Padre retired to the extensive study. There, they drank aged Spanish sherry, smoked Cuban cigars, and studied antique seafaring charts laid out on the large wooden table in the center of the room. In the many blank spaces of their antique maps were drawn mighty krakens and other mythical sea beasts. In the four corners were great, bellowing, cloudy faces of the Four Winds. Surrounding them were floor to ceiling bookshelves with old leather-bound tomes that laid out the development of human thought and experience for over five centuries.

Despite being, in all appearances, an ancient, rustic mountain lodge, it had every modern convenience. There was a very sophisticated air purification system that prevented any smoke from rising to the sky and revealing their presence. The air was dehumidified and set at the right temperature. The kitchen was as well-equipped as any of the best high-class restaurants. They did not skimp on any creature comfort. The lodge was completely self-sufficient with gas, electricity, and water.

Dinner was at 2100 sharp. They gathered, standing at their places around the long table, dressed in their finest. They stood and waited, as was their custom, for ten minutes until Juan came out and joined them at the head of the table. Once he took his seat, everyone else followed, except the Padre, whose melodious voice intoned a benediction in High Latin. Everyone took this with the utmost seriousness and understood every word.

After the Padre sat down, Juan rose and gave his annual speech:

"My dear brothers, we gather once again around this table at this special time of year. The gods blessed us when we found this most special treasure, a treasure that we cannot share with anyone else. As you know, we must partake of the wondrous waters in the sacred Fountain below us once a year. In so doing, we choose an age and that is the age we will be until the next time when we can choose again.

"I always choose forty-two, the golden age for a man, when he still has his physical health, but also the gravitas that only age can give. Some of you prefer to experiment with different ages, but I constantly choose the same.

"Nonetheless, we must pay a price for our eternal youth. We are rendered incapable of producing progeny. I consider that a more than fair trade, as I would never want to see my children grow old and die before my eyes. I had four children from my first wife, who now lay at rest beside their mother. A parent should never have to see that.

"With no time and age limit, we have all become very wealthy through various business ventures, especially real-estate. Given enough time, it is obvious what the path of development for cities is. We just bought and waited. Sometimes we had to wait 100 years or more. Who wants to relate the story of how we discovered our Fountain, as is our tradition?"

Juan sat down and the Second Mate rose. "It was during our second voyage to Florida. As we all did in those days, we searched through every forest, swamp, and mountain for gold. But what we discovered is worth far more than gold. Through our interpreters, we asked each native village we came to: where was the gold? They consistently answered the same. They had none, but the next village certainly did.

"Thus, we always were pushing deeper towards the darkness of the Florida swamps. Until one day, we arrived at yet another village and we received the same answer. Except this time, one of the villagers secretly told us of a special Fountain, forbidden by the tribal elders. They believed it was essential for the health of the tribe to have the population renew itself with every generation.

"However, this young man secretly partook of the magic waters. He guessed he was nearly 400 seasons old, or about 100 years, as we calculate them. The elders suspected him already and would probably decide to torture him to death at the next tribal gathering in a few months. He offered to tell us of the forbidden Fountain if we would help him escape.

"He revealed this wonderful Fountain that lies beneath us and its magical secret. Of course, we did not believe him at the time. We marked it carefully on our map and drank of it, anyway, just in case there was any truth to it. We swore an oath of secrecy and that we would always be together. None of us could live apart from the others, so we could ensure that no one else would ever find it. For if the world would discover it, there would not be enough water in the entire region to slack the endless thirst.

"Ah, but what of the tribesman? What did we do with him? Our wise Capitán here offered him to join us. He replied he would rather be taken far away, far away from the temptation of the magic waters. As he saw it, they were both a blessing and a curse.

"At his refusal to join us, several of us wanted to kill him to preserve the secret in case it did turn out to be true. But our kind Capitán decided we were not heathens who reneged on our dealings, unlike our barbaric countryman, Pizarro, and what he did to the King of the Incas. No, you offered to take him to Puerto Rico to live out his life with a heavy sack of gold to ease the transition. He took a local wife, had a large family, and lived well until his final days.

"You explained that no one would believe a bizarre legend from a lone native even if he did want to change his mind. Yet, he never did, proving, you made the correct decision."

At this conclusion, everyone rose with a crystal wine glass in hand and cheered their benevolent Capitán. They served themselves a wonderful banquet and the old Spanish wine flowed freely. One by one, each descended the narrow stairs alone to the cavern. Dim electric lights illuminated the path to the deepest point where the cavern opened up like a cathedral with a ceiling many stories high. In the center, bubbled the Fountain surrounded by strange moss that glowed a bright blue. The surrounding stalagmites created strange statues of alien gods that smiled benevolently from above.

Beside the Fountain was the eternal chalice that the tribesman told the old gods placed there when they walked the land. Strangely luminous gems that formed mysterious symbols covered the golden chalice. He had told them that only that cup would work its magic. No one knew if the benefits of youth came from the properties of the chalice or the waters, or maybe both were required.

A few of their mates would rush to gulp down the sweet water. Others would first contemplate life and its mysteries before doing so. Juan invariably went last, as he always took the longest time. Sometimes he would take hours, especially after a death of a beloved wife earlier that year. This was when his crew would wait nervously in silence. In the end, he always drank from the miraculous chalice.

No one could ever lie about taking the waters as they produced a blue hue around the individual for some hours afterwards. After the annual ritual was completed, they would drink a barrel of their heavy Spanish wine until the sun rose.

The remaining days of their retreat would involve more fine eating and regaling of stories and experiences, often hundreds of years old. It was a time to not only restore their youth, but also to reaffirm their deep personal bonds of friendship. According to their tradition, on the last night of their annual retreat, their Capitán Juan Ponce de León would retell the story of how they discovered the Fountain.

CHAPTER FOUR

The Discovery

"I'll start from when I returned to Puerto Rico to protect the Royal Charter that our Majesty King Ferdinand gave to me in May 1518. I spent the next two years rebuilding my home and plantation from when the Caribs burned it to the ground during one of their raids, while I was in Spain. I had to resettle my family and spend some time with my wife, angry with me for being away for such a long time.

"Even so, I had to fulfill the command of our late King to establish a colony on Florida's shores. I gathered you and many more, over 200 in total, including artisans and farmers, animals and implements to build a settlement there. We left in January 1521 on two ships.

"We arrived at the site I had chosen near Port Charlotte on the southwest coast. At first, everything went well. I negotiated a peaceful coexistence with the local Calusa tribe. They allowed us to establish a small fort, a storeroom, and houses. Leaving everyone else behind to carry on building our settlement, I took this band of merry men here present to explore the interior.

"We rode our horses for a few days eastward, passing several tribal villages along the way. Each became more hostile the farther we continued. Also, the terrain was becoming more difficult to pass with horses. We stopped at the last village, considering whether we should continue into the dark fetid swamps that we now know as the Everglades.

"Do you remember the village headman? He was a suspicious, shifty character. He took our presents, but even so would shift between tolerating our presence to threatening us. It became so bad that the second morning we were there, we awoke to being surrounded by several hundred of his armed men. That would have been a very dangerous fight, as they were so close to us already.

"I must say that quick-thinking is my forte. Before the chief could give the order to attack us, I pulled out a chicken egg and held it high so everyone could see it. This caused quite a lot of wonderment. At first, they thought it was a weapon and stepped back from us.

"Even more to their astonishment, I pulled many more from our food stock together with some bacon, onions, and garlic. The chief was expecting me to produce some kind of magic, which is exactly what I did. I fried up, right in front of all of them, a big skittle of scrambled eggs. I filled up a plate and invited the chief to sit and have breakfast.

"No one can resist the smell of bacon cooking with onions and garlic, even our modern vegetarians and vegans are sorely tempted. He sat down and together the two of us shared a wonderful breakfast. He ordered someone to bring a few nicely ripe tomatoes and we became, if not friends exactly, at least good acquaintances.

"For the next few days that we stayed there, we ate the same breakfast together. One time, he brought what looked like duck eggs, leeches, wild garlic, and wild boar meat. I tried to reproduce scrambled eggs, but the eggs just did not come out the same. I even tried making an omelet with them, which I thought was far worse, but the headman loved it.

"He gave us many gifts, mostly food. But he insisted I take a nicely carved ritual pipe of his own, which I still have sitting on my fireplace mantel. That was an honor. He invited us to build our settlement there, but being so far from the sea made that impossible.

The one thing he did impress on us was the futility of continuing east, further into the swamps.

"From the swarms of mosquitoes, snakes, and alligators, we needed little convincing. So, we packed up our horses and started our journey back to our settlement on the coast. The entire tribe came out to bid us farewell. The headman gave me a hug. He was probably secretly glad to see us go. The local maidens were starting to show interest in us.

"We had gone about six hours and stopped for lunch. We were having our siesta afterwards when our man, Semoya, reached us. Once all the villagers returned to their daily activities, he followed us, running most of the way. He had learned some language of the Taínos, due to him being the main trading contact for his village with the outside world.

"We invited him to eat and rest with us. He clearly had something serious in mind to exert himself like that. And, indeed, he did. He told us of our wonderful Fountain and its incredible properties. He offered to take us there and how could we refuse? Of course, we did not believe him at first. Whatever it was, it was worth the trip.

"He led us on a very indirect route so as not to tip off his village. It was a very serious secret that, if the headman discovered we were going there, would have attacked us with no mercy. We traveled a day north, a day east, and finally another day south until we reached this very spot, about 500 years ago.

"Antón already described the details during our dinner of renewal. You all know them well. So, I will continue with what happened next.

"We did take him with us back to our settlement. I remember we debated very much during that week of traveling back. Was his story true? We were highly doubtful. Yet within a day, we noticed that we had indeed changed. We took on the attributes of the younger age we chose when we partook of those sweet, blue-glowing waters, just as he told us.

"Now we had another dilemma. How to arrange our lives to take in this new life-changing event? Each one of us was lost in thought over the remaining few days of our trip as we contemplated what to do next. The last night before we would reach the settlement, we had to decide.

"That dinner was a silent one. We all stared into the campfire, our thoughts lost in the dancing flames, trying to discern the best path forward. By then, we were full of the vigor of the younger ages we had imagined when we drank the glowing blue waters. Would we be thankful for the onetime extra fifty or sixty years of life and be satisfied to continue our normal lives? Or would we become addicted to the vim and verve of youth forever?

"My decision was easier than most of you. I was much older than any of you. I was staring at old age, literally in my face. I didn't like what I saw. Furthermore, my children were strangers to me. I had spent so little time with them as they grew up.

"My wife and I were estranged; despite all the time we were together after my last return from Spain. I learned that she had taken lovers in my absence, practically any sailor who passed by. In her heart, she could not accept the ideal of womanly virtue that we would expect from our Spanish wives, if we had any. Don't laugh, Tiago!

"As for me, I decided to fake my death and continue my life of adventure as an unknown character in the tragic play of Spanish colonialism in our New World. I would return every year to the Fountain to renew my life. I asked all of you to sleep on it and tell me your decisions in the morning.

"The next morning, I began by telling you my decision. I would fake my death and would need the help of some of you to achieve this. My plan was to pretend that the Calusas attacked us. I was hit by a slow-acting poisonous arrow in my thigh. This would give me time to arrange for the settlement's continued development and for our return.

"I asked you, Jaime, to stab me lightly in my thigh. But you did it so hard that it took me six months to walk right again. Our native friend gave me a powder that their shamans used when they went on their spirit wanderings. This powder lowered their blood pressure so much that the body's metabolism barely functioned.

"To all appearances, they were dead. The body would be cold and there would be no discernable breath. Their spirit wanderings could go on as long as two or even three months. They didn't need to eat or drink anything. He recommended that if I did use it to only use enough to last less than a month as, in his experience, for longer periods, the shamans never were quite right in the head after they awoke.

"I kept it, but fortunately, thanks to your help, I didn't need to use it. I would have hated to gain everlasting life at the cost of my mind. Fortunately, our glowing-blue water reinvigorates our brains as well.

"As it turned out, things did not go exactly to plan. When we approached our settlement, the Calusas were really attacking. They had killed all our livestock and uprooted our newly planted fields. They had nearly broken through into our fort when we arrived.

"We charged them from behind on our horses. I remember poor Semoya clinging desperately to me as he tried to hold on behind me. He was shrieking terribly. He had never seen a horse two weeks before, and now he was in the middle of a cavalry charge.

"Well, as you all know, we broke the Calusa's attack. They retreated, but clearly our settlement was no longer viable in the face of a hostile neighbor desperate to remove us. I continued with my plan. I retreated into my cabin. My wound was bleeding terribly from the cavalry charge. It was easy for everyone to believe my story after such a desperate attack.

"I decided that we abandon the settlement and return to the nearest port of Havana. I would 'die' shortly after we returned. Thanks to our Padre Pedro here, it was arranged quickly and smoothly. Late at night before the burial, you guys found a body from where and how I never want to know and placed it dressed in my clothes into the casket.

"Later, those loyal to my memory moved that poor bastard's remains to Puerto Rico to be buried at the Church there in San Juan. Some of you have visited it. Not bad. I think they did a good job to praise my memory, though I could never understand who the carved stone woman was supposed to represent.

"We dispersed after that with the agreement that we would all meet ten months later in Havana. Every one of you returned, though I know many of you were still quite doubtful about the whole thing. Semoya gave us a map of how to get to our Fountain from both the west and east sides. We chose to return from the east, as we were too familiar to the hostile Calusas to try the familiar western path.

"After accomplishing that, we decided to stick together from that time onward. We built a little hamlet by a peaceful Ais tribe on the coast north of today's Miami, who willingly traded with us. The women enjoyed our company, and the tribesmen enjoyed all that we could offer. But after four or five years as peaceful fishermen and farmers, were we satisfied with such a pleasant quiet life? Of course, not.

"We stole an armed caravel from Havana harbor one late night. We preyed upon the small merchant ships trading local products like rum, grain, and leather between the colony ports. Yes, call us what we were. We were pirates. But you have to admit it was fun until we met that stupid captain of the merchantman Santo Simeón.

"He was transporting cheap grain, for god's sake. As we neared his surrendered ship, I told him clearly that we only wanted the cargo. After we transferred that, he and his ship could go free. Any normal captain would have agreed. But, oh no! His men opened fire with their crossbows just as we approached.

"Poor Martin and Alejandro were hit. You guys remember them? They were good boys. They died in front of us, as we helplessly watched. I burned the merchant ship and killed the murderous captain. But those two showed clearly that our Fountain could protect us from old age and disease, but not from violent sudden death.

"We decided that the quiet life by our peace-loving friends was the far better one. And so it was. We worked beside them, hunting and fishing. Sharing what little we had, we soon became honorary members of the tribe. We learned their language and explored the entire interior of Florida, making friends with the natives as we met them.

"But after forty years of not aging and, despite the warm affections of their women, we never produced any children. They started to suspect that maybe we were spirits and not men. Which would have been fine, but for whatever reason they decided that we must be malignant spirits, rather than benign. People always assume the worst. The women stopped visiting, and the men stopped trading with us. We were ostracized. Fortunately, our motherland, Spain, came to our rescue.

"In 1565, we learned that a growing colony was established at Saint Augustine. We moved there, settled down, and prospered to this day."

Everyone sank into silence as they remembered their shared experiences, their shared adventures, their shared lives.

CHAPTER FIVE

Isabel

The autumn sun was high, and the sea breezes were cool. With an iced down Zombie in a large Tiki-type mug sitting on the glass table in front of him and a wide umbrella behind keeping the sun at bay, Ponce de Léon relaxed on the beach behind his house. It was low tide and before him was a group of young people frolicking in the waves or playing frisbee about fifty feet away. He watched them distractedly. His thoughts wandered to review his strange life.

It was already two years after the interment of his wife. Ponce de Léon felt that his heart and mind had recovered. He could concentrate on life again. His normal restlessness was reappearing. That always worried him. So, he threw his energies into his many businesses and philanthropic activities.

With enough patience and time not being an issue, it is easy to make a fortune. All one needs to do is study the geography of any location. It is usually clear what path economic development would take. For a city on the coast like Saint Augustine, clearly real estate development will follow the coastline. Buying empty and reasonably priced land ahead of this path is as simple a successful business model as there can be.

To this purpose, they created a joint-stock company, an S-type corporation. All their investments were done in the company's name, so no individual investment could be traced back to them. The owner of the company was a trust fund that included every member of the crew in equal proportion.

They were all trustees of this fund, with Ponce de Léon acting as a kind of Quaker Clerk, as all decisions were decided unanimously, not by voting. In this manner, though decisions took generally much longer, at the end, no one was ever disappointed in the outcome. It was the only way their cooperation could survive without factions and dissenters.

Anyone could propose a new investment and present it to the group. After many flops and failures, they decided to keep with what they knew best. Though real estate was easy to understand, they did other things, according to individual interests and experiences.

For example, they all knew the Caribbean extremely well. But no one knew it as intimately as Antón. He had sailed and piloted ships to every island and coastal region of the Caribbean. In 1518, he piloted Juan de Grijalvain's four-ship fleet, becoming probably the first European to sail along the coast of Mexico. A year later, he piloted Hernán Cortés' eleven-ship fleet and 500-man army to the Yucatan, to start the campaign that would defeat Montezuma and the Aztecs.

Ponce de Léon befriended him in 1512 while preparing for his first voyage to Florida. Antón knew the currents, every hidden reef and shoal. He knew every port with their demands and offerings. It was natural for him to start and build a very successful regional shipping company.

They were all very wealthy. Money was no object. Though treated with the utmost seriousness, business ventures were more for providing meaningful distraction for those with time on their side. What other choices did they have?

Some may object to these capitalist endeavors and say they could develop their sensitive, creative sides. But these were rough men of the dangerous age of sail and no holds barred war. If they ever had any sensitivity, that was long extinguished after their first taste of combat.

What about being loving family men, concentrating everything on their families? That was a sensitive subject for those who would always outlive their wives, their children, their grandchildren, etc. How about developing a long and illustrious career in science or industry? What would their colleagues think at their retirement party about their strange colleague, who was invariably the same age?

No, being anonymous was the key to everything they did. So, what fits perfectly into anonymity? Charitable donations. Ponce de Léon found this the most interesting activity of all. It was his chief motive to create more wealth. After deducting all living expenses from his annual income, he kept 10% to grow his businesses. He would support many worthy causes with the remaining 90%.

Avoiding anything political, he chose progressive causes across the spectrum. They had to be serious, backed by science and common sense. Even after that filter, there were still thousands available all around the world. Sometimes, he would make one-off gifts for specific projects. He paid for the renovation of the old church in his hometown. He gave a foundation to support a museum there about his early life because he thought it was important for later generations to feel proud of where they were born. They, too, could do something important and make their mark on the world, as he had done.

As their captain and the architect of their great fortune, Ponce de Léon had the complete respect and obedience that only those born and raised in the feudal Medieval Iberian Peninsula could have. He proposed rules of conduct that were accepted by everyone in their unanimous Quaker way:

They could do nothing illegal. Spending years in prison would prevent them from taking their annual draught of reinvigorating waters. They learned very early that the waters only work on location and are worthless taken outside the cavern.

They all took a vow of secrecy. They could not even hint to anyone about the key to their longevity. This included the most intimate soulmates, no matter how tempting.

They were to conduct themselves with the utmost respect and kindness to everyone. They were to be excellent neighbors and citizens, living with a low profile above all reproach.

They were to do nothing that would pose any threat to life, whether through physical accident or disease. In the case of disease, the Fountain's waters would cure them if they could survive until their next annual trip to their secret retreat. But the waters could not bring someone back from the dead or replace a missing limb.

There were many others, but these were the most important. If anyone was slipping, the others were quick to notice and would pull him back from the precipice. Sometimes it was difficult. For several years in the 1970's, Jose would always choose an age in his early 20's, though he ordinarily would have been in his 50's. He went to the disco dance clubs every night, going home very drunk at the break of dawn with a different young woman. He would just make it to the annual retreat, relying on the waters to clean him up, which they did.

A car crash one night put him in the hospital for six months with nothing more than eight broken bones and no permanent damage to a twenty-two-year-old body that might have killed an older man. Ponce de Léon placed him in rehab for eighteen months afterwards with a private assistant that was really a guard to keep him from sneaking out. When he realized he would miss the annual retreat because of this, he saw the light and turned his life around.

This led to another rule that everyone agreed. No one was allowed to choose an age below thirty-five, unless they were originally younger than that. If so, they could not choose an age younger than they already were. This removed the temptation for the older ones to live like reckless teenagers. The younger ones never had this temptation to live it up while they can, knowing they never would have to face the decline into old age.

Ponce de Léon shook his head as he remembered that emergency. Every century had its own particular crisis. For example, in the 18th century, he adamantly refused any business

34

venture that involved slavery. That caused a lot of bitterness, but in the end, they came around to the immorality of it.

In the 19th century, it was the debate about whether to remain in Florida after the US acquired it. They decided to stay, despite strong misgivings about Yankees and their culture. Later, it was the Civil War. Because of the issue of slavery, Ponce de Léon prevailed to convince everyone not to take part in the war in any way. Finally, in the later 20th century, it was the crisis of sex and drugs. He wondered what would be the crisis for the 21st century? Probably it would be something having to do with the internet or virtual reality.

Suddenly, he was yanked back into the present when a frisbee flew at him and knocked his icy drink across his bare chest. Soon afterward, an embarrassed young woman ran up to him. She took off the towel that she had tied around her waist, apologized profusely, and tried to dry his chest. Her barely legal bikini revealed exactly the body that Ponce de Léon was most attracted to: athletic, slim, tight, with proportions closer to boyish than matronly.

It was easy to raise his eyes to take in her intriguingly beautiful face. The first thing he noticed was her brown eyes. They had both the innocence of youth and a touch of life that had already experienced a touch of sadness. One day, the one would overshadow the other, but the bloom of youth was still the dominant then. Her face showed that she was actually closer to late twenties than early.

Her hair and skin were the attractive cinnamon color of the Portuguese women he had known. Though they shared the same Iberian Peninsula, they differed from those of his homeland, whose hair and eyes were usually jet black. He recognized that there is beauty in all peoples, but this woman, busily and earnestly drying his chest, was special.

"Oh, my dear sir! I am so sorry. Your drink! I spilled it all over you! Let me dry you."

"Don't worry about it. Really. I needed a bit of ice to cool me down. I can just dive into the waves to clean off."

"You're not angry with me, are you?"

"Angry? No! Not at all. You don't need to dry me, really. I'm fine."

"How can I replace your drink? There's no bar around here, and as you can see, I have no wallet. What can I do to make it up to you?"

Oh, my dear lass, I can think of something you could do! "It's no problem at all. I'll just call my assistant over and he can make me another. He's right over there on the veranda."

"Are you sure? OK... By the way, you have such a wonderful accent. You're not from the US. Where are you from originally? How did you end up in Florida with such an impressive house? I so love men with foreign accents. You're not a drug lord, are you? No, no, sorry. I didn't mean that. Why do I have to say such stupid things to interesting men?"

Her face blushed with embarrassment. Blushing young women were nigh impossible to find in the US for at least fifty years. It was all he could do to not take her in his arms right then, kiss her, and tell her everything was fine.

"Hey, don't worry about it. It's easy to think that a rich man with a Latin accent, sitting on a Florida beach in front of his mansion in the middle of the week with nothing to do, would be a drug lord. I don't mind taking up the challenge to prove to you I'm not a stereotype.

"However, I will not do that nor answer your question of how I came to be here, unless you sit here and have a cool drink with me. What will your cool drink be?" Juan knew from a sales class he took once that the assumptive close works most of the time.

"OK. I'll bite. Do you happen to have a cool Chardonnay from California?"

"I'm sure I can offer you a cool Chardonnay from anywhere you like."

He turned and motioned over his assistant.

"Jorge, a glass of our finest Chardonnay for our new friend here and another Zombie for me, but use Curacao instead of the cherry brandy. And bring some of those Spanish almonds."

Jorge bowed slightly and turned towards the outdoor bar on the veranda without saying a word.

Her friends were standing at a distance, staring at her, wondering what was going on. She waved them away. Not to worry. Everything was fine.

CHAPTER SIX

First Governor of Puerto Rico

Juan Ponce de Léon showed no mercy to his native foes in war time. But in peace, he treated them with the dignity and respect that any person deserved within the confines of the colonial exploitive feudal system of the encomienda. He learned their language and their ways. He gave total respect and love to his Taíno wife, Leanora, and she returned it with total devotion.

He did not subscribe to the common belief of his compatriots that the pagan natives were only good for exploitation, worse than beasts of burden. One had to pay for a horse or an ox, so they had value. The native slaves were captured or simply given to a landholder as part of the land grant on which they lived. They had no economic value.

He disagreed with the Church fathers like Saint Benedict, who once wrote: "nothing brings more joy to a Christian heart than slaughtering pagans". This joyous statement was later updated by Saint Dominic, who wrote: "nothing brings more joy to a Christian heart than slaughtering heretics." Both founded powerful and influential monastic orders, the Benedictines and the Dominicans, respectfully. Ponce de Léon's much more enlightened attitude would prove very pivotal in his life.

Soon after establishing his new frontier town of Higüey, he established a trading center for the regional Taíno. From the visiting native merchants, he learned that gold flowed in the rivers of the large island to the east. Ponce de Léon knew it from being on the voyage when Columbus sailed along its southern coast before continuing on to Hispaniola. Columbus had named it San Juan Bautista, but it later became known as Puerto Rico.

After only a year, Ponce de Léon's natural restlessness was showing. He would take long walks in the forests alone for hours, instead of concentrating on the details of the growing town. Other times he would stare out at sea in silence. Leanora knew what these signs meant. No matter what she could do, it would be in vain. Her husband had already decided he needed a new adventure.

The Spanish Crown gave Vicente Yáñez Pinzón, the Captain of the La Niña on Columbus' first voyage, the exclusive rights to Puerto Rico in 1505. But as of 1506, he had done little to exploit his monopoly. So Ponce de Léon decided to take a closer look for himself. In that same year, he took a secret voyage to investigate. He discovered that indeed, it was a fertile golden island worthy of his attention. Unfortunately, there was nothing he could do but patiently wait for an opportunity.

A year later, Pinzón's commission expired. After a respectful time had passed, Ponce de Léon enquired to the King if he might make an official exploratory voyage to the island. The King granted his request in 1508. Ponce de Léon at once prepared a ship with fifty men. He arrived shortly at a bay where he established a base with a fort and storehouse that would become San Juan, the capital of present day Puerto Rico. They planted some crops but spent most of their time looking for gold, which they found in substantial quantity.

In 1509, Ponce de Léon returned to Hispaniola with enough gold to persuade his superior, Ovando, to make him governor of the entire island. Ovando did so quickly, backed up with a royal appointment from King Fernando himself. Ponce de Léon promptly packed up his family and moved to the much larger pastures of Puerto Rico.

Ponce de Léon wasted no time in attracting settlers to his new domain and started rapidly developing the island. Perhaps

Puerto Rico was large enough to contain his restless urge for discovery. But fate would not give him that peace.

Diego Colón (Columbus in English), the eldest son of his deceased father, Christopher Columbus (Colón in Spanish), had been fighting in Spanish courts to allow him to take over the rights and privileges of his disgraced father. When the disgraced Ovando was removed as governor in the same year, Colón prevailed and, despite strong misgivings, the King had to appoint him as Viceroy of the new colonies.

Despite the courts confirming Ponce de Léon as Governor of Puerto Rico, Colón replaced him with Juan Cerón, one of his lackeys in the same year of 1509. However, the King reaffirmed Ponce de Léon's position as Governor. Ponce de Léon quickly arrested the appointees of Colón and sent them back to Spain in chains. The conflict between the two became quite personal. Yet, even with royal favor and support, Viceroy Colón managed to prevail and by the end of 1511, Colón reinstated Juan Cerón and removed Ponce de Léon. So much for absolute monarchy.

King Ferdinand forbade any further retribution to Ponce de Léon, who remained with his family as a private citizen of the colony of Puerto Rico. He had no choice but to seethe at this unfortunate turn of events. The King felt sorry for his favored loyal subject, wronged by the vagaries of the legal system. As fate would have it, Ponce de Léon did not have long to fume.

Rumors of fabulous as yet undiscovered islands to the north reached the King's ears. Being unexplored, they were outside the purview of Colón. In early 1512, the King issued a contract to Ponce de Léon that granted him exclusive rights as Governor for life of all the islands he discovered that centered around the area called Benimy, which included the Bahamas and the still officially undiscovered Florida. He had three years to carve out his domain. This fortunate event would change his life forever.

CHAPTER SEVEN

Flowers on Easter

It took a year for Ponce de León to finally set sail after King Fernando gave him the right to govern any new lands he discovered. It took all that time to build and outfit three caravels, as well as to hire a crew and gather the supplies required for a possible year of exploring. Finally, on March 4, 1513, a very impatient Ponce de León and his crew ventured forth towards unknown waters to the northwest. According to the royal charter, he only had two more years to discover new territories and establish outposts where he could carve out his governorship.

Ponce de León met Antón de Alaminos in the local tavern one evening shortly after receiving his royal charter. There was a celebration that filled the place with recent settlers, mostly farmers and shepherds. Antón recognized a fellow adventurer and offered Ponce de León a seat at his table. Many, many pints of ale later, they became best friends. He told Antón his plans and together they crafted a roadmap to bring those plans to fruition, starting with Antón being the First Mate, navigator, and pilot of the fleet.

He named his three caravels: the San Cristobal, the Santiago, and the Santa Maria de la Consolacion, keeping the tradition of naming ships after saints or women. They were sixty-five feet long. Like all caravels, he built them to be highly maneuverable and seaworthy. They did not have a high carrying capacity, but they were perfect for exploring unknown shallow waters.

What made caravels especially impressive was the use of triangular lateen sails, used by almost all modern yachts. Triangular sails set parallel to the hull allow the contrary winds to pull them forward. They used the same aerodynamic principle for the shape of an airplane wing, causing the air to lift the plane, keeping it aloft. A lateen sail was basically a vertical airplane wing. The keel below the ship kept the wind from blowing the ship sideways, leaving the only option to move forward.

Alas, the winds are a fickle thing. They often change their angle. This requires sailors to constantly change slightly the angles of the sails left to right relative to the hull to keep the sails tight and full of wind. If the wind changes its angle even more, sailors must make large changes to the angles of the sails relative to the wind called tacking. Thus, the ship sails into the wind in a series of diagonal maneuverings.

The caravels had two masts with an aftercastle at the stern, which occupied the back fifth to quarter section of the ship. It was the size of an additional large room that contained the captain's cabin and provided a raised space above where the helmsman could steer the ship with more visibility. The sailors' sleeping quarters and cargo space were below deck in the hold.

The draft of his caravels was relatively shallow at eight to ten feet. This allowed the caravels to approach much closer to shore and even sail up rivers. There were no docks and wharfs where Ponce de León planned to take them.

Each ship had six swivel cannons, four mounted on the railings of the aftercastle and two at the bow. They were breech loading and cast iron. They were loaded from the back like modern artillery and fired a ten-ounce lead ball against the side of an enemy ship or a larger number of smaller balls as grape shot against enemy sailors.

The balls and gunpowder were preloaded into beer mug shaped shots that were prepared in advance, like cartridges for rifles. The cannon had three chambers where the mug-shaped cartridges

42

were placed with wedges, allowing the cannon to fire three shots in quick succession. They could swivel left to right and, to a lesser degree, up and down.

Ponce de León had a crew of 200 spread across his three ships. He loaded his ships with sacks of grain, lead and iron ingots, chickens, casks of water, and casks of rum with other tradeable items. The whole cargo was less than 200 tons. Provisions for the crew would be salted fish and beef with hard biscuits, but only after the fresh food gave out. They drank watered down beer. The alcohol in the beer killed the nasty things water of that era could have. People did not know why drinking 'straight' water was dangerous, only that it was often deadly.

While his crew was loading the ships and otherwise preparing their voyage, Ponce de León had to hide his intentions from the hostile new governor of Puerto Rico, Juan Cerón. The Captain of the Port Guard found Ponce de León on the wharf overseeing the activities of his little fleet.

"Just where do you think you're going with those three ships?"

"Captain Diaz, I have decided to take up trading. You know, sailing among the island colonies buying and selling whatever makes sense. I'm getting bored just sitting here watching the grain grow."

"Oh really? With so many sailors, too?"

"Most of them are passengers."

"Passengers?"

"Just ask them."

"Knowing you, I have my doubts. But…"

"But you can't stop me. That is correct, Captain. Now, if you would be so kind as not to interrupt our work with your groundless suspicions and those of your boss, we need to get back to work."

"Fine. But the Governor is very curious about your intentions to subvert his authority. Don't be surprised if one of his ships follows yours."

"Subvert his authority? Even after he usurped mine thanks to that perfidious Columbus family? No, not at all. That is the furthest thing from my mind." Ponce de León gave his most charming smile.

Captain Diaz frowned, growled, then walked away to report to Governor Cerón.

After all the preparations were complete, Ponce de León announced publicly that they would start the voyage after Mass on Sunday. In fact, his ships slipped out of the harbor shortly after midnight on Thursday. By the time Governor Cerón realized what had happened, they had an eight-hour head start to hide their direction from any following spies. They sailed northwest along the northern coasts of Puerto Rico, Hispaniola, and then Cuba before swinging north towards the Bahamas.

Ponce de León made a point to stop at every one of the small but growing colonial settlements along the way, buying fresh food for the crew and selling small amounts of whatever they had in the cargo. It was a necessary subterfuge, as lying to a Governor was not looked on lightly. Nonetheless, he did not want to waste too much time on it.

Many of the Bahama Islands were already well-known, including San Salvador Island, where Columbus made his initial landfall on his first voyage of discovery. To the Spanish colonial masters, the Bahamas were useless, except as a source of native slave labor. Many years of slave-raiding had seriously depopulated the islands. Once established as governor, the first decision Ponce de León would make would be to protect his tribal population from predators and end slavery in his domains.

They sailed passed many islands daily to both their west and east. Often, they passed empty rotting fishing villages whose inhabitants were now working in the plantations and mines of their new Spanish masters, if they had not already died from overwork and disease. Very rarely, they saw small fishing canoes who paddled away as fast as they could, most likely in terror at the sight of the approaching ships.

They mapped any new islands they passed as potentially falling under the authority of Ponce de León's Royal Charter as newly discovered territory. They occasionally stopped to collect fruit, wild game, and fresh fish. But nothing interested Ponce de León to stop for more than a few hours. He had bigger ambitions and rumor had it that a much larger island was somewhere to the northwest.

Three weeks after setting out, they passed the last of the Bahamas. Before them was open ocean. Any direction but south was uncharted waters. Ponce de León decided to sail directly west until he found land. That would have put them somewhere between Port St. Lucie and Vero Beach on Florida's east coast. But something still unknown to them was gently carrying them far to the north: the Gulf Stream.

They sighted land late on April 2, 1513. Being the time of Easter and the coast being much more verdant than the Bahamas, Ponce de León named it La Florida after the common Spanish name for Easter of La Pascua Florida, floral Easter. The 'Pascua' was dropped, but the 'Florida' remained.

He noted in his captain's logbook that the latitude was thirty degrees and eight minutes. That latitude was far north of the one he noted when they turned due west from the last island of the Bahamas at twenty-seven degrees and three minutes. It was a great mystery that had to wait to be solved. In the meantime, a great coastline disappeared into the distance, to both the north and south.

Ponce de León anchored his three ships less than 100 yards from shore. He could smell the fragrance of the spring flowers carried aloft by the cool night breeze. It was so tempting to row ashore and spend the first night by a campfire on the beach. Considering that they had no idea what might meet them, he decided to wait until morning.

He was so excited he could not sleep that night. He realized he had discovered what he was searching for: a large, lush land to build his own colony and make his mark in history, the mark of a de León. If his father and Uncle Pedro could see him now. He smiled and slipped into slumber.

The landing party of twenty rowed to the beach. Ponce de León planted the flag of Castile and claimed the land for his mentor, King Ferdinand. He looked all around him and smiled. This was a land worthy of his new governorship.

They had their first breakfast on the wide, fine, white, sandy beach. Hours later, they built a camp at the tree line where the beach ended. Many more crewmen came ashore. Everyone was curious and excited, as if they were young children at their first Carnival. They marveled at any new bird, flower, or tree they found.

For five days, small groups of six or seven explored in every direction. Occasionally, they would meet the native inhabitants, who would flee deeper into the forests. There was no possibility of trade. So, they collected and hunted whatever looked edible and returned to their camp by the beach. Antón compiled their separate maps into a single one of the entire area.

Ponce de León was impatient to expand his claim, but was faced with a critical decision. Like everywhere else the Spanish explorers had discovered to that point, he decided that this new floral Florida was an island, too. Sailing all around it would make the most solid claim possible. He considered his two choices: sail north or south around the island.

Despite his restless and adventurous spirit, he was not rash. After several hours of consideration and discussion with Antón, he decided it would be safer if they sailed south toward Cuba. If anything went wrong, they would be closer to safe harbors. If he had decided to go north, his small ships might have been eventually crushed by the ice in the Northwest Passage of Canada as he continued to sail around the vast island that would be his.

So, south they sailed. A day later, they met the Gulf Stream head on, where it is the strongest between Florida and the Bahamas. No matter how they tacked with the wind's force behind them, it was no match for the strong ocean current, which pushed them backwards. Two of the ships took shelter in a cove, while the third one, the San Cristobal, was swept out of sight.

Ponce de León knew it was hopeless to go after it. All they could do was wait to see if the swept away ship could find its way to rejoin them. Meanwhile, Antón studied the powerful current. Ponce de León wrote the conclusions in his logbook, making it the first known discovery of the Gulf Stream that would prove so important for trans-Atlantic travel to the current day.

After two days of anxious waiting, the San Cristobal sailed into view and rejoined them. The ship's pilot added his observations of the Gulf Stream. Ponce de León decided they would sail close to the coast to avoid the opposing current. That suited his aim to map the coast and making occasional trips ashore. After a celebratory dinner by a beach bonfire and a good night's sleep on stable dry land, they continued south.

CHAPTER EIGHT

Carving Out His Personal Domain

The going was slow as they anchored and went ashore every day or so to explore inland for a half a day's walking distance. They did not discover anything of note until they spotted a large native town at the mouth of the Miami River. They made a small base on the shore of the Biscayne Bay and ventured to visit the natives to establish friendly relations with his future subjects.

The town was of the Tequesta people. They all fled into the forested interior at first sight of the three strange and huge monsters moving upon the water. Ponce de León waited ten days, hoping they would return. They did not. Ponce de León explored the town and forbade his men from taking anything.

They encountered a large mound. They guessed it had important religious significance and left it alone. There were no signs of any agriculture. Judging from what they saw, the natives ate fruit, berries, and game found in their area. The main part of the diet came from what they captured at sea. They lived in raised huts on wooden stilts with thatched roofs.

After ten days, Ponce de León lost patience and continued south. They passed other coastal villages. All the natives fled in panic at the sight of the ships. Quick inspection of the empty villages indicated the same tribal people lived there.

Soon they met a long chain of small islands stretching to the west, away from the Florida mainland. The depth between the islands was less than the keel of their ships. At times, the keel would scrape along the sand below until it became stuck. This would cause general panic as they certainly did not want to run aground and need to abandon ship.

Ponce de León would calmly tell the crew to bring the long oars and row their ship back to deeper waters. The decks were close enough to the waterline to do this. Eventually, after very slow going for a week, they found a passage that allowed them to continue north.

They sailed in a general northeasterly direction until they made landfall at Charlotte Harbor on Florida's west coast on May 23, 1513. There they met the Calusa, the overlords of the tribes of southern Florida, including the Tequesta people of the Miami area. They did not flee and were not interested in trading. Their only interest was to drive these probable slave raiders away.

Despite Ponce de León's best efforts to maintain peace, conflict ensued. For the next three weeks, diplomacy ended with violence. The Calusa usually outnumbered them ten to one and were armed with longbows. The Spanish arquebus matchlocks and crossbows evened the odds. Eventually, the conflict devolved to threats and general fulminations, as both sides kept out of range of the other.

Ponce de León decided this would be the best location for his first colony, if only he could win the confidence of these stone age tribal people and turn them into productive prosperous subjects. He meant them no harm, nor intended to enslave them. He would pay for their produce as any governor in Europe would do.

If they would only become productive and not just rely on the subsistence of the land. By being productive, Ponce de León meant for them to produce a saleable surplus, or even cash crops for which they had no use except to sell. This ran completely contrary to the native way of thinking.

All Ponce de León wanted was for them to learn to grow cash crops and raise livestock. Everyone would prosper. Surely, they could see the wisdom in that. He could care in the least if they converted to the Church. He only required them to be peaceful, law-abiding, and productive members of the new society. Alas, they were not getting the message. Ponce de León decided he better leave things alone for a while, let tempers subside, and try again later.

They sailed further north, discovering Tampa Bay. When the coast turned westward with no sign of curving back east like a normal island coastline would, Ponce de León began doubting whether La Florida really was an island. If so, there was no indication of how far he should continue exploring. He turned around and sailed south.

Once he had returned near to their first encounter with the stubborn Calusa, he sailed southwest across the uncharted open ocean to where he expected the west coast of Cuba to be. Perhaps he would find a more hospitable and more civilized native people who understood better the benefits of profitable peaceful commerce.

Sailing far west of the last of the Keys, they found Dry Tortugas Island. There was no water or even much plant life. What they did find were hundreds of turtles. Because of this, he named them the Tortugas, Spanish for turtles. It was called 'Dry' because of the lack of water. After a fine turtle feast on the sandy shores and a night sleeping by a bonfire, they continued their course back home.

Continuing their progress south, they expected to meet the coast of Cuba in a few days. But the strong eastward currents pushed them back towards the southern side of the Florida Keys. Ponce de León decided they would just return the way they came via the Bahamas. When they approached Grand Bahama Island, they encountered a Spanish caravel commanded by Diego Miruelo, a lackey of Diego Colón.

Ponce de León's first suspicion was Viceroy Diego Colón sent Diego Miruelo to spy on him, trying to find his three ships somewhere still in the Bahamas. This dark thought caused him to fume as he watched the ship in the distance. Antón calmed him by pointing out that Miruelo was too many months behind them to know anything about their voyage. He probably was just another

Spanish slaver, hoping to squeeze a few more slaves from the tragically depopulated Bahama Islands.

It was already too late in the day to continue, and the dark menacing clouds of a storm were brewing nearby. They anchored in a protected cove of a small empty island. That night, the whistling winds and rough waves still rocked their ships, such that sleep was hardly possible. The next morning, the storm had subsided, and they continued their way.

As irony would have it, the storm caught Miruelo unprepared. The winds had blown his ship aground, breaking it in half. He and his crew were stranded on the rocky islet with their hapless native captives. Ponce de León's little fleet found them waving, jumping, and crying to be saved. Ponce de León considered what to do.

He was so tempted to leave them to their fate, representing two things he loathed: the slaving of the natives and Viceroy Diego Colón. In the end, he decided he had to at least save the hapless natives. In doing so, he could not just leave the Spaniards behind.

His ships were too close to leave without being identified anyway. If another passing ship saved them, Ponce de León would become a pariah and could never crew another ship again. Not coming to the rescue of shipwrecked sailors was a major taboo.

Before doing so, he ordered one of his ships, the Santa Maria, to continue exploring the Bahama Islands in a northeasterly direction. Once he had Miruelo and his crew onboard, they could do nothing but return to Puerto Rico.

The rescued Spaniards hugged whatever member of Ponce de León's crew was within arm's reach with tears in their eyes. Even Miruelo was thankful for the 'Christian' behavior of the rival of his benefactor, though he would not show it. The rescued native Bahamians huddled in the bow, completely bewildered by the whole thing.

Once Ponce de León learned from Miruelo where he snatched the innocents, the first thing he did was to return them to their island. Miruelo was enraged at the loss of his valuable cargo but could only fume over it. As for the islanders, they could not believe that another white devil would save them. Perhaps there was hope, after all.

From there, they sailed back to their home port in Puerto Rico. They arrived home on October 19, 1513, over eight months after they set out. The Santa Maria eventually returned safely on February 20, 1514, after sailing deep into the Atlantic, finding nothing noteworthy. Ponce de León had what he needed: a claim to a very large colony, probably larger than anything discovered until then, even bigger than Cuba.

Ponce de Léon could only shrug his shoulders at the ungrateful Colón's lack of recognition of saving Miruelo and his crew. For his part, Colón only seethed in anger, having no power to stop Ponce de Léon from making his own self-financed voyages. Ponce de Léon and his loyal crewmates refused to disclose any details about their discoveries to Colón. Colón could do nothing openly, as Ponce de Léon clearly had the support and favor of the King.

Nonetheless, Colón undermined Ponce de Léon at every turn. Ponce de Léon suspected that he was even trying to steal Florida from him. This prompted Ponce de Léon to return to Spain to cement his claims and discoveries, as was proposed by the King. His trip to the royal residence in Valladolid was the first time he had returned to his native land for 20 years.

King Ferdinand received him warmly, granting him a knighthood with his own coat of arms, the first of the Spanish colonizers to be so honored. The king affirmed Ponce de Léon's governorship of Florida and the Bimini islands of the Bahamas with a new royal charter that defined all the details, including the splitting of the profits between Ponce de Léon and the royal treasury.

The Carib peoples were attacking the Spanish Caribbean colonies at this time, even burning to the ground Ponce de Léon's home in Puerto Rico. In response, the King gave Ponce de Léon three ships and crew with orders to defeat the Caribs and bring peace to the royal realm once again.

While the ships were being prepared, Ponce de Léon had to register all his discoveries with the Casa de Contratación in Seville, which served as the main coordinating bureaucracy of the Spanish colonies. There, he would help enlarge the Padrón Real, the secret maps of Spanish discoveries that every Spanish explorer had on board his ship.

On the way, he stopped at his birth town, Santervás de Campos. It was just as sleepy as he remembered it growing up. His parents died even before he started his military career in the campaigns to drive the Moors from the Iberian Peninsula. He visited their graves along with many unknown siblings who died as babies.

Their simple graves were crumbling and overgrown. He gave money to the local caretaker to care for their graves as the parents of a new Knight of the realm deserved. Later, when he had to cut all ties with his past, he would discontinue this, and nature would reclaim what was rightfully hers.

In May 1515, he returned with his little fleet and began military operations against the Caribs. Barely a year later, King Ferdinand, Ponce de Léon's great benefactor and friend, died. Ponce de Léon had to return again to Spain to confirm his rights and royal agreements. He spent nearly two years accomplishing this.

In the meantime, his contacts informed him that Colón had already made two unauthorized voyages to 'his' Florida. Fortunately, the brave Calusa warriors repelled them, too. Nonetheless, he decided he had to act quickly. He returned to Puerto Rico in mid-1518. He would soon make a discovery that would change his life forever.

CHAPTER NINE

Introductions

"Before we start sharing our life histories, shall we learn each other's names? Mine is Juan."

"Mine's Isabel. So nice to meet you, Juan."

"Isabel? You must have a Latin root in your family. In the English-speaking world, that would normally be Elizabeth."

"Indeed, I do. My grandparents came from the Azores in the 50's. My mother, who has a Scotch-Irish background, wanted to name me Elizabeth, not for the Queen, but for her grandmother. But my Azores grandmother persuaded my parents that Elizabeth Beatriz Alves Silva de Santos did not quite fit. So, Isabel I became."

"I once knew a Queen Isabella. She was such a gentle and compassionate soul. I would have gone to the gates of Hell for her. In a way, I kind of did…" Juan closed his eyes and went silent for a few moments.

"Queen Isabela or Queen Elizabeth?"

"Sorry. No, she was the wife of a mentor of mine. Everyone called her 'Queen'. But back to you. Seems I already know a lot about you just from your name. I guessed you had a goodly amount of Portuguese blood in you from your cinnamon-colored hair and eyes."

Jorge quickly returned with the requested items and placed them on the low wooden table in front of them.

"Hey, Jorge, our new friend's grandparents came from the Azores. Let's honor them by bringing us a wheel of that São Jorge cheese I bought last week."

"Very well, Capitán."

"Captain? Are you a captain, too? A captain of what?"

"Oh, that's just what my friends call me. We're not friends yet, so just call me Juan."

"But there must be a reason they call you that."

"Well, I was a captain once. I spent many years at sea. I had a modest ship of my own and many of my friends here were part of my crew."

"A modest ship of your own? Where did you sail?"

"Mainly across the Atlantic, around the Caribbean islands, and the coasts surrounding them."

"Was this a sailing yacht for tourists?"

"A sailing yacht for tourists? Hmm, no. It was more of a commercial ship, trading between the various ports not served by the larger shipping companies. In fact, I have been to all nine islands of the Azores. Which one was your grandparents from?"

"They're originally from Terceira, from a small town called Biscoitos. I've never been."

"We used to stop by Praia de Vitoria on our way back to the Caribbean. They have a nice little harbor there. But that was a long time ago. So, what brings you to our beautiful beach?"

"My friends had some vacation time and decided to come here. They asked me to come with them. I decided I needed a break and joined them. One of them rented a house in town for two weeks. I don't have a regular job. I'm a student."

"A student? You don't look so young. Do I have to ask you your age?"

"My age? I have no problem telling you my age. I'm twenty-nine. And no, I'm not that kind of student. I'm a PhD candidate at the University of Chicago."

"Forgive me. It's just that teenagers look and act so grown-up these days. I can never tell. A PhD student at the University of Chicago? Looks like we are well on our way to a conversation. What's the subject of your studies?"

"I decided to use my Portuguese heritage and study comparative literature, focusing on the Portuguese and Spanish literary cultures. So, I learned to read both Portuguese and Spanish. I learned to speak Portuguese from my grandparents but had to learn to speak Spanish on my own. Are you Portuguese? I can't quite place your accent."

"Spanish, actually."

"Ah! Maybe you can help me with my Spanish? So sorry. That was being too presumptuous on my part."

"No, you're not being presumptuous. But that wouldn't be a good idea, anyway. My Spanish differs greatly from what they teach you in school. My grammar is terrible, and my accent is way too different from proper Spanish. I would rather help you with your Portuguese. Most of my Portuguese I learned from the good people of the Azores. I could probably have an interesting conversation with your grandparents."

"Sadly, they're no longer with us. Let's stick with English."

"So, what are you reading now?"

"I'm reading Camões' 'Os Lusíadas'."

"Ah, Camões, Camões. He was a great traveler himself, a poet retracing the voyage of Vasco de Gama to India. He wrote a wonderful tribute to the Portuguese people and their great age of discovery, opening the world to Europe. 'Os Lusíadas' must make you proud of your Portuguese roots."

"You really surprise me! You know a lot about him. What else can you tell me about him? Anything not found in books? It would help me understand him."

"Not found in books? Well, he was once the favored poet of the Portuguese Court and that meant a lot then in terms of wealth and opportunity. He fell out of favor, they say, because he had a penchant for pursuing high-ranking ladies at Court who were really out of his social reach. That didn't stop him from trying, though.

"I heard in some cases he was successful in his amorous pursuits, and this brought his fall from royal grace. Later in life, when he finally ended up in Lisboa, he had a Malaysian slave he brought back from Asia. He was so proud but poor that he sent his slave to beg for them both in the marketplace. Portugal's most revered poet died in disgrace and poverty. So typical of many great men."

"You're right. I never came across that in my research. But what do you mean 'you heard' and 'they say'? Did you make all this up?"

"No, it's all true. I learned it somewhere from a very reliable source. I don't remember now."

"Then I guess I can't footnote it in my research. Too bad."

"That was for you to understand him better, which is what you asked for."

"OK, fair enough. It does seem to fit in with his romantic poet nature. What other interesting tidbits can you give me?"

"Tidbits? You're not a cat at my table. I would gladly wine and dine you like a visiting princess from a faraway palace visiting her devoted subject in the provinces."

"Oh, dear, my fascinating man, that is very tempting. But you still haven't answered my question. If you're not an infamous drug lord, how did you end up here with all of this?"

"Clearly, if I were an infamous drug lord, I wouldn't tell you. And if I were, I would have a dozen cell phones surrounding me. Besides, how do I know you aren't a secret FBI agent?" He winked at her.

"Did you just wink at me? That was the first time a man did that to me. That makes me feel like I'm in an old Bogart/Bacall film. Except, I guess I would be the one doing the winking. How delicious! Well, do go on. Don't try to change the subject."

"OK, OK, fine. But you should know I really don't like talking about myself. I come from a family who was on the lowest rung of the royal hierarchy of Castille. Before we fell off completely, my parents managed to have me raised by a noble family higher up the ladder.

"I became educated, but not just tutored in the normal subjects of school. I was tutored in the art of war, which included horseback riding, the use of weapons, strategy, and tactics. Most importantly, I was tutored in the etiquette of being a noble gentleman. How to interact with others both above me and below me. How to act at the Royal Court. In short, how to succeed in a monarchy."

"You were home schooled in all that?"

"Home schooled? Oh, I guess you young people of the US would call it that. We called it 'being tutored.' We don't do 'home schooling' in the old country."

"Well, excuse me. So, you're from old money. Go on."

"Yes, that's it. I come from old money."

"But that doesn't explain how you ended up here."

"My family moved here in the early days of this fine city's history when it was still a small outpost of the great Spanish empire. They grew and prospered with the expanding city. I suppose you could say they made some smart real estate decisions."

"Your family has been here for 500 years? But then how is it you still speak with such a heavy Spanish accent? It doesn't add up. I'm leaning back to the drug lord theory."

"That's simple. They made great real estate investments and other financial decisions, but they made very poor marriage decisions. After it was all said and done, they simply died off. I was the last of the blood relatives. About twenty years ago, a trust administrator found me and told me of my good fortune.

"I was a simple captain of a small tramp steamer carrying goods between the minor ports of the island world of the Atlantic and Caribbean. I gladly accepted my new lifestyle. And here I am today. I haven't been on a steamer ever since."

"I guess that's plausible, incredible, but plausible. But how is that a noble one, such as yourself, so well tutored and trained to take your rightful place at the Royal Court, ended up as a captain of a little freighter? Try explaining that to me."

Ponce de Léon was becoming annoyed with her interrogation, though he had been through similar questioning many dozens of times before by curious women. He was tempted to end the conversation and send her on her way, but every time his eyes wandered to her tight bikini, just barely holding everything in place, his temptation changed to something else. He took a deep breath and continued.

"You clearly are not knowledgeable about life at Court. The entire ladder of nobility is constantly fighting for the King's favor. When someone receives his favor, the others scheme for his downfall. When someone achieves success, the others are jealous and try to make him fail. The backstabbing is terrible.

"I was an excellent example of this. I had received the King's favor due to success from my own abilities and efforts. Immediately, everyone at Court schemed to bring me down. They succeeded, and I left that life. I am happily far from their petty evil-mindedness. Those infernal damn bastards!" Ponce de Léon's anger flashed as if it had happened just yesterday.

"OK, OK, calm down. You're here now, enjoying life on a sunny beach with a cocktail and conversing with a young woman who is becoming very interested in you. That can't be all bad, can it?"

"No, you're right. I guess it's my Latin passion rising to the surface."

"No problem. I suppose Latin passion is more than a stereotype. So, if you're the last of your noble line, do you have children? You have to preserve this wealth in the family, don't you?

I mean, after 500 years; it would be a shame to lose it all to strangers in the end."

"Alas, I had children. Unfortunately, life on the sea is not good for family life. They became estranged from me, as did their mother. We all went our separate ways. I think they all died, the last I heard."

"They all died? How terrible! I'm so sorry."

"Yeah, it is terrible. But that's life sometimes. I'd rather not talk about it. You have my story now. Now let's talk about you."

"Not much to say, really. I'm third generation Portuguese-American. They say the third generation becomes 100% American. That's true with me. Except for eating salted cod at Christmas and speaking decent Portuguese, I guess I'm as American as they come.

"My cultural heritage is why I chose my major at university. I have been a student my entire life. I don't have much experience with living and seeing the world, though I would like to change that. In fact, I'm becoming impatient to do so. But where to start?"

"I guess you could start with a trip to your grandparents' hometown in the Azores."

"You know what? That is exactly what I've been thinking. I think I'll just do that. There are so many Azorean immigrants in the US that there are many direct flights from the US to there. Have to plan it, though. I'd prefer to not travel alone. I always think it's better to share experiences with a special someone else."

"Why don't you go with your boyfriend?"

"Boyfriend? Hah! That's a laugh. That's exactly my problem. They're all boys! I've been disappointed every time and quickly, too."

"Oh, I'm so sorry to hear that." Juan was definitely not sorry to hear that. He continued, "You must be so lonely without a mate. Tell me, what kind of man are you looking for?"

"This will sound silly, coming from a modern American girl. I must admit I always admired my grandfather. Yes, he was a simple, poorly educated, very traditional, stubborn, male chauvinist. But oh, how he treated my grandmother! So tenderly and with the utmost respect, even after sixty years of marriage.

"I would be offended and turned off by all those things that infuriated me about him, if it weren't for that tenderness. Ah, yes. If I could have the respect and tenderness without the other things, he would be my dream man. Unfortunately, no such man exists today. So, I'll continue to be alone in my loneliness."

"Now, Isabel, such men do exist. You just haven't looked hard enough."

"Yeah, I have to believe they do…" She smiled at the thought and silently stared out to sea.

"Look, it's getting late. Will you give me the pleasure of dining with me tonight?"

"Oh, dear. What time is it?"

"It's already 5:30."

"5:30! I completely lost track of time. I need to go. I'm having dinner with my friends tonight. They must be worried about me. My dear Juan, it was so…" She jumped up as she prepared to end the conversation.

Ponce de Léon grabbed her hand.

"Wait! You can't just leave as abruptly as that. How long are you staying here?"

"It's supposed to be two weeks, but if I like it, I'll stay longer. I can do everything I do with a good Wi-Fi connection." She allowed him to continue to hold her hand.

"Give me your phone number and let's try to meet sometime while you're still here. I greatly enjoyed talking with you. You're a very fascinating young woman, don't you know?"

"I'll tell you what. Give me your phone number and we'll see where things lead."

"Yes, that would be better. That's how your grandfather would have done it. Here's my phone number. I very much look forward to your phone call." He gave her his best enchanting smile. She was duly enchanted.

"Yes. Let's indeed see where things lead." She blushed a little.

She squeezed his hand, leaned over, and gave him a kiss on the cheek. Her blushing face became even rosier. She suddenly turned and left. After running for ten seconds, she abruptly stopped. She turned to him, waved, and continued at a gentle pace, with her maidenly hips swerving from side to side. It took several minutes for the hot electric grip on his heart to subside.

CHAPTER TEN

Uncle Pedro

"But Mamá, I don't want to go live with Uncle Pedro. I want to stay here with you, Papá, and the rest of our family. No! I won't go! I'll run away and come back here."

"Fernando! Come talk to your son. He doesn't want to go live with Knight Commander Guzmán."

Juan Ponce de Léon's father entered the living room, picked up his young son, and carried him outside. He sat him down on the wooden bench in the garden. It was a warm Spring day with bees humming among the newly blossomed flowers and fruit trees. His father sat beside him.

"Son, you're already eight years old. You're no longer a small child. There is so much for you to learn. And the time is now for you to learn them. First, never forget you are a descendent of a king, King Alfonso IX of León. That's the origin of our name 'de León'. Always carry your name with pride, but most importantly, you must live your life so as to bring honor to our ancestors and to yourself."

"Yes, Papá, you have told me that many times. I remember it well."

"Good. Now, for the part you probably won't understand well. The next few years are critical for you to prepare for your future when you'll be a father yourself with your own family. You only have a few paths open to you.

"You could be a peasant like the ones who work our fields or like the luckier ones who have a little field of their own. They eke out a living from the unforgiving soil that surrounds us. That certainly is not a life for the descendent of a king."

His words clearly showed that he scoffed at the idea. That was not a choice for his son.

He continued, "Another path is to devote your life to our Lord and the service of the Church. Here you can do two things: you can lock yourself in a monastery where you will pray all day and still labor like a peasant anyway in exchange for a place to sleep and eat. Or you can become a priest at a small church in a small town, trying to lead small people to their salvation like sheep to their nightly pen. You know how Padre Sebastián lives. Is that a path for you?"

He clearly had little respect for the trappings of the Holy Catholic Church.

"Or you can choose the path of Knight Commander Guzmán, the path of glory and action, the path of a military man. In this case, you can either be a footman in the King's armies, used like fodder for pigs, stealing a few coins from the pockets of your slain enemies on the battlefield like a thief. Or you can become a gentleman officer and a leader of men like your uncle, who has earned glory for his name, the respect of his men, and honor from our King. Which path would you prefer? It's time for you to choose."

"Papá! I don't want any of those things. I want to stay home and be like you. Why can't I follow in your footsteps?"

"Ah, now that is the second thing you must learn today. It pains me to explain this to you, but clearly, I must. Fate has not been kind to us. The Almighty, in His benevolent wisdom, is clearly testing us or maybe punishing us for the sins of our forefathers. We can never understand the mysterious workings of our Lord.

"But the simple fact is our life will take a drastic turn for the worse. I will need to sell most of our land in the next few months. I hope to at least keep a few fields of my own and the flour mill. Don't worry. We will survive on the strength of our family name. We'll still have some influence in this small town of ours. But your future will be grinding wheat into flour for the rest of your life. I only have little time to find positions for your brothers and sisters.

"Now here is the good news. Your uncle Knight Commander Guzmán has graciously accepted you into his service as a member of his household, but not as a servant. I could not agree to that. No, he will educate and train you to be a military leader of men and how to succeed in His Majesty's service. You will learn to read and write, as well as all the other liberal arts fit for any noble gentleman.

"Uncle Pedro is away on campaign against the Moors of Grenada. When the campaign season ends in September, you will go to him and start your passage to honor and glory. We will not force you. If you insist on staying with us, that would be fine. That gives you the summer still. But this summer you will not play with your brothers and friends, as you did in the past. A miller has no time for play. You'll work in our flour mill. You'll learn what your future will be. At the end of the summer, you must tell me your chosen path of your life."

Juan stared at his feet, speechless. The usually bright and talkative boy sat in silence with his mind racing in turmoil. He was on the brink of crying.

"I'll leave you now to think all this over. Take the rest of the day to consider the few paths you have. Go visit Padre Sebastián and understand how he lives his days. Watch how the workers in the fields fill their days. You don't need to visit the mill. You will start working there tomorrow from daybreak to nightfall." His father smiled sadly and slowly trudged away.

After finally collecting his thoughts, Juan considered what his father had told him. He knew that the boys of his age with peasant parents were already working the whole day beside them. As for Padre Sebastián, he slept in a small room attached to the old stone church, on a pile of straw on a narrow wooden bed. He would kneel for hours on the stone floor with his back bared, whipping himself until he bled. Besides, the Padre was always trying to hug him and get him to pray together in his private quarters. That just did not seem right and proper.

At dinner that night, Juan stood up and solemnly told his parents that he thought about it and had decided to stay and learn how to be a miller.

His father put his hand on Juan's shoulder. "I don't think you made the right decision. But I'll respect it. You'll start working at the mill tomorrow. As my son, I expect you to work harder than the others. You need to go to sleep soon after dinner. You'll need it for tomorrow." His father gently pressed him back onto his seat and motioned him to eat.

The next morning, shortly after breakfast, when the roosters started to crow, Juan's father led him to the mill. The sun had not even broken through the horizon, and the pre-dawn chill was something new for Juan. His father gave instructions to miller António. He was to treat his son no differently from anyone else.

So, all day, every day, Juan worked at the mill, except for Sunday. But rather than play on that day of rest, all he wanted to do was sleep. He led the donkeys in circles around the grindstone, grinding the grain into flour. He had to feed them and clean up after them. Juan was too small and weak to help with the heavy sacks of grain and flour. He would have preferred that to the mindless, boring drudgery of leading donkeys in circles for fourteen hours a day.

One Sunday after Mass and the Sunday meal, Juan dropped to his knees and cried. He did not want to be a miller, but a military man like his uncle. Juan's mother's eyes pleaded silently with her husband. After five minutes of sobbing, Juan's father finally broke the silence.

"Really? How do I know you're not just being lazy, shirking the important training for your future life as a miller?"

"No, no, Papá! That is no life for me. I understand that now."

"Prove to me you're being sincere. You can't change your mind afterwards."

"I am sincere, completely! Please, please tell me how I can prove it to you?" He kneeled, staring at the floor, trying to stop the tears from rolling down his cheeks. After all, military men do not cry, but the tears continued, just the same.

"All right, fine. I'll tell you what I'll do. Every officer in His Majesty's army can ride a horse. I will teach you how to ride. I'll give you just two weeks. If you don't take it seriously and can't ride after that time, back to the mill you go. I will ask Knight Commander Guzmán to accept your brother instead. How does that sound?"

His mother gasped at such a short time to learn how to not only stay on a horse, but to bend it to the rider's will. Fernando shook his head quickly at her with a look indicating the discussion was over. As for Juan, he stood up, wiped the tears from his eyes, and solemnly assented to his father's offer.

The next day, his father led him to the stables and chose one of the smaller horses for Juan. After some basic instruction, he helped his son on to the horse. On his own horse, Fernando led them toward the horses' favorite meadow. Juan's horse sensed where they were heading and galloped off. With a slight lifting of his hindquarters, the horse easily tossed Juan onto the ground.

"No, no, son! Control the horse. Show him you are in command. Every action must be done with decisive authority. Every movement of the reins, every movement on the saddle, every movement of your feet in the stirrups, all must be performed like the leader you're to become."

Juan was tossed off several more times that day. His father said nothing, but his disappointed shake of his head spoke volumes. Every time, Juan climbed back onto the horse and tried harder. Finally, his father told him to not get back on but to take the reins and see if he could at least lead the horse back to his stable on foot. Juan tried to hide his tears of frustration, his tears of failure.

The next morning, his father called him for breakfast. Juan was so sore from falling onto the ground a dozen times that he was so tempted to quit. But then he remembered the dreadful drudgery working at the mill. He forced himself up from bed and back to training how to ride the terrible beast. At breakfast, Juan's father reminded him of the great El Cid and his many famous exploits. There were statues of him in many surrounding town squares. Every child knew his tragic but heroic story.

His father concluded with the question: "Do you think the great Cid walked through his adventures? What is he sitting on in all the statues in his honor? Well, what?"

"A horse, Papá, a horse. I promise I'll do better today."

And he did. At the end of the two weeks, he could control his horse even at the gallop. It was empowering to bend the enormous beast to his will. Trot, then gallop, turning to the left, to the right, stopping, starting. The power, the speed, the wind blowing through his hair, it was simply exhilarating.

Fernando took a more personal interest in his son, who could now ride with him to inspect the fields, check on the mill, visit nearby towns, have picnics by country streams, just to be together. He knew that when he delivered his oldest son to the Knight Commander, he would probably never see him again.

The summer passed all too soon. Juan came to know his father for the first time in his young life. His attitude turned from fear and respect to affection. It was still not love. Love between father and son was still centuries away. Overcoming the conflict of the roles they were required to play was too overwhelming for them both. The same held true for mothers and daughters. However, love between mother and son was normal, as was affection between father and daughter.

The fateful day came when the messenger arrived, informing them that the Knight Commander was expecting his new page within the week. Fernando was gripped with remorse when he read the message, but he knew he was doing the right thing. He loaded his family into a simple carriage for the eight-hour journey to the Castellan capital of Valladolid. The distance was only fifty-two miles, but it could just have been 1000 miles away. It was rare for someone to travel even ten miles from their villages.

Uncle Pedro treated them kindly and with generosity. He showed them their quarters for the night in the big manor house, where they could rest before the feast that was prepared in their honor. The Knight Commander invited many of his fellow Knights of the Order of Calatrava, of which he was their commander. This was a great honor to dine with so many heroes of the wars with the Moors. Uncle Pedro led Juan by the hand and introduced him to everyone as his new page, who would learn to be a squire in his service and eventually be a knight himself, a Knight of the Order.

The next morning, after breakfast, Juan's family lined up and said their farewells to him. His mother, crying the whole time at losing her oldest son, hugged him closely until she had to acknowledge that this was best for the boy and released him. She would lose her son, but he would gain an honorable life. It was a sacrifice that a mother could understand. Juan stood by Uncle Pedro, his mind in a fog, overwhelmed by everything.

The Knight Commander took Fernando aside and confirmed their agreement. Juan would still be Fernando's son, but he would serve as a page in the household of the Knight Commander. In exchange, Juan would be educated as a noble gentleman and trained as a military leader of men.

He concluded, "Fernando Ponce de Léon, I know this must be hard for you, but it's the best for the boy. These straitened times must be tough for you. I would not have accepted this arrangement if it were not for our blood ties. Here, take this. This should help you arrange something for your other children. If the Lord wills it, have a safe and peaceful journey back home."

With this, he placed a heavy sack of coins into Fernando's hands and hurried away before Fernando could refuse. He called for the eight horsemen, who would escort them on their home journey. Fernando knew that his welcome was coming to an end. He squatted down before Juan, squeezed his shoulders, and left him with the words: "You have taken your first steps on your path to honor and glory. You may forget your family one day, but never forget that you are a Ponce de Léon."

His family settled in the carriage and slowly disappeared into a dry cloud of dust. Juan watched them disappear into the distance. Uncle Pedro quietly returned and patiently stood by Juan with his hand on his shoulder until his family was out of sight.

Then, with a pat on the back, he said, "Juan, this must be a lot for you to take in. You have learned the important lesson that nothing in life is certain. Change can come at any time. But come. We have no time to waste. This is the first day of your new journey to great triumphs and wonderful adventures."

CHAPTER ELEVEN

Infatuation

The next morning, Ponce de Léon awoke to the buzz of a small plane flying overhead. He had a very restless night, tossing and turning, all the while thinking about Isabel. As hard as he tried to put her out of his mind, her beauty and sing-song voice constantly crept back in. He turned over and noticed the bedside clock was already past 0800. Time to get up. He could always take a nap later.

He started his day as normal: breakfast on the back veranda overlooking the morning waves with seagulls weaving above them with their high-pitched squawks. He poured a second cup of his favorite Guatemalan coffee and picked up the New York Times that arrived every morning at his doorstep. He tried to read the headlines of the latest political scandal deepening.

The lines blurred. They made no sense. After rereading them five times, he gave up. He simply could not concentrate. His mind drifted back to her. Laughing at himself for being so taken by a woman... again. He wondered what was wrong with him. But his line of enquiry always ended with her, like a mental dead end.

So, what was it about her? That was the question that made more sense to ponder. Sure, she had a perfect body. But the beaches of Florida were full of beautiful young women looking for some adventure during their Spring Break with bodies that would make an old man wish for younger days. It was not just her unblemished skin, her cinnamon eyes and hair, though they helped, too.

Isabel was clearly well-educated. She had the intelligence and self-confidence to engage in witty conversation about subjects that mattered. She was an expert in her field. Yet, her life was mainly found in books and the world of the intellectual. It would be a wonderful challenge to show her the world and educate her in the ways of life. He was an expert in those.

But no, it was something else. He leaned back in his chair, closed his eyes, and gave in to his mind's desire. He replayed their conversation, but ignoring the words spoken. After fifteen minutes, he opened his eyes. He had the answer.

Her face was fresh with the innocence of youth, yet there was a sadness lurking in her eyes. It was the sadness that is the residue from one too many of life's disappointments. This sadness gave her eyes a knowingness that revealed there was much more of it deeper inside her. And then there was the innocence, too. She was still in the confused state between knowledge and dreams, probably how Adam and Eve felt after partaking of the forbidden fruit.

Her voice confirmed this. Her tone of voice held at times the sparkle of an excited little girl describing to her father what she saw at the zoo that afternoon. At other times, there were shades of the temptress, knowing full well her powers over an older man, a femme fatal, using innocence as a lure. What was even better, she was totally unconscious of any of this. He guessed she had one, maybe two, older men in her life who lit a spark within her that wanted to burn with more ardor. By the gods, he wanted to get her in bed!

Isabel clearly had captured his body's interest. But that was never enough. She had done something even greater. She captured his mind's interest. She intrigued him. What to do next? Is there even a next thing? She had his phone number, while he did not have hers. He could only wait for her to contact him. But would she? Why would she?

His day was wasted as he both waited for her call and persuaded himself that she would not. He pulled his phone out about every twenty minutes. Did she call? Was his phone on silent? Maybe she sent a text message? No. Maybe his phone was not working, but there was a strong signal. Maybe her phone was not working. Maybe she forgot to bring her recharger.

To force his mind off the merry-go-round of impotent frustration, he went for a swim in the ocean. He could not bring his phone with him into the sea. Perhaps the salt water would force him to get a grip and stop his silly adolescent anguish.

The swim worked. He managed to pull his mind away from something he had no power to resolve and onto something more mundane. He read the latest real estate report for Florida, concentrating on his next real estate acquisition. He found a few and put them through his analysis, a spreadsheet full of formulae that would indicate a potential winner or not.

Sitting down to the divine dinner that Jorge had made: clams in garlic and white wine, followed by a steak of swordfish, grilled rare with asparagus. Jorge also placed beside him a bottle of the same California Chardonnay that she had the day before. That was all that was needed to spark a flood in his mind with thoughts of her.

Clearly, they were not having dinner that night. It was late by US standards. He never ate dinner before 2000. She was certainly not the late-night dance club type. They were not to meet at all that evening. He sighed and was about to ask Jorge for a second bottle. But then he considered what if she did call him before she went to sleep, laying in her bed, thinking about him, thinking about him lying next to her? He certainly did not want to sound anything but his suave mature man of the world voice.

What could he do? He went for an hours-long walk on the beach under the pale moonlight, letting the sound of the waves sooth his disappointment. Staring at the reflection of the moonlight stretching across the quiet sea calmed him. As he always did in such circumstances, he became philosophical. Putting everything back in order in his mind, he was ready to go to sleep. He returned to his bed, drove her out of his mind, and slept soundly.

The next morning, he awoke to the faint smell of bacon sizzling in the kitchen downstairs. Jorge was making breakfast. Five minutes later, he was sitting on his veranda in his bathrobe, watching the sun slowly drift higher on the horizon. In front of him sat a plate with a large mushroom and cheese omelet and a smaller plate stacked with bacon. There was a basket of warm fresh bread made with spelt and butter ready to melt into the bread's rough surface. The first Guatemalan double espresso of the day was placed beside him as soon as he lifted his fork.

Many doctors would not approve of such a large daily dose of cholesterol. But then, those doctors do not rejuvenate their bodies once a year, cleaning and detoxing them to be as pristine as a newborn baby's. The body weight would return to what is perfect for the age chosen when the glowing blue liquid passed the lips. He could eat and drink whatever he wanted as long as it did not kill him before the next annual retreat.

After Jorge cleared the table, Ponce de Léon unfolded the New York Times and caught up on the latest sorrows of the world. For his second double espresso, he continued reading for the rest of the morning the third novel, Only After Dark, by his favorite author, Thomas H Murray. He was so engrossed in the story that he forgot the hour until his stomach reminded him it was approaching lunch time.

Living a life of leisure does not mean looking leisurely. It was way past time to get dressed. Ponce de Léon rose from the table, carrying his book and empty coffee cup into the house. He filled the rest of the time before lunch, checking emails and the other flotsam that the ocean of the internet tosses up to his conscience.

Jorge normally served lunch at 1300 and that day it was grilled lamb with mint sauce as they eat it in New York and Philadelphia. Baby potatoes and grilled aubergine moistened with olive oil poured on top rounded out his lunch. By 1400, he was ready for his afternoon walk along the beach. The sea breeze and the ocean waves were perfect for keeping everything in perspective.

Back home by 1500, he busied himself with whatever piqued his interest. He was studiously ignoring his cell phone. He normally put it on silent mode. At the end of the day, he would check his voicemail. If there was no voice mail, then the call was clearly not important. He accepted the world only on his terms. Yet, even so, the world would sometimes barge into his life without being invited.

Sometime late that afternoon, Ponce de Léon's peaceful silence was broken by a woman's voice calling his name from the veranda. "Juan? Juan? Are you there?" After a few seconds, he realized that was the voice of the woman that he had driven from his mind. She had forced herself back into it.

He rushed to the open sliding doors that led down to the veranda and stepped out. There she was, dressed in an evening gown with her high-heeled shoes in one hand and a small stylish purse in the other, somehow looking even more radiant than he remembered her in a bikini. She had walked along the beach in her bare feet so as not to destroy her shoes to the place she remembered to find him.

"There you are! Why don't you answer your damn cell phone? If you're not interested, then just answer your phone and tell me. It's damn rude to not answer and ignore me." She clearly was upset, but was dressed as if things might just work out after all. Her rouged, pouting lips made his heart leap.

He quickly descended the stairs to her. "Oh, my dear Isabel! I'm so glad to see you!" He explained his cell phone habits. "I held my cell phone all day yesterday, hoping you would call. But you never did. I naturally concluded that you weren't interested after all. Today I decided to return to my usual daily routines and habits. Normally, my phone is on silent mode. So, why didn't you call?"

Realizing the silly misunderstanding, she dropped her pout and smiled. "My cell phone lost all its power, and I forgot to bring my recharger. After searching all day, I found a place that sold the one that fits my phone. But it was already too late. I didn't want to disturb you."

"Oh, you could never disturb me. Let's not just stand here. Come in! Come!" He took her by the hand and led her into his home. He said to himself, This is exactly why I dress myself every day. Never know who might show up at my doorstep.

Before she stepped in, she brushed off the sand from her feet and put on her shoes, swaying gently as she followed him to wherever he was leading her.

"Come sit here on the sofa. Jorge! Come here. Jorge, we have a very special visitor."

Jorge quickly appeared. "Tell Jorge what you would like. The same the first time we met?"

"No. I'll have whatever you suggest is best at this time of day in your wonderful home."

"Late afternoon is the time for sherry and aged goat cheese."

"That sounds wonderful."

Jorge nodded and turned to the kitchen. He knew what to prepare.

"You're quite elegantly dressed. Not exactly beachwear."

"This? Well, yes, it's definitely not beachwear. I thought I might try once more and just show up late enough in the day to see if I could invite you to dinner at the place of your choosing. You know, like in the old-fashioned way before telephones, since they clearly were not working."

"You probably don't remember those days, but it would be considered most unseemly for a young woman to show up at the doorstep of an older man. You would have a reputation to protect, and the entire neighborhood would titter about it for the rest of the year."

"Oh, no! I'm so sorry. Did I do it all wrong?"

"No, don't worry. We happily no longer live in those days. Young women are all so liberated now, and no one cares what they do anymore."

Jorge arrived pushing an elegantly carved wooden cart with crystal decanters of golden sherry surrounded by small plates of various kinds of cheese, thinly sliced presunto (smoked ham), and water crackers with sea salt and cracked black pepper. He poured out two glasses and slowly retreated.

Ponce de Léon placed one of the glasses in her hands. "I doubt you ever had anything like this." He clinked her glass. "Salud! Or, as your grandfather would say, saúde! To your health."

She took a sip, smiled, and sank back into the thick leather sofa. "You're right. I've never had anything like this. I'm afraid the range of my life experiences is so limited."

He took one of the small silver forks and stuck a piece of presunto (thinly cut smoked ham) on it. "Now, try this. Coming from the Azores, I doubt your grandparents ever had the joy of tasting presunto. But because you are my guest, you now have the pleasure."

She took the fork and placed the savory ham in her mouth and let it melt with all of its delightful flavors around her tongue. "That's simply divine. It's times like these that I am so happy to have avoided the popular fad of my generation to be vegans or whatever it is they're not eating this week."

"Ah, you successfully passed my vegan test. Just teasing. You did not run out the door offended at the sight of a plate of meat and dairy products. As I tell vegans and vegetarians, the only reason these domesticated animals exist at all is because they have an economic value. And they have an economic value only because we buy their products to eat."

"I know vegans who make exceptions to eat fish."

"Do they think fish grow on trees at the bottom of the sea? If anything, they should take issue with eating a wild animal who was not raised to be eaten, but to swim freely in their natural habitat, free of fishermen and fish markets."

"Yes, you're right, of course. Maybe they think of fish as a lower life form than mammals and don't quite count."

"Fine, but is a fish a lower life form than a chicken or a duck?"

"Of course not. But they would add that herds of cows and sheep produce methane, which is bad for the environment."

"You mean gas? Let me tell you, there is much more methane gas produced by the population of our cities than all the world's herds combined."

She continued playing the devil's advocate. "Another thing they would assert is that the amount of land and other resources that herds require are far more than growing plants."

"I've heard all these arguments before. The land that sheep, cows, and goats graze on is not at all suitable for growing anything else. The land is dry, only suitable for thin grass. It's not an apples-to-apples comparison. What it would take to irrigate and fertilize that land to make it suitable for anything else would greatly surpass what is required for our hooved friends to live on. Ten thousand years ago, we already figured out what use was best for what land."

"Juan, trust me. You're preaching to the choir. I see you're a thinking man, my favorite kind." She smiled.

"Yes, I am a thinking man, and that's not always for the best. Most people don't think beyond the first layer of the onion. Most of the time, they don't want to know what's just below the surface, let alone what's buried deeper. I guess life's simpler that way. Glad to hear we're on the same page. So, now we can change the subject. Tell me more about yourself. Where were you born, how were you raised, whatever you would like to share."

"There's not much to my story, at least not much yet, and I intend to change that. I was born in Newark, New Jersey, near where my Azorean grandparents first landed. There is a sizeable population of Portuguese and now Brazilians there. But it's an ugly city, full of warehouses and a very busy airport. The rail line from New York to points south passes through with the elevated tracks dominating the city's main thoroughfare, slicing it in half from north to south with a clattering, dreary, dark rail line."

"Yes, I've been there. But at least you can get a plate of that wonderful Portuguese salted cod, called bacalhau, from one of the many superb Portuguese restaurants there. They say there are more recipes for it than days of the year. But you're right about the train tracks. They should have put that whole thing underground years ago. Go on."

"My grandparents and even my father were so embedded in their traditions. My mother joined in as something quite exotic to her. As for me, I was third generation and could not relate, really. I had enough of the three 'F's' of Portugal: Fado, Fatima, and Football (Soccer). My father was a manager of one of the myriads of warehouses. It would have been scandalous for my mother to work. She was happy to play her role.

"I was raised in a dingy lower middle-class family in a house the exact same size and style as all the others on my street, with a small garden and a swing set with a sliding board in the backyard. Newark is not a small town sitting in the shadow of New York across the river, but it sure seemed that way to me. So, at age eighteen, I jumped ship for Chicago and its great university. And I've been a student ever since."

"I'm sure there's more to it than that. But I get the picture. So, what is it you want to do in life, continue on the path of academia, become a professor of Iberian Studies somewhere?"

"Yeah, if you asked me that last week, that's what I would have answered. But lately the thought of being an Iberian Studies professor at some small college in Kansas, teaching Don Quixote and elementary Spanish year after year, has given me a suffocating feeling, exactly like Newark used to do.

"My social circle is full of the same academics with the same prospects. The best we can come up with for a vacation is a nice Florida beach for a week or two. None of us has the means to try anything more adventurous.

"But you, my dear sir, are completely different from anyone I've ever met. I see different worlds and eras floating in your eyes. I feel you could open doors to life for me. Doors that I could only dream of stepping through. But please understand something very important. I don't give a rat's ass about a big house and car with unlimited money. Not at all. What I want is to see, no, experience life while I still have my youth. If I'm being too forward or silly for you, then no harm, no foul. I will just finish this glass of ambrosia and be on my way."

Isabel sat back in silence, prepared to be shown the door. She never had opened herself to a man like that before, and he was nearly a perfect stranger. She kicked herself for blurting all that out, thinking: how foolish I must sound.

Ponce de Léon was surprised by the young woman's plea to live life, to live it to its fullest. It was the desperate cry from a sensitive mind still full of a child's curiosity to explore the world, but also sensing that time was not on her side. Her cheeks appeared to be blossoming with the blush of youth, but in fact was the blush of embarrassment.

Her eyes were tightly closed, as she hoped not to be ushered out the door. She was clearly interested in whatever he could show her. She gave her best pitch, and the ball was fast approaching him. What to do?

He decided to swing. "Well, dear Isabel, that is quite a lot to take in. Let's continue with a few tentative steps and see where we end up. Would you like that?"

She opened her eyes with her face radiant with excitement. "Oh, yes, I would!"

"Fine. So, first things first. We will have dinner together, but at no other place than my dining table. Jorge is the best chef in this town, and we could do no better than eating right here. But it's still too early for dinner. Let's continue our chat."

"We have so much to talk about and you have so much to teach me. Let's continue by you telling me about your place of birth and youth."

"That's fair. I was born in a small town, Santervás de Campos, in the province of Valladolid, in Spain. I guess you could say my family was also middle class, starting as upper, but due to a series of unlucky events, sank slowly to the lower level of that class. We were farmers in a small agricultural town that was losing its population every year. I was the oldest of six.

"My parents were good people, though I think my father was probably too hard on me and my mother too soft. When I was eight, hardship hit my family and my father sent me to be raised by my uncle, who was an important military man in the hierarchy of things. I followed in his footsteps and joined the army while still a teenager.

When I got out, I found a life on the sea and journeyed my way through with adventures and experiences, both good and bad. But they have all made me the man I am today. I think it's time to refill your glass…"

CHAPTER TWELVE

A Page in a Knight's Court

Crowing roosters woke young Juan from his deep sleep. The excitement of the previous day's events, the separation from his parents, harkening his new life, exhausted him. The sun's first rays were seeping in through the cracks in the wooden shutters. The sounds of the other boys stirring awake reminded him of where he was.

He looked up at the still dark wooden rafters above him and wondered what was next. He was already home-sick and missed his familiar straw-stuffed bed. Stifling the tears welling up, he remembered his father's parting words reminding him that he was a Ponce de Léon. He felt an indistinct pride but was not sure what it really meant to have such a surname. The fear of the other boys seeing him cry was a much more powerful deterrent.

There were sixteen boys, aged from seven to fourteen, who each had a hard wooden bed with just a folded blanket serving as a mattress. The beds were in two rows along the walls of the barracks-like building. There were two fireplaces at each end where the older boys slept. Juan was one of the youngest and, so, he slept in the middle, furthest from the fireplaces. Being still September, they were not needed yet.

Soon Juan would learn that he lived in a military world where hierarchy was all important. The higher one rose in the ranks, the more small perks they would have, like sleeping closer to the heat of the fire. Everything was designed for one to strive to a higher level in the order of things. In all of medieval society, it was the military that was the most merit based. So, training and learning better than the others was valued. Juan was starting a year later than the few seven-year-olds sleeping by him. Being older, he had to prove himself better than the tykes.

They were pages in the service of a great knight. They would carry on such duties as a child could perform, but always with the intention that the service was part of his growing into his future role as a knight. He never performed any drudge work such as those who worked in the kitchen, in the laundry, or on the sprawling grounds.

He would carry messages from and to the important adults managing everything or even to close destinations like to town. He would help his lord dress, clean his armor and weapons, care for the horses and hounds, serving him at events like hunting expeditions, and basically be at his beck and call for anything else. None of this was demeaning. It was a great honor.

Juan found himself assigned to the stables and the kennels to care for the denizens of those places. He loved animals and thought it was the best of all possibilities. Besides, he intended to have his own stables and kennels one day and needed to learn all about caring for them. It was an endless cycle of feeding, cleaning, walking them. He learned how to saddle a horse and care for it before and after long rides. He mastered how to clean and buff saddles, and taking care of all the other parts that would encumber a medieval horse, like stirrups, bridles, reins, etc. Luckily, there were other boys tasked with doing the same.

In exchange for half a day of service, the rest of his days were filled with training and studies. He trained in the use of the arms of the age, starting with the sword, first wooden, then blunt metal ones, and eventually the real thing many years later. He trained to feint, block, thrust, slash, and the other tactics to maim and kill an opponent. Then came pikes, maces, and axes.

He learned to care and train hawks, to care for armor, and to ride horses. Fortunately, his father's challenge to avoid working in the flour mill put him way ahead in this area of training. He could ride nearly as well as the older boys and much better than the younger ones. The hardest part for him was the hawks: nervous, independent, highly intelligent birds with exceptionally sharp beaks and talons.

To hold rank in polite society required one to be educated. The personal priest of his uncle's family had an assistant monk who was tasked to teach reading and writing in both Latin and the Castilian Spanish of the royal court. However, being literate was not nearly enough. He learned to sing and play musical instruments like the lute and the recorder. He learned how to write poetry and put it to music. His favorite class was mastering the game of chess.

Over the years, he would receive the rudiments of what was called a liberal education. Though he could not compete with the university students, at least he would understand enough to say something intelligent if faced with any of the seven subjects: grammar, logic, rhetoric, arithmetic, music, astronomy, and geometry. His uncle considered himself a renaissance man and hired the best experts he could find in their fields of study, while not overstepping the boundaries of what the Church considered acceptable.

The days and the seasons passed quickly. By the time he was fourteen, Juan was the finest horseman, chess player, poet, and musician of his cohort. He could hold his own in armed combat. He overcame his distrust of hawks, and they did the same of him. He developed a close relationship with the third hawk he was given. The one weakness he had was that he could never quite get the hang of hounds.

Uncle Pedro took a keen interest in Juan and trained him personally, much to the jealousy of his mates. This often led to all manner of pranks and conflicts with them. But since Juan was better at hand-to-hand combat than the others, after many fisticuffs, their jealousy turned to admiration. He became their unofficial leader. In return, he would share with them what his uncle taught him.

The Knight Commander noticed these things from a distance. He was secretly pleased to see that his young nephew was already becoming a natural leader of his peers. Considering Juan's general excellence in his training and studies, during a formal ceremony in the manor house assembly room in his fourteenth year, Juan was raised to the rank of a squire.

Everyone of Knight Commander Guzmán's large household gathered in the great hall. Many knights of the Order came, too. Juan kneeled on the stone floor before his uncle's feet. After numerous exhortations and benedictions, Juan felt his uncle's hands gently on his head. Juan felt a surge of energy pass through him, an elation at the honor of being a squire, one step before becoming a knight in the Order.

His uncle took him by the hand, raised him to his feet, and turned him to face the cheering throng crowding the hall. It was the happiest day of Juan's life. It occurred to him that he had not thought of his family for several years. And yet, there in the back, was his father's face, barely visible through all the faces bobbing before him. It was unmistakably him.

As everyone slowly moved to the feast room, Juan tried to squeeze his way to where his father had stood. But he was nowhere to be seen. Was he mistaken? He preferred to think he was not. Suddenly memories and the longing of homesickness filled his heart. He was too old to cry and would not dare, in any case. He felt it would be better to be alone and go for a long walk, remembering his childhood, lost in nostalgia. But that would have to wait.

Uncle Pedro found him. "What are you doing here by yourself looking so sad? This is a great day for you, a day to celebrate. What's wrong?"

"Uncle Pedro, did my father come today to see the event? I thought I saw him in the back of the crowd?"

Knight Commander Guzmán considered how to answer that. If he told his nephew 'yes', he took the risk that the boy would become homesick and lose concentration on his training, or even worse, want to return home. He did not want to risk losing his rising protégé.

If he replied 'no', then the boy may become sad or angry that his family had forgotten him. This may lead to homesickness and wanting to return home to force them to remember him. In the end, he decided to play it safe.

"I really don't know, nephew. I didn't see him. If he came, he didn't tell me and, in any case, he seems to have left already. Come, you are wanted at the feast table. We cannot start without you. We have some important guests. Let's not keep them waiting." He gave a reassuring pat on Juan's back.

Juan smiled and rose. He decided that he should concentrate on the present and his future. The only fact of his past that he never forgot was that he was a Ponce de León. Walking beside his uncle, he banned any trace of nostalgia and homesickness from his mind.

Knight Commander Guzmán held the modern equivalent rank of General. He was the son and grandson of two Grand Masters of the Order of Calatrava. The Order was the first monastic military order founded in Castile by the Cistercian monks in the twelfth century. A military order was an order of monks who organized themselves as knights to defend Christendom against heretics and pagans, in their case the Muslim Moors who once ruled most of the Iberian Peninsula. They were similar to the Templar Knights.

The knights lived as monks, taking the vows of their religious order. Initially, this meant a vow of poverty and chastity. Centuries later, they received papal dispensation to marry, but remain chaste. Then the rules became to be chaste only three days a week. By Uncle Pedro's time, no one cared to ask how many days of chastity they followed. Indeed, it would have been considered a rude, even a vulgar question.

With every success in war, the King would give them, in true feudal practice, more lands and the people who lived on them. By the time Juan became a squire in the Knight Commander's service, the Order had land and towns with a population of over 200,000 and the income from them. Clearly, the vow of poverty was lost somewhere along the way. But they could field an army of 2,000 knights at short notice.

As the tide of history turned against the Moors in the Iberian Peninsula, the Castilian kings used the Order to maintain their power in the many dynastic wars against their fellow Iberian Christians. A few generations after Knight Commander Guzmán, the Order would slowly disappear into oblivion, becoming by modern times a sad caricature of their once glorious past.

But when Juan was a page and squire, there were still wars to be fought driving the Moors from their remaining stronghold in Granada to the south and a major dynastic war between Afonso V King of Portugal and Ferdinand King of Aragon for the prize of the Kingdom of Castille. All these conflicts were successfully concluded by 1493 when Juan would join Columbus' second voyage to the New World. A voyage that would drastically change his life.

Squire Juan still had much serious training to do before he could take part in these momentous events. First, he moved into the squire's quarters in a part of the manor house, where each one had their own room and a charcoal burner for warmth. They were very similar to monk cells. They were expected to live like monks, chaste, pure, with nothing to their name.

Many of Juan's fellow monk squires would find solace in the arms of the various household milk maids, laundry girls, and kitchen lasses, who sought temporary escape from the drudgery they were sentenced to. They doubted the promises the squires made that they would make honest ladies and wives of a Knight of the Order, but it was still great to dream of a better life. Juan never indulged. Being discovered meant instant expulsion. Juan had more important dreams to follow of his own.

As a squire in the Knight's service, he continued his training and studies from his days as a page to an even higher level. He was now a knight in training. As such, he performed duties much more significant and worked even closer to his benefactor and master.

Juan was the favored protégé of the Knight Commander and not because he was a nephew. Juan had proven himself to be the finest page and soon the best squire in his service.

Juan carried his uncle's shield or sword during important ceremonies. In processions, Juan carried the banner of the Order. He made sure the pages did an excellent job caring for the horses, properly placing the saddle placed before his uncle mounted up, cleaning his armor, sharpening weapons, and generally oversaw the activities of the pages. Juan would also dress his uncle in armor, which was impossible to adorn by oneself.

Juan rode his own horse, always prepared to give it to his uncle to ride, if anything happened to his uncle's horse. This meant that Juan's horse was equivalent to his uncle's. Juan was always by the side of Uncle Pedro at any official event. Juan's favorite event was the excitement of the annual tournament. It was all there: the pageantry, the crowds, the mock but highly dangerous combat between different teams of knights on foot, and most importantly, the jousting to determine the most honored place in the hearts of all, to be praised and sung by bards for years later.

CHAPTER THIRTEEN

And So It Began, Again

"Dinner is served, Capitán." Jorge announced in a near whisper, standing behind the sofa.

"Well, let's go see what Jorge whipped up on such short notice."

Juan led Isabel to the formal dining room where the table could sit thirty. As with all the other furniture in his home, everything was solid wood of an exotic type. The dining table was mahogany. One could also find items made of ebony, rosewood, teak, brazilwood, cherry, ironwood, cedar, etc. Two great crystal chandeliers hung above the table, illuminating the room. Candelabras on the table and large candles, each on their tall carved wooden stands, lit up the room in a golden glow.

"Oh, candles! This is turning into a romantic evening." Isabel was clearly impressed by everything.

Jorge served at a slow pace a seafood soup, a taurine of couscous and lamb, roasted asparagus, concluding with a chocolate mousse.

They continued their conversation. "Tell me about this incredible collection of antiques that fills your home. They all appear to be many hundreds of years old, from Spanish colonial to Art Nouveau. It seems you haven't bought any furniture for over 100 years."

"Furniture designers lost me with Art Deco. As for the antiques filling my home, well, most are family heirlooms. The

Spanish colonial furniture has been in the family since we first settled here nearly 500 years ago. Many of the things hanging on the walls, like those pikes and shields, for example, have been around as long as the furniture.

"I admit they make my home much darker and ponderous than modern interior decoration, but I just can't rid myself of them. I tried to lighten things up with more of an Art Nouveau look. Perhaps I need an interior decorator to explain to me what I need to do. But even so, I would be loath to rid myself of these things which all have their own story. None of the older items were bought in a store but came to my family in various ways."

"Oh, no. Please don't change a thing. I wasn't complaining. If anything, your taste deserves praise. This is your home and not any interior decorator's. It should be exactly as you like it, no more nor less. Do you know the stories of these things? I'd love to hear some."

"Why, yes, I do know the stories, as they have been passed down to me. For example, those pikes and shields on the wall there were used in the defense of St. Augustine against English raids in the 1600's. A cabinetmaker who settled here from Seville made this dining table in 1763. The mahogany wood came from Honduras.

"That ornate pipe on the fireplace mantel was a personal gift from the headman of one of the Calusa tribes on the western side of the Everglades to one of my early colonial ancestors. He had spent years of friendly persuasion through trade and diplomacy to forge a peace treaty with those prickly people, succeeding in the end through personal friendship, but mainly by completely ignoring religion. He was also one of the few representatives of the Spanish crown to deign to learn to speak their language.

"There must be more to how he won over the chief."

"The secret was through food. My ancestor cooked a fine omelet in the best Spanish way for the chief with whatever he had on hand. For the next morning's breakfast, the chief made his version of an omelet for my ancestor, using what local ingredients he thought would make it better. It was quite delicious, actually, though it could have used more salt."

"More salt? I love your special personal touches in your stories. You embellish your stories with the most amazing details."

"Embellish? That's how it came down to me, anyway. The painting of the nude laying on a divan in a jungle hanging above the fireplace is by Henri Rousseau. It came to the family by marriage in 1912. Jacqueline was her name. She was the daughter of one of France's successful industrialists and the wife of the Mayor of Paris.

"After the mayor resigned from office in disgrace, he fled with his early teenage mistress and his embezzled fortune to the Amalfi Coast of Italy. Jacqueline divorced him. Being a free woman, barely out of her teens herself, she decided, after the stifling, musty air of the political salons of Paris, she needed the fresh winds of adventure. She decided the US was adventurous enough without being too far from civilization when she would need it.

"She ended up in St. Augustine at the behest of her father, who wanted to explore certain real estate opportunities that Florida presented at the time. That's how she met my great grandfather. She fell in love with his combination of old world sophistication and his new world daring adventurousness. Well, that's what she told him, anyway. I guess he had a way with women.

"They married and she brought this painting into the family. She was quite a passionate woman. He had little energy to do anything else. Alas, she died of yellow fever at thirty-four..." His voice fell into silence.

"You seem sad. You really are a sensitive one, feeling sad for your great grandfather's loss."

"Yeah, well, I get carried away sometimes. Shall I continue?"

"Yes, but please, nothing sad."

"OK, fine. The chandeliers came from Bohemia in the early 1700's. They were bought for the family home that was in the center of the city. The city condemned the house as unlivable 200 years later. The city government bought it and gave us this land on the beach, which was quite undeveloped at the time. I consider it a fair deal, as the old house was indeed falling down."

"The dinners these chandeliers must have seen!"

"My grandfather told me a story regarding a dinner in the old home. It goes like this: His family was on good terms with the city mayor. He held a feast to celebrate the mayor's reelection. After dinner, everyone retired to the veranda for cigars and port.

"Mice lived within the walls and had holes where they could go in and out. One such mouse was hungry and saw all the crumbs and bits of cheese which had fallen on the floor under the table. He ran under the table and started eating the tasty morsels. Suddenly, the family cat sees him and chases him back into his hole, nearly catching him.

"The mouse is still hungry but does not dare to try again. After some time, he hears the family dog barking. Because the family dog would always chase the cat away, he knew it was safe to go out to eat some more. He runs out of his hole and is immediately grabbed by the cat. The cat glares at him, squeezing his claws ever so tightly, and says to the mouse, 'Isn't it great to speak foreign languages?'"

Isabel laughed so hard she nearly fell off her chair. "Oh, that's great! I wasn't expecting that. I thought you might tell me a true story."

"It is true, exactly as my grandfather told me."

"Come on! How can that be?"

"The cat told him all about it."

This brought more laughter. Ponce de León enjoyed immensely the effect his joke had on her. It pleased him to bring her such pleasure. As for her, the wine, the food, the candles, and her charming host slowly had their effect. She decided she would have to see more of this intriguing, worldly man.

She also knew that the only thing interesting about her was her maidenly charms. She had to play the age-old game to ensure his interest beyond just a dinner and a night together. Regardless, he was rising quickly in her estimation.

"Dear Juan, it really is getting late, and my friends must be worried. I told them I would be back two hours ago, and it's nearly midnight. So, I will bid you a good night. Will you call me if I give you my phone number? If you aren't too bored with me, perhaps we can meet again tomorrow?"

"Isabel, there would be nothing I would prefer to do than meet you again. Why don't you call me when you're ready? I would drive you back, but I had more wine than any driver should have. I'll call you a taxi."

While waiting for the taxi, he showed her more rooms on the ground floor: a study, a library with floor to ceiling bookshelves, a guest bedroom, the kitchen, etc. The taxi driver interrupted them with his phone call, announcing his arrival. Ponce de León opened the gate from beside the front door so the taxi could drive up to the front door. As he showed her out, she suddenly hugged him and kissed his cheek. She whispered, "Thank you for a truly wonderful and completely delightful evening."

The perfume of her hair brushing his face and her breasts pressed firmly against his chest filled him with desire. He answered with a whisper, "Until tomorrow."

She nodded with a serene smile and entered the taxi. She waved to him as the taxi pulled away. Oh, dear. What am I getting myself into? He murmured to himself as the taxi disappeared into the darkness.

Later that night, Ponce de León tossed and turned, unable to sleep. It was not because of the excitement of a new relationship with a beautiful special woman, but rather the dread of it. He had traveled that road dozens of times and it always ended in sorrow. He decided he would have none of it. It would be better to face immortal youth alone. With that problem resolved, he fell into a deep sleep, until the sea gulls and the waves under a late morning sun awoke him.

He happily went about his day. Blissfully ignoring his cell phone. During his after lunch walk along the beach, he let out a long sigh and his chest relaxed. It was best to be free of emotional entanglements. The experience of the night before was a close call. He asked himself why he so easily falls for the first beautiful young woman who knocks on his door? A smile crossed his lips as he was relieved that wisdom overcame passion.

Back in his study, he was internet surfing for several hours. A random question would pose itself in his mind and he would research it. This would, in turn, produce another subject to research until finally he was learning something that was far removed from his original enquiry. It was one of the most enjoyable ways to spend his considerable free time.

Sometime after 1600, Jorge knocked on the open door with Ponce de León's cell phone in his hand. "Your cell phone is ringing, sir."

Before his mind could respond, he leaped from his chair and grabbed his phone. He answered. It was her. His heart leaped. So much for wisdom.

"Hello, my dear gentle Juan. It's me. How are you today? Did you sleep well?"

"Isabel! It's you! Well, yes, of course, it's you. I mean, it's so great to hear your voice. And yes, I did sleep well. Thanks for asking. How about you?"

"I didn't sleep at all well. Was thinking about you and all your wonderful stories. Oh, how I would just love to hear more! And, of course, learn more about you, too. I was thinking that we could have dinner tonight at the new seafood place by Vilano Beach. It would be my treat. Please say yes."

"I would love to dine with you this evening. But on the one condition we do so at my favorite restaurant of all, the one in my home. Jorge is a far better chef than any restaurant by a beach. Also, it would be impossible for a guest to my city to treat me to anything. I will send a driver to pick you up, at say seven?"

"You are making it very difficult for me not to take advantage of you and your generosity."

"My dear young lady, you can take advantage of me whenever and however you want. What do you say?"

"If you put it that way, I can't refuse. I accept. Seven it is. Here is my address …"

And so it began.

CHAPTER FOURTEEN

Mademoiselle Jacqueline, the French Wife

As he did every Sunday, Ponce de León spent the afternoon at his family crypt, remembering his many various wives. He would kneel before each casket and remember the grief and the joy each woman gave him. That Sunday, he kneeled most of the afternoon in front of the final resting place of Jacqueline.

He met his only French wife outside the office of his real estate attorney one April morning in 1912. He had just signed the papers for ownership of a large citrus grove. Though her voice was steady and respectful, her anger showed through.

She was very agitated with one of the real estate agents, who shared the same office as his attorneys. What struck Ponce de León the most was her strongly accented English. It was so beautiful to his ears that he had to stop and listen, ignoring the actual words. He noted there was nothing so beautiful as a French woman speaking English, except maybe a southern woman from Arkansas.

"My dear sir, I specifically told you that my father wants to buy agricultural land. You are only showing me residential land on the beach!"

"Yes, Miss Jacqueline, but the value of oceanfront land will rise and is rising as we speak. I have over twenty-five years of experience in Florida real estate. It would be a much better investment. You just need to explain that to your father. He seems to be a man of the world and would understand better than a ..."

"Better than a woman? That's what you were about to say, wasn't it?!"

"Now calm down, missy. Don't get all emotional. I meant no offense, but there are things that women just do not understand as well as men. Commerce and the ways of the world are such things. Don't you have any brothers? Perhaps your father should have sent one of them. I don't want your father to make a mistake with his money because his daughter just won't see reason."

"Will you stop calling me 'Miss'! I am a full-grown woman. I have seen and experienced much more of the world than you have. As you can see, Mr. Roberts, I am trying to stay calm, but I am losing my patience!"

Just then, Ponce de León decided he should intervene. "Excuse me, madam, I could not help but overhear your conversation. Perhaps I can help."

"Good morning, Mr. León, sir. I am late for another client. Please help the young missy, if you can." Mr. Roberts speedily escaped the irksome female, leaving her in the excellent hands of his partner's best client.

"Good morning to you, too, Jeromy. I'll see what I can do." Turning back to Jacqueline, "I overheard you are interested in buying some agricultural land? What kind specifically? Before you answer that, let me explain that I am not a real estate agent. I will earn nothing from whatever I show you. I am a real estate investor like yourself, but with wide knowledge of real estate in Florida."

"Well, Mr. León, is it? What do you suggest?"

"It depends. Citrus fruit like oranges and grapefruit are growing in popularity in the northern cities. If you prefer not to rely on the vagaries of the weather, then cattle raising is another alternative. I happen to own land of both types."

"Before we go any further, I would not dare take the gentleman's time without recompense. How can I compensate you for your time?"

"The only compensation I would desire would be to spend a day listening to your beautiful French accent."

"Do you speak French? We can speak that, if you think my accent is too thick."

"Indeed, I do speak French, as well as Spanish, Portuguese, and Italian. But then you would be listening to my accented French."

"Impressive, but you're right. We French are quite critical of foreigners speaking our language. So, as you North Americans would say, 'it's a deal'. Let's get started. Lead the way."

Ponce de León had read about the self-confidence and independence of modern French women. The first one he met was a perfect example.

"Yes, madam, right this way. My car is parked right over there." He motioned to one of the few cars parked on the quiet street. It was a new Rolls Royce Silver Ghost equipped with the newly invented electric starter. His driver was wiping the wind shield.

"That? Why, that's the same car my father bought. That's an impressive coincidence. Now let's get one thing straight. You are not to call me 'madame' anymore. My name is Jacqueline, and I am so glad to make your acquaintance."

"Please call me Juan. It just so happens; I bought more citrus groves and was planning to go visit them now. So, first, I'll show you my citrus groves to the south, some distance from the coast. I also will not show you any of my beach front properties. We will have some lunch, which I have already packed in the back. After that, we'll go visit my cattle ranch in the interior to the west of here. We should be back before dinner."

"That would be a wonderful plan. I also trust later for dinner that you can introduce me to the best restaurant this town can offer. I hope it's not French either." She took his hand as he helped her into the back seat. He sat down beside her, and they started their adventure.

It was Spring, so the citrus trees were in blossom, and their delightful fragrance filled the air. Their blossoms buzzed with honeybees. It was already time for lunch. The driver spread a blanket in the shade of an especially perfumed orange tree. He pulled out the enormous picnic basket, opened it, and laid out lunch. It was more than enough for the three of them and three others besides.

He pulled out smoked salmon, Italian cheese and olives from the immigrant's market, baguettes (lucky choice of bread), a mushroom and duck paté, and various other dainties. From a small icebox, he produced a still chilled chardonnay. Another basket produced all the cutlery, plates, napkins, and wine glasses.

'You continue to impress me, Juan." She purred. "I was expecting cold cut sandwiches, not this! Is this how you normally eat?"

"Just because I'm a farmer doesn't mean I have to eat like one."

"A farmer?" She laughed. "Oh, Juan, you have already proved you are much more than that."

"Shall we start? I'm quite hungry. I hope you are, too."

"Yes, but what will your driver eat?"

"Why, my dear, he will eat with us, of course. He has a name, too. Jose, this is Jacqueline from Paris. She will be our guest for the day."

Jose bowed his head, "Enchanté, madame."

Jacqueline was embarrassed over her faux pas. "Of course, you're right. I'm so sorry, Jose, to show my European snobbish classism. It's refreshingly absent here. It would be impossible for my father to have a picnic under a fruit tree in a field in any case, let alone with his driver. That would be scandalous!"

"Unfortunately, things would be different here if Jose was a black man working for someone else. Fortunately, I don't care what color someone's skin is. I treat everyone with the same respect that a member of humanity deserves from another. I've seen too much of life to think differently."

"Yes, that's true. I've seen a lot of that here. The little traveling I have done has shown me the same."

"Now, I have a question for you. Why did you so quickly accept my invitation? How did you know I would not just take you out to the forest and have my way with you? I could have even left you for dead."

"That's simple. I looked into your eyes and saw a sensitive and kindhearted man. I have learned to judge a man by his eyes, not by their color, but by what they reveal of the inner person. Besides, I can't think of a better man than you to ravish me stretched out on a flat rock in the wilds of Florida."

Ponce de León suddenly found himself in uncharted waters. He was speechless at the forwardness of the beautiful young woman sitting so close beside him. His only reaction was to take a few sips from his wineglass to recover his composure.

She giggled and kissed him on the cheek. "I'm so sorry. This is the time to be all business-like. Let's talk about such things at dinner tonight. Jose, pass me that plate of salmon."

"Um… Yes, I agree. Let's stick to why we're here. Do you see all those honeybees? I'll soon set up a honey operation here. The honey from these orange blossoms is simply divine."

Later, they had a romantic dinner of seafood and champagne overlooking the ocean. He did not invite her home that night, nor the next one after another day together sailing on his yacht to Jacksonville and back. After the third day together, she invited herself. She told him that if a man had three chances with a woman and refused her unspoken offers, he was clearly not worth her time. After considering that strange explanation, he graciously proved that she was indeed not wasting her time.

So began a wonderful relationship full of love and spontaneous adventures. Life was full of things like exploring the interior of Florida on horseback and sleeping together by campfire, sailing for months among the Caribbean islands, sleeping on empty white sand beaches, sailing up the Amazon, shopping for Mexican tiles in Veracruz, etc.

Though she resisted at first, finally she relented to show him Paris. It was shortly after the First World War. The streets were full of young men missing their legs, arms, even their minds. He had been to Paris before, but he wanted to see her Paris, the Paris of her happier days. But she could not get past her city recovering from its depressingly hollow pyrrhic victory.

It was a tenuous victory won by the horrors of the endless fetid trenches, the thundering artillery barrages that would drive men to madness, and the creeping deadly gas. Then there were the machineguns. The great invention of the mechanical industrial age where one boy could scythe down hundreds of other boys as they tried once again to run across a hundred yards full of decaying body parts, barbed wire, bomb craters, and mud mixed with the blood of those who tried before to take the opposite trench.

If they managed to cross no-man's land, they would try to kill the equally young boys they encountered by any means possible: pistols, knives, shovels, even their bare hands. A million teenagers would die in a matter of months, like what happened during the Battle of the Somme in 1916, just to change the front lines by just a few miles in one direction or the other.

Things were always peaceful at her father's estate near Fontainebleau, to the south of Paris. Life there during wartime might as well have been on another planet. War was good for business, and this war was particularly good for Jacqueline's father. Her army-aged brothers never had to experience the hell just 150 miles away. Her father disgusted her, but he was still her father. She tried to show Ponce de León the best face of Paris and her family as she could, but she clearly was becoming more upset with each passing day. He cut short their time there and took her home to St. Augustine, promising her they would never cross the Atlantic again.

But throughout everything, their life was full of love and affection. A lot of lovemaking in the most spontaneous locations: on the beach, in the forest, in a sordid hotel room, in the back of the trusty Silver Ghost, in a broom closet, in short, anywhere they found themselves when the feeling moved her. It all ended when she caught yellow fever during a trip through the Panama Canal and after twelve years together, she died at the young age of thirty-four.

Ponce de León smiled at her stone casket and the incredible memories they had made together. He smiled, even as the tears streamed done his face.

CHAPTER FIFTEEN

Together at Last

The taxi dropped Isabel off at Juan's front door right on time for her invitation to a pre-dinner sherry hour. A fire crackling in the fireplace set the right mood. Miles Davis' Some Kind of Blue filled the house with the sounds of his magical trumpet. She was duly impressed, thinking every evening should start exactly like that.

The mood did not call for them to sit on separate sofas. She rose from hers and sat beside him. Soon she snuggled against his shoulder, stroking his hand. "How did you know I love the music of the greatest titan of jazz?"

"You just seem to be a Miles Davis kind of girl. Seems that I guessed right."

"Right as usual. This is how I imagine the start of a perfect evening would be."

"Well, then, we'll just have to continue making it perfect, won't we?"

Dinner was another wonderful gourmet creation, with Juan regaling her with his endless font of stories and anecdotes. After they emptied their last glasses of Port, Isabel rose and took his hand. "I believe it's time to make this evening even more perfect. I think I remember you showed me that your bedroom is this way. Come, gentle Juan, come with me."

She indeed remembered well where his bedroom was. They shared a passion that was dormant for quite some time in both of them. She made love to him unlike anyone else since Jacqueline 100 years ago. With the little experience Isabel had with men, she clearly had been paying attention. Between sensitivity and imagination, she gave him the best gift she could, the gift of passion and pleasure.

He did his best to keep up with her. In the end, he laid back panting with his heart racing to recover from the intensity of their climax. It was experiences like this that made Ponce de León want to continue living with all his physical attributes functioning perfectly.

A golden glow of warmth flowed through him, happy that they had consummated their relationship. Now they could get down to the serious effort of falling in love. For love was what he desired most. He had not had the warm glow of being in love with someone who loved him, at least equally in return for what seemed too long. The fine woman lying beside him with her eyes tightly closed and a grand smile on her lips would be just the one to share love with.

"Oh, by the gods, Isabel! That was incredible! I am so happy that your Frisbee landed in my lap."

"My dear Juan, I am so glad that I landed in your lap." She snuggled close with her head on his chest.

He slowly stroked the back of her head. "I hope this is the start of a wonderful relationship."

"Juan, I think this is the start of a beautiful friendship."

"You just quoted the last line of my favorite movie, Casablanca."

They discussed that wonderful movie with Humphrey Bogart and Ingrid Bergman, the kind of actors they just do not make anymore. An hour later, Ponce de León looked at the clock and exclaimed, "Oh, Isabel, look what time it is! Your friends must be worried about you."

"Don't worry. They aren't. I already told them I wouldn't be sleeping there tonight. Do you mind terribly if we sleep together, listening to the rhythm of our breathing, as we lay with our legs and arms entwined?"

"There would be nothing better I would want to do. But how did you know we would end the day like this?"

"Come on, Juan. I'm not as naïve as I look. I saw the desire in your eyes from the first time I tried to mop up the spilled drink from your chest that the fateful Frisbee had caused. That desire had only intensified with my every visit. We just needed a little tip over the edge. Miles Davis and a crackling fire did it for me. Besides, I know of the unspoken rule of the third date."

"The rule of the third date? What might that be?"

"Many men give a woman three dates and if by the end of the third date nothing happens, he moves on. This was our third date." The explanation echoed what Jacqueline told him so many years before, but in reverse.

"Yes, so it was. But I understand why a man would not want to 'waste' his time with a woman who only wants free dinners when he's looking for something more. Listen to us. This conversation is sinking into a direction I'd rather not follow. Come, let's shower together and fall asleep in each other's arms."

And so started Ponce de León's newest adventure in love and devotion. For the rest of the week, she remained with him. They filled their afternoons with making love to the sounds of waves and seagulls, with the warm sea breeze blowing across their flaming bodies. Breakfast was on the terrace above the ocean with the sun rising in the eastern sky, listening to the joyous music of Vivaldi, followed by walks on the beach.

They discussed plans for when her vacation ended. She preferred to rent her own place and maintain some semblance of independence. He offered her to stay at one of his furnished apartments in the city center. She accepted only if she paid rent. After discussing that ridiculous idea, he agreed in the end that she would provide the wine for their sumptuous Saturday dinners.

From the following week, she only visited him for dinners and breakfasts on weekdays, returning to her apartment during the day to continue with her PhD thesis. She was inspired to finish it as soon as possible and get her degree. She wanted urgently to close that long overdue chapter of her life, so she could start a new one, experiencing life the way it should be. Life beckoned to her with a man who understood it well. There was no better guide to life than Ponce de León.

There was just one caveat. Ponce de León had to be alone every Sunday afternoon when he would spend the day visiting the crypt of his previous loves. He and his men had bought the abandoned church about 100 years before. It came with the old cemetery. They practically rebuilt it. It was their private church where Padre Pedro conducted the services of marriages and funerals, never baptisms. Padre Pedro accepted the men were not church-going believers in any traditional sense. The church was practically unused most of the time, maybe only once a year for Easter near the time of their discovery of Florida. To them, masses and confessions were not necessities of life.

Though Ponce de León had been an official instrument of the imperialism of both the Spanish Crown and the Church in his early pre-Fountain life, the idea never enamored him. He had spent too many years living with the natives of the Caribbean islands and Florida, surrounded by their beliefs. The truth of the matter was that he did those things to satisfy his own sense of adventure and accomplishment. His father's words always echoed in his ears, to never forget that he was a Ponce de León.

With all the evil and nastiness that exists in the world, Ponce de León knew that there could not be one all-powerful, omnipotent God. There either were many gods or none. He had seen too much of life and death to think there was an all-powerful, all-knowing benevolent God perusing the world from above. He could accept a Great Spirit, like a Nature Spirit, similar to what the native peoples believed. That was the extent of his belief system. Yet, he understood perfectly well the need for rituals marking the important milestones of life.

He always returned from his time of remembrance at the crypt in a very morose mood. He would skip dinner and spend the evening locked in his study, alone, as he slowly returned to normal. Clearly, he could never explain to any woman where he went and why. It was just a quirk about him they would have to accept, and they did, though curiosity would always remain.

A month after their wonderful consummation, they became very relaxed and easy with each other. Their relationship was full of passion, but more importantly, they were caring and respectful of each other. They were nice to each other. Being nice was the foundation for a long-lasting love. Even passion falls to embers, eventually. Love was what endured.

At Thursday dinners, they would discuss what special part of Florida far off the beaten path he would share with her on the coming weekend. They would leave late Friday afternoon and return late Sunday morning. Isabel accepted that for some reason Sunday afternoons and evenings were his private time. She continued her own academic work during that time. She estimated that concentrating on the main thread of her dissertation and ignoring all side paths, she could finish in about six months.

The end of May was approaching. Isabel asked him if he would be interested in watching the Memorial Day parade through the center of town with marching bands and floats celebrating the culture of that part of the world. It was the first time he surprised her.

"No, my lovely, I don't do parades. I certainly don't celebrate anything military."

"But this celebrates the end of the Second World War in Europe. That's something that should be celebrated, don't you agree? Besides, it signals the beginning of summer in the minds of people."

"I know what it represents. I just don't do parades. I prefer to celebrate in my own way the things worthy of celebration. All those uniforms: the police, the national guard, even the boy scouts, all remind me of the horrors of war. People become something different when they wear a uniform. They lose themselves and fuse into an organization that has values and goals different from their own personal values, if they dared to think about it."

"Oh, I get it. You told me you were in the military before. Is that where you get your anti-military principles? Have you ever seen combat? Have you ever experienced the horrors of war, as you call them?"

"No, no, of course not. Spain wasn't in any conflicts when I was doing my national service. I was just a grunt, keeping my head down, and patiently waiting for my national service to end, like a prisoner waiting for his jail sentence to be over. I am much too peace-loving to ever fight in a war, certainly never in any combat situation. I guess it's just the principle of the whole thing."

"The principle? I like parades, the pageantry, the spectacle. Oh, come on, Juan. Let's go."

"You're free to go by yourself. I would never insist on something you feel is important. It simply is impossible for me to go. If you insist I go with you, I'm afraid we may have our first disagreeable moment. I really don't want that."

"Oh, very well, my precious man. It's simply not that important to me. Let's go somewhere nice instead." She rose from her chair and hugged his head tightly against her breasts. This always had a calming effect on him.

"Great idea. I tell you what, let's make it a longer weekend. I'll do my Sunday thing on Memorial Day. I think it's more of an appropriate day for me, anyway. Here are some ideas. Tell me which one appeals to you…"

CHAPTER SIXTEEN

The War of the Castilian Succession

The year was 1475. The weak King Enrique IV (Henry in English) of Castile died with only one child, a daughter, Joana, as his heir. Her mother, Enrique's Queen, was the daughter of King Duarte of Portugal (Edward in English). Enrique IV had a half-sister, Isabella, who also had a claim to the throne. They shared the same father, King Juan II of Castile (John in English). To make things even more complicated, there were widespread rumors at the time that Joana was not the King's daughter, but rather was the daughter of a nobleman that the Queen took as her lover.

Eventually, Enrique agreed Isabella would be the heir if she married according to his will. His will specifically excluded King Ferdinand II of Aragon. She secretly married Ferdinand anyway at age seventeen. Isabella had gained for her cause a powerful ally of neighboring Aragon. Meanwhile, the supporters of Joana persuaded King Alfonso V of Portugal to marry his twelve-year-old niece. She now had her powerful ally of neighboring Portugal.

The stage was set for yet another nasty dynastic war over the succession of a kingdom. It was really a civil war between two Castilian women, with powerful allies both within and outside Castile. The powerful noble families of Castile chose sides, according to their personal interests.

One of these powerful interests was the Order of Calatrava, the order that Juan's uncle Pedro was a Knight Commander. The

Order was divided into three groups with one group in Aragon and another two in Castile. Pedro Gíron was the Grand Master in the years leading up to the war. Ironically, King Enrique IV considered him to be so important that he gave his half-sister, Isabella, in marriage. On the road traveling to his wedding to the future Queen of Castile, he died, thus changing the history of Spain.

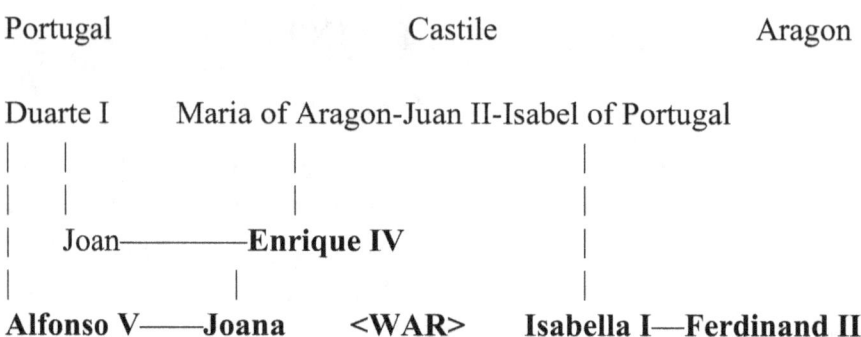

Portugal   Castile   Aragon

Duarte I Maria of Aragon-Juan II-Isabel of Portugal

Joan————**Enrique IV**

Alfonso V——Joana **<WAR>** **Isabella I—Ferdinand II**

Note: This gives a taste of how complicated royal genealogy is and how everyone was related to everyone else. "|" means a parent-child relationship. "-" means a spousal relationship.

In an order of monks with vows of celibacy and poverty, things could be different with the popes' acceptance, indeed connivance. This was the case with Grand Master Pedro Gíron. His illegitimate son, Rodrigo Gíron, became the next Grand Master. The Gíron family was an eminent Castilian family descended from Portugal. The Grand Master chose the side of Joana. Many knights disagreed and took the side of Isabella.

Knight Commander Pedro Gúzman had to choose sides. Was he to follow the head of his order to whom he swore allegiance or to many of his fellow knights who took great offence to the idea that the position of Grand Master could be inherited and take the side of Joana?

Afonso, the King of Portugal and brother of Enrique's Queen, invaded Castile in the beginning of May 1475 and joined up with Joana, his niece. They married a few weeks later. The pope's dispensation and acceptance endorsed the unusual union.

By June, their army captured much of the northwest of Castile. The Grand Master himself captured the large city of Ciudad Real. With this success, he sent messengers in July appealing for the Knights to join him to support the cause of Joana.

Knight Commander Pedro Gúzman delayed his response until the Autumn harvest was brought in, three months later. But now it was time to decide. He had been preparing all summer for war. There was no option to stay neutral. He bolstered the defensive works of his castle. He gathered his knights and men-at-arms. They numbered 400 mounted and armored knights with 550 crossbowmen, swordsmen, and spearmen. Everyone gathered in the central square of his castle, both the armed followers and everyone in his household. He shouted to them from atop the walls.

"You all know why I gathered you here. It is time for me to decide which side to throw my support. The Grand Master has ordered me to join his side supporting the King's daughter, despite the King himself designating his sister as the rightful heir. Many of my fellow Knights of the Order have rankled how the bastard son was designated as heir by his father as if we were just like any other typical noble family.

"As everyone knows, Joana is most likely not even the King's daughter. So, how can I follow one bastard to support another? I have decided to support our late King's sister as the rightful heir to the throne. I will support Queen Isabella. Tomorrow we will march to aid her husband, King Fernando, in the region of Zamora and Burgos. Since our cause is the just one against the usurpers, God will grant us victory! To victory!"

Everyone below shouted in unison for several minutes the words "To victory!". Swords, lances, and banners all rose into the air. Later, they all joined together for a grand feast. Up before the next day's dawn, they set out just as the sun started its ascent. It was the end of October 1475.

The Knight Commander brought his squires with him. They rode their horses a respectful distance behind him. Juan was fifteen years old and was tasked with carrying the great man's shield. One carried his lance; yet another carried his helmet. Another carried the banner of the Knight Commander's family coat of arms, while another squire carried the banner of the Order. In total, six squires accompanied him, the ones deemed most capable and skilled.

On the way, scouts reported that there was a camp of the Count of Baltanás with 400 spearmen who were still unaware of their approach. The Knight Commander asked his squires for his helmet, lance, and shield. They were to ride behind him, protecting his back. He sent the crossbowman to set up at the tree line about fifty yards behind the enemy's camp. The spearmen would position themselves behind the crossbowman to protect them from any attack.

The knights and squires quickly approached from the front, leading their horses dismounted through the tall grass. When all was ready, they quickly mounted and formed the charging formation. The Count's men were taken by surprise and hastily set up a defensive position against the knights. Knight Commander Gúzman rode close to the camp and bade the Count to parley.

The Count approached on his horse. He knew his spearmen were very effective against mounted knights and was confident of any outcome.

"Ah, it's Knight Commander Gúzman. Have you come to join me to defend the honor of our rightful Queen, Joana? If this is the case, why not just say so and not form up your knights as if you would be so foolish to charge a camp of spearmen?"

"Count of Baltanás, sir, I see you are enjoying your after-lunch siesta. You really have not chosen well a place to do it. You didn't notice us until we were practically on top of you. Actually, I have come to bid you to join me to defend the honor of our late King's sister, Queen Isabella. Let's march together to throw the meddling Portuguese out of our country."

"You would have me aid the scheming King of Aragon and the conniving King's half-sister, instead? Is that the choice you are offering me? Your knights are welcome to charge our spears and have your horses fall beneath you."

Knight Commander Gúzman told the squire next to him holding his banner to raise it, signaling the crossbowman and spearmen hiding in the woods to advance towards the rear of the camp.

"My dear Count, you really need more military experience. You see, you are surrounded. My crossbowmen behind you will cut down your spearmen with their bolts as my knights sever their heads from the front. Come, let's resolve this according to the rules of chivalry. Tell your men to throw down their spears and we can discuss this amicably."

The Count realized that the Knight Commander had outfoxed him. He had no choice but to submit. It was a minor victory, but a good omen for the start of their campaign. His men gathered the dropped spears and tied up the unarmed men of the Count's. The Count invited the Knight Commander into his tent.

They started by discussing how much the Count would pay to ransom himself and his men. The Knight Commander's offer was twenty-two pounds of gold for the Count and the same amount for the 400 spearmen. They haggled and, in the end, they agreed to twenty-six pounds for the Count's freedom with his promise to stay neutral for the remainder of the war and his 400 spearmen would join the ranks of the Knight Commander.

With that amount of gold lost, the Count would need quite a few years to make it back. In the meantime, he could not afford an army of any size. As for the Knight Commander, he gained enough to pay for six months of campaigning and an enormous increase to his forces. With this small matter resolved, they and the other knights all gathered in the grand tent for a feast.

The next day, they continued their way to Burgos to join up with King Ferdinand's army. Knight Commander Gúzman asked his squires: "Tell me, squires, what did you learn from our little victory yesterday?"

The other squires were slow to answer. After a respectful pause, Juan answered, "Smart tactics can win victories with little or no blood spilled."

"Yes, Juan, indeed you're correct. You must be able to size up any situation at a moment's notice and act decisively in whatever way that will give you the greatest advantage. You haven't seen actual combat yet. I have and I can tell you that a charge against spearmen in a defensive position would have been crazy. Our horses would have had spears in their chests and our knights would have fallen to the ground. With their heavy armor preventing easy movement, they would be easy prey for hundreds of spearmen and their knives. I expect you, Juan, and all you others will be veteran fighters before this is all over."

They arrived at Burgos by the end of November and joined the siege. They set up camp overlooking a section of the city walls. There was nothing to do but wait until the defenders ran out of food and surrendered. Or for the besiegers to start running out of food, forcing them to assault the walls. King Ferdinand was not present.

In the beginning of December, the key Joana-allied city of Zamora rebelled and besieged the Portuguese garrison in the castle sitting on a hill above the center of the city. Fernando and his army entered the city to help with the siege of the castle. Meanwhile, King Afonso gathered his forces, including the forces of the Grand Master, at the city of Toro. By the end of January, his son, Crown Prince João, arrived with his forces, doubling the Portuguese King's army.

Meanwhile, Knight Commander Gúzman and his army of 1350 were ordered to continue with the siege of Burgos. After nearly two months of sitting by fires all day and sleeping in tents in freezing temperatures at night, his soldiers began to dwindle. Some died from illness and disease. Others simply disappeared into the night. Finally, on the last week of January 1476, envoys from Isabella arrived and negotiated the surrender of the city in exchange for a complete amnesty.

With that victory, Fernando ordered the besiegers to march quickly to his aid at Zamora. In the middle of February, Joana's armies marched to relieve the siege at Zamora. They besieged Fernando and his army in the city, who were in turn besieging the castle manned by the Portuguese garrison. The winter weather was bitter cold with freezing rain nonstop for ten days, and disease was appearing in the besiegers' ranks. Juan was happy to be finding warmth within the stone walls of a warm house. Outside it was much colder and wetter than Burgos.

King Afonso decided to return to Toro and wait until the Spring. The siege was lifted, and the Portuguese garrison surrendered in the castle. Fernando decided it was time to go on the offensive and pursue the retreating supporters of Joana. They met up at Toro on March 1, 1476. Afonso decided to give battle outside the city. He had slightly more men than Fernando. Between the Knights and his very able son and heir, Afonso had every likelihood of victory.

CHAPTER SEVENTEEN

The Battle of Toro, 1476

It was dusk on March 1, 1476, when the two armies faced each other in a field across the Douro River from the Castilian city of Toro. Juan could not understand why they would fight an hour before nightfall. He did understand that it was not his place to ask questions, but to follow orders. This was his first experience with actual combat in one of the most important battles of his homeland's history. He was barely sixteen and fear gripped his heart when he saw the enemy formations across the short distance from him.

Both kings divided their armies into three parts, as battles had been fought for over 2000 years. There was a right wing, a left wing, and a center. The Portuguese King Afonso and his knights of the nobility occupied the center. The Portuguese Crown Prince João, with his elite army of chevaliers, arquebus artillery, and javelin throwers, occupied the left wing. The Archbishop of Toledo, one of Joana's Castilian allies, commanded the right wing.

King Fernando and his knights of the nobility held the Castilian center. Three noblemen with heavily armored knights commanded the left wing. They were the strongest units fighting for Isabella's cause. Six units, each with their own commander, made up the right wing. Knight Commander Gúzman commanded one of these units and that is where Juan found himself that day facing the best of the Portuguese army under one of their ablest commanders.

Both armies were nearly the same size with about 8000 men each. King Afonso had a bit more. The forces comprised about a third knights, a third pikemen, and a third crossbowmen. Prince João also had javelin throwers and arquebuses. The composition, the organization, the tactics, the weapons, etc. were the same for both sides. The only two things that differentiated the individual units in each army were the skills of the leaders and the elan of the fighting men.

The Knight Commander organized his crossbowman in front and the pikeman behind them with the knights mounted in the back. The Knight Commander and his fellow knights wore plate armor with a lance, sword, and shield. Juan and his fellow squires were mounted, too, but wore a metal helmet and thick padded leather armor with the same weapons. They were at a respected distance from their lord, but still could hear the Knight Commander's words.

Juan's fear turned to the excitement of finally using what he had been training for the past eight years. He felt the comradery of his fellow squires and was inspired by the veteran knights of the Order. He would follow his uncle to the ends of the earth. He would gladly join the charge of the enemy when the order was given. Yet, the darkness quickly was descending and, even worse, the sky was full of menacing black clouds.

The overall commander of their wing, Álvaro de Mendoza, asked King Fernando if they could attack. The answer was to proceed as long as all units advanced together. Álvaro de Mendoza attacked first, before the signal was given to the others. The Knight Commander asked out loud what everyone else was thinking. "What is he doing?"

A few minutes later, another unit began the advance, until all six were advancing separately from the others. Facing them was a relatively new weapon, the arquebus. This was an early firearm that was fired by a single soldier using a metal support stuck in the ground. This support was required to aim with any accuracy at all.

Those armed in such a way would put the gunpowder in first, followed by the lead ball. There was a long rope that was always lit on one end. This is what the soldier used to ignite the gunpowder through a hole in the gun. It took a minute to reload, and the accuracy was terrible. They depended on a mass of lead balls fired at the quickly advancing enemy knights at close range, less than 100 yards   . This meant that they could fire twice before the enemy was upon them. The pikemen would then step up to fight the enemy. The javelin throwers would throw their weapons while the arquebuses were reloading.

The Knight Commander ordered his men to advance, even before receiving any signal. They could only succeed by advancing together. The two opposing armies were about 250 yards apart. The knights proceeded slowly towards the enemy lines, saving the energy of their horses, until they reached a distance of about 100 yards. Meanwhile, the footmen followed as quickly as they could.

The arquebuses and the javelins withered the Castilian units before they could make contact. Other units had already reached the enemy lines. They were being slaughtered piecemeal. Something had to be done. Knight Commander Gúzman ordered the charge against the enemy flank before them. Juan spurred his horse forward at the gallop, trying to keep up with his uncle. Juan remembered the horse race with his father eight years before. He was as determined as then to succeed.

Then the bullets slammed into them. One ricocheted off Juan's helmet and nearly knocked him off his horse. He saw many knights, their horses, and even his fellow squires fall to the ground. Many were trampled by those behind them. By the time they reached the enemy line, many were left dead or disabled strewn across the ground behind them.

The arquebus was now useless. It was the pikemen's turn to fight. But the weight of the charge with their lances lowered slammed the pikemen, forcing them back. By this time, the footmen arrived, and the fight became savage. Juan was slashing with his sword while fending off the pikes with his shield. His mind was so full of adrenaline-filled concentration that he heard nothing of the great din of screams and metal hitting metal. His vision narrowed to just the man he was fighting.

Juan's sword cut through a man's neck so that his head, though still connected, flopped against his shoulder. Blood spewed up like a fountain until he fell forward into the cold dark mud. Juan thrust his sword through another's face, killing him instantly. Suddenly, a pikeman thrust his weapon into his horse's chest. Juan went down with his horse.

As he landed, an enemy jumped on him with his knife nearly at Juan's throat. The Portuguese soldier's face was so close to his that Juan could smell the garlic he had eaten with lunch. For a second, he looked into the eyes of his killer and saw his own. Juan was face to face with death. A calmness flowed through him as he thrust his knife into the armpit and into the heart of his assailant.

Throwing off the now-dead body, he jumped to his feet. He saw his uncle surrounded by enemies hacking at his armor. Off a horse, an armored knight was so heavy he could only move slowly. Juan ran the few steps and thrust his sword into the back of the closest attacker. Meanwhile, another had leaped onto the Knight Commander, trying to pull him onto the ground. Juan mortally stabbed him in the side, allowing his uncle to regain his stance.

Together, they killed the others. As the Knight Commander was catching his breath, Juan grabbed a riderless horse and gave it to his uncle. The enemy was slowly surrounding the remainder of his men. If this happened, all would be lost. The other units were in equally dire straits. Some were already running away.

Juan helped the Knight Commander onto the horse. His uncle gave the order to retreat. Juan grabbed a fallen lance before his uncle pulled Juan up behind him. The few remaining knights hacked a hole through the tightening noose, and the surviving footmen ran quickly behind them. Many dropped their weapons to run faster.

Prince João ordered his elite knights to cut down the routing Castilian army. Some chose the Knight Commander as their prey.

Juan fended them off with his lance while his uncle concentrated on urging the horse to flee faster. Then the sky intervened. It started to rain. The thick darkness of night made the chaos of the battlefield even more so. The rain signaled to the pursuers that they better reform back with the main body and see what new orders they may receive from their victorious leader.

The routing right wing completely disintegrated. They stopped running when they met up with a Castilian unit that was securing the rear. The Knight Commander regrouped his men and tried to rally them. But he knew the battle was over for them. Fernando's army retreated to Zamora. After a few days of recovering, answers started coming to the many questions from the chaotic battle.

The Knight Commander and his men recuperated in the market area of the city. The men-at-arms pitched tents by the stone walls that sheltered them from the late winter winds. The knights and squires found space in the nearby tavern, either in rooms for the higher-level knights or on the dining floor for the rest. The Knight Commander gathered his knights and squires in the tavern, where there was a warm fire, decent food, and plenty of wine. They were about a quarter less than before the battle, with many others wounded.

Various heavy, roughhewn wooden beams supported the high ceiling of the tavern. Countless arm sleeves over myriads of years had rubbed smooth the tabletops. Smoked legs of ham hung from the ceiling above the long counter that served as the bar with their cloven hooves swaying with the draft just above head level. Against the back wall were rows of large wine barrels on their sides cradled in racks with their inviting tap spigots set within easy hand reach. A heavy closed door hid the kitchen, but the smells of roasted meat and heavy stews revealed the source of their hearty winter meals.

Knight Commander Gúzman rose with wine cup in hand. "My dear countrymen, I will share with you what I know about what you are all wondering about, namely, what just happened. Clearly, we and our fellow units on the right wing were routed. We all know that much to our great shame. But what about the battle as a whole? We knew very little at the time of battle about what was happening elsewhere. Fighting in a dark rainy night can only create chaos on the battlefield.

"In the center, King Fernando defeated the Portuguese King, who fled the battlefield. Our left wing held its ground, but with no definite result. King Fernando left the battlefield and returned to Zamora while we were still fighting the Portuguese. I'm sure he had his reasons. As you all know, the rules of warfare, the leader who remains on the battlefield is the winner. That, plainly, was Prince João of Portugal.

"So, what comes next? That's up to King Fernando. From the reports I've seen, both sides lost about ten percent of their forces. There is nothing decisive about that. King Fernando, the defender of our Queen, still has his army intact. He has forced the Portuguese back to Toro. He's probably waiting to see what the Portuguese do next. The initiative is theirs. Meanwhile, we will continue to serve him as we swore to do until the ultimate victory is ours.

"Despite our poor results, you all showed incredible bravery in a terrible situation. I toast you all!" Everyone stood glumly, raising their cups in response. "My orders for you now are to drink, eat, and be merry. Tavern master, please send another barrel of wine to my men resting in the tents outside. Make sure they do not lack for food. Squires, come sit with me at my table. Let's discuss the battle and what we learned from it."

Uncle Gúzman indicated for Juan to sit beside him. Juan noticed that, including him, there were only four squires left of the original six. For a few days after the battle, his mind was in a daze, traumatized by the violent carnage he had just participated in. He was just now slowly coming to his senses. The wine helped.

"Cheer up, lads! We survived. Yes, running away like we did is a true shame. But the war is not over. We still have a chance to regain victory and honor. This was your first taste of combat and war. This is what you have been training for all these years. Tell me. What did you learn from this?"

Juan, as was his custom, waited until the others spoke. They gave vague answers as they would to the schoolmaster when they were not prepared for class. Juan waited a respectable few minutes and then answered.

"Knight Commander, sir, in truth, what I learned was that nothing that we studied applied for what I experienced during the battle."

"Oh? How so, Juan?"

"Well, sir, everything happened so quickly. I had no time to think about stances and form. When I fell from my stricken horse, an enemy leaped on me, trying to cut my throat. My only thought was to survive. I felt no glory when I stuck my knife into his side and pierced his heart. I only felt relief when I saw his eyes, so close to mine, slowly glaze over and his grip on me loosening. The fact is my mind was not thinking at all. I was just doing."

"Juan, that is exactly what your training is supposed to do. All the practicing of forms and stances allowed you to act without thinking, even if you did not actually do them exactly as you learned. That is what kept you alive. Anything else?"

"I'm sure that the results of the battle in the grand scheme of things matters. I'm also sure that I would feel the elation of being victorious. But I can't help thinking that in the end, after so many have been killed or permanently maimed, life will be the same for us, no matter who sits on our thrown. I mean, how would life be different if our Queen is Isabella or Joana, our King Fernando or Afonso? What does it really matter if..."

"Careful, Juan, careful. You are treading in dangerous waters. You clearly have not learned the first and most important lesson of military men. Never question your superiors. You follow orders unto death if necessary. Currently, our orders are to follow the will of King Fernando of Aragon.

"A warrior must be strong in body and mind, united in one resolve. If the mind is plagued with doubts, the warrior is weak, no matter his strength of body and military skill. If you cannot bend your mind to your will, then you are useless as a squire or a knight. You are free to leave my service and return to your father. Is that what your mind would prefer?"

The shock of that possibility clarified Juan's mind with a start.

"No, sir, no! There is nothing I want more than to continue in your service. I will control my mind better in the future. Please forgive my childish thoughts."

"They are not childish thoughts, just not a warrior's thoughts. You have chosen the path of the warrior. Your mind must be as strong as your will. I will give you a piece of advice, Juan, and to all you other squires. What we do in battle is for our King and his glory. But that is not all. We are also doing it for our own honor and glory. With honor and glory, you will rise in the estimation of your peers and reach positions of success. If that means power and wealth for you and your family, then so be it. That is the second lesson, only slightly less important than the first one."

"Yes, sir. I understand better now. I will not question anymore."

"Juan, you must understand there is nothing we can do to change the scheme of things. There are kings and nobles. There are peasants and laborers. There are merchants and the trained craftsmen of the guilds. Then there's us, the tools of the wills of our superiors. We all have our roles to play. There is nothing you nor I, nor, the truth be told, even the kings can do to change the world we live in. The sooner you accept that fact, the happier you will be, and the further you will go in life. Am I making myself clear?"

"Yes, sir, perfectly clear. You are a man of the world and understand far more than me. I have not seen or experienced much in life. Everything you have said makes perfect sense to me. Thank you, sir, for taking the time and interest to set me right."

"I have great expectations for you, Juan. I see in you the potential for greatness. It would be my honor if I could have any part in your success. Now, I can give you an order, but I prefer to give you a suggestion. Eat, drink, and relax; recover from the horrors we just experienced. Remember those who did not make it. But be glad that you have. The night is very young. Now I have matters to discuss with my knights."

Only the four squires remained at the table. The other three crowded around Juan, whom they held in the greatest esteem. They saw what Juan did to save their lord and benefactor in the heat of battle. He was their hero. One of them stood and raised his glass to Juan, toasting him and his bravery. Then the others all stood and began to sing a favorite drinking song, a song of honor and praise sung when saluting a mate.

The Knight Commander heard them and stopped all conversation at his table. He also stood with his glass raised and joined the singing. Afterwards, the morose group of humiliated soldiers shook off their defeatist demeanor. The entire tavern erupted in loud conversation, uproarious laughter, and general merriment until late into the night.

CHAPTER EIGHTEEN

The Calusas

"OK, Isabel, I have an idea. You are so fascinated with my old Calusa pipe. Let's go visit the descendants of the few remaining Calusas left. They live on the Miccosukee Reservation a five-hour drive from here. But I prefer taking the longer scenic route by turning inland at Fort Pierce. It's a half an hour longer, but it's worth it. We could leave Friday afternoon and start back on Monday morning. They are my friends and they remember the story of my ancestor."

"That sounds absolutely wonderful, Juan! What a great idea!"

"It's a trip completely off the beaten path. I'm sure no one you know has been there or ever would go there. It's not a place for tourists. In fact, the trip always makes me sad. But it should be interesting for you."

"Sad? Why does it make you sad?"

"The Calusa were once a powerful people who controlled all of southwest Florida. They resisted any European influence, including traders and missionaries. They were defeated when their enemies adopted the culture of their Spanish conquerors and their firearms.

"Now, they have all but disappeared. There are just a few dozen left from a population of over 10,000. Almost all the natives of Florida were gone by the early 19th century, mainly due to disease from contact with the Europeans. That is when the Seminoles pushed south to escape the rapacious Georgians, when Florida was still a part of Spain. The few original natives who remained were absorbed into the Seminole tribes."

"No. Let's not go. I don't want the love of my life to be ever sad. Let's go somewhere completely silly, like Disney World."

"I don't do Disney. That would make me even worse."

"Don't do Disney? Why ever not?"

"Let's just say their sense of reality and mine are completely different. Besides, it's a kind of silliness that's way off my silly meter. It'll be wall-to-wall people this weekend, anyway."

"Your sense of reality is different? How so?"

"I'll give you one example of many. In the world of Disney, animals are smarter than people, children are smarter than adults, and women are smarter than men. Also, I'm not a fan of rodents and I don't do goofy."

Isabel laughed for a full minute. "Oh, you are too much! Fine, I agree you're not the goofy type. Let's go visit the once mighty Calusa. Your ideas are always better than mine."

"I'm glad you agree. Anyway, they always do a good job trying to cheer me up. They should be sadder than me, but they aren't. They've made peace with the world long ago. So, it's decided.

"I'm not sure if my ideas are always better than yours. I have no monopoly on wisdom. Though I do think at times we have very different tastes. I mean Disney and Memorial Day parades? Sweet Isabel, sometimes you make me wonder." He said, shaking his head.

"No, no, my precious! Don't think that, ever! Just imagine that my life is a book with only one chapter out of a hundred to be written. I am currently just starting chapter two and you, my dear sir, are the author. I cherish the idea that we will write the last chapter together." She leaped up and enveloped his head and shoulders tightly in her arms and bosom. Her tears were wetting his hair.

"Oh, my dearest Isabel. Please don't cry. I will rise to the challenge of being the co-author of your life's book. I promise to make it the most interesting and happiest story ever." He turned in his chair and pulled her to his arms, kissing her tears away. Love always has a way with words.

The day of their trip came soon enough. She spent the night with him. They had a late brunch and were on the road before 1100. The Memorial Day traffic would be another reason to get off the interstate as soon as possible. A five-hour trip would likely be seven or eight hours.

In the event, it was two hours just to get to Daytona Beach, which normally took less than one hour. He thought to turn inland on US 4, but that was the way to Orlando with Disney and all the other amusement parks. The traffic would be even worse. With a long exhale, he continued with the original plan.

He stayed calm by playing all the early Santana albums. The time went faster as he faced the challenge of educating Isabel with the ways of Santana of the late 1960's and 70's. He explained such mysteries as the meaning of the lyrics to 'Oye Como Va', the meaning of the title to the song 'Samba Pa Ti', the history of the songs like 'Black Magic Woman' and 'A Love Supreme', as well as many other mysteries to the uninitiated.

Time passed quickly. Isabel was genuinely interested in everything he had to say about Santana or about anything at all. Juan was a fount of wisdom to her. He always had a reason for everything he had to say. He always thought before he spoke.

The song 'I'll Be Waiting' from the live album 'Moonflower' was just ending when he finally parked the car in the middle of a hamlet of eight doublewide prefab houses placed in a circle, under the only trees for miles around. They had been driving for nearly an hour on a dirt road through scrubland after turning off West State Road 84. The curious inhabitants quickly crowded around the car. They clearly had very few visits by outsiders.

The small crowd parted like a sea before Moses when an old man approached slowly with the help of a cane. He had a wonderfully warm smile on his face. "Juan? Juan? Is that you? Come out and give me a hug."

He was the headman of the small group who still called themselves privately the Calusa People. Juan smiled and nodded to the nervous Isabel. They opened their doors and stepped out. Indeed, Juan's first action was to give the old chief a great bear hug.

"Juan, how long has it been, twenty years? My, you haven't changed a bit. How do you do it? Come. Bring your things. You will stay with me. Dinner is almost ready in our community hall. We all want to hear your wonderful stories and, even more importantly, you need to introduce us to this wonderful radiant woman you brought with you." With one arm around Juan's shoulder and the other leaning heavily on his cane, he led them to the best tended house.

After they unpacked their things and refreshed themselves, they rejoined the chief of his small tribe on the back porch.

"Come, sit down, Juan. I was so happy to receive your phone call, telling me about your visit. Our entire tribe was excited by the news. You and your ancestors hold a very special place in our hearts. Here, try this. It's our latest home-distilled special drink. It's not moonshine as we can legally make it, according to the rules of the reservation. We can even sell it. But now, tell me, who is this sweet young woman you brought with you?"

"Chief Hardy, this is Isabel, my new special friend."

"Welcome, Isabel. Any friend of Juan's is a friend of ours. So, Juan, what brings you to our little isolated corner of the world?"

"It's been a while. Your ancestor's pipe holds a place of honor above my fireplace in my dining room. Isabel has taken quite an interest in it and its history. We were thinking of making a special trip for the holiday weekend and I thought of you. So, here we are."

"Ah, so she knows the illustrious history of that special pipe. It's one of the best stories between our peoples. It's my responsibility that my people learn it and continue to pass it down through the generations like it has these 500 years. We have about an hour before dinner is ready. We've prepared something special for you. Hope you like it."

"I'm sure we will." They spent the next hour catching up on all the main things from the previous twenty years.

Dinner in the communal hall was indeed very special. Suckling pig, roasted venison, and a large stew of seafood, which included papaya with various nuts and berries. It was all washed down by the special self-distilled liquor. Dinner was followed by traditional dances, music, and singing in the original Calusa language, which no one could really speak anymore, but sounded beautiful, nonetheless.

After dinner, the menfolk gathered around an open pit fire behind the communal hall. After settling into their chairs, Chief Hardy produced an ornate tribal pipe, puffed on it to light it, and passed it around, first to Juan. Isabel sat with the older women inside, preferring to continue drinking, rather than smoking with the men. Their laughter floated out through the open doors. The outdoor stereo system was playing Redbone's 'Come and Get Your Love'. The ambiance was perfect.

For their part, the men spoke little, content to enjoy the contents of the intricately carved magical wooden pipe. The contents were a combination of tobacco and hashish. Juan never really liked the tobacco part, as it sometimes gave him headaches. The calming effect of the hashish more than made up for it.

"Juan, did I ever tell you how we started smoking hashish, rather than just the cannabis leaf, which grows like a weed around here?"

"Yes, Chief, you did. It came from when your father was a soldier stationed in Morocco in the 1950's. He thought it was a brilliant innovation and brought it back here."

"That he did, Juan. And we've been enjoying his innovation ever since." They all started laughing over the word 'innovation'. Clearly, it was time for laughter.

"Did I ever tell you the one about the chicken farmer, Chief? No? A chicken farmer had a rooster who was getting old, so he bought a young one and set it down in the chicken yard.

"The old rooster said to the young one, 'Look, we can fight this out. Yes, you might win, but I will do you some serious damage. Or we could race around the hen house here. If you beat me, I will go on my way peacefully. But if I win, you'll do the same and leave us alone. I just ask that you give me a five-foot head start.'

"The young cock tilted his head back and laughed. 'Five feet? I can beat you, even if I give you a ten feet head start, you old fart.'"

"'No, no, five feet's enough.' And he counted out the distance in front of them."

"So, they started their race. Suddenly a shot gun fired, and the young rooster dropped dead.

"The farmer watching from his porch yelled, 'Damn it! That's the fifth gay rooster I bought this month!'"

Chief Hardy laughed so hard he fell off his chair. Many minutes later, the final chuckle ended.

"OK, here's one for you, Juan. An elephant walks into a bar. He sees another elephant well ensconced at the bar watching the game on the TV. The first elephant sits down next to him and asks, 'What's the score?' The other elephant runs out of the bar screaming, 'Oh, my God! It's a talking elephant!'"

This brought on another five minutes of stoned laughter. Juan was glad he made the trip. He had not laughed so hard in a long time.

The next morning, breakfast was served again in the communal house.

The Chief greeted them: "I trust you slept well, Isabel? How was yesterday evening? I hope the women folk were not being too silly for your educated tastes. You know what they say about the country in the girl."

"Oh, Chief, I had the most wonderful time. I am honored to be your guest. Juan is showing me so much that I never would have experienced on my own."

"Glad to hear it. Now here comes something special. This omelet is from the recipe that Juan's great ancestor taught ours when he diffused their misunderstanding we had at first contact with the European world. You like it?"

"Yes, it's exactly how I like it."

"Now this second one is from the recipe that our ancestor came up with in response. You'll notice it's similar, but with some significant differences. We use ground walnuts mixed with blueberries. Grilled fish is tucked inside. There are two changes from the original recipe. We now use chicken eggs instead of wild duck eggs and we put some salt in it. What do you think of this one? It might be an acquired taste."

"Well, Chief, I've already acquired it. I'll try making it when I return home and will make it with duck eggs. There's a farmer's market near where I live that sells all sorts of unusual things."

They retired to sit in a large circle behind the communal house, enjoying their coffee. The stereo was playing Erik Satie.

"Isabel, I can tell from the look on your face how surprised you are to hear the beautiful music of Erik Satie in the middle of nowhere Florida. I learned to play Satie on the piano. We can be quite cultured and educated like anyone else. We're not a bunch of savages." Everyone laughed at that.

"Of course, you're not. I admit that I've had very little contact, no contact really with the native peoples. Juan tells me you are not a Seminole or a Miccosukee, but here you are living on a Miccosukee reservation."

"I guess you could call us honorary members of the Miccosukee Alligator Alley Reservation. We native folk need strength in numbers, no matter what our tribal history is. No, they and the Seminoles are foreign to this land. They were pushed south from Georgia and Alabama by the white folk in the 1800's.

"We and all the other First Peoples of Florida were pretty much all killed off by then. Between the Spanish diseases and slavers carrying us off to work and die in Cuba, all of us, no matter the tribe, were only a few hundred spread across Florida, hiding in whatever remote corner we could find. We, the Calusas, alone numbered well over 10,000 when Juan's ancestor first found us.

"We controlled all of southwest Florida, even the Keys. Our specific sub-tribe came from far northwest of here. Most of the current native reservations are not even close to where the tribal lands once were. The whites put us wherever they deemed useless lands to them. We couldn't all fit in Oklahoma and some enlightened whites did not believe that a good Indian was a dead Indian. And so, we survived.

"What is killing us now is our drift away from our traditions and heritage. Drug abuse, alcoholism, unemployment, domestic violence, and the tug of modern life in the cities are all taking their toll. Last night was a special celebration for your visit. I hope you don't think we're all a bunch of boozers and stoners living off the federal government.

"I can only speak for our little band here. We take life and our heritage seriously. We don't take government subsidies nor the easy money from the corrupting casinos, but work for our living. In fact, I doubt you know we are ranchers. As you can see, looking out there that it's not all oranges and grapefruit in Florida. Florida ranks tenth in the country for cattle. We tribals have some of the largest beef herds in the country."

"Oh, please don't mistake my ignorance for prejudice. I generally refuse to form an opinion about something I know nothing about." Isabel hastily interjected.

"After lunch, I'll take you for a tour of our little slice of paradise."

The weekend passed too quickly. Isabel was sad to leave the warmly generous and hospitable small band of surviving Calusas. On the long drive home, Isabel could talk of nothing else. She wanted to visit them regularly, maybe once a month. Juan was non-committal. He was worried that maybe he went too far with that visit.

They were indeed wonderful people, but he could not maintain a long-term relationship with anyone there. The chief did not press him on why he appeared to be the same age as the previous visit twenty years ago. Why would he? But if he visited again in twenty years, the chief would be in his eighties and Juan would still be in his early forties. That would raise eyebrows, for sure. He exhaled deeply while thinking 'careful, Juan, careful'.

As if right on cue, Isabel asked, "Chief Hardy believes in the story of your ancestor and the omelets. You even have the same name. Are you really a direct descendent of the great explorer?"

"My father thought I was. That's why he named me as such."

"Wouldn't it be cool if you could trace your lineage all the way back? You would be an honored citizen of Florida."

"No, I don't think that would be a good idea. I'm as honored here as I want to be."

"Oh, come on, Juan. I would do all the work. You just have to confirm what I find. It would be a great genealogical detective project. Research is what I do best."

"Isabel! No! I'm not interested, and I don't care to know. Genealogy is ridiculous to me. Yes, I agree, we should all know where we came from. But to trace generation by generation back to a famous person is silly. What does it mean anyway? That's like a little lizard telling me he is brontosaurus on his mother's side. How does that relate to the little one who lives under a rock today? You'll find that there are a few things I believe strongly in, though it may not appear logical to you, like military parades and Disney. Genealogy is one of them. Sorry, dearest, best to drop the subject."

"Well, only if you insist. I still think it would be fascinating, especially for the history of Florida. You know, like one of those old Michener novels."

"Let's change the subject. We'll soon pass a place that I used to visit many years ago. I wonder how it's changed. Interested?"

"Of course. I'm interested in everything about you."

Juan took the next exit off the highway and drove to the coast. He turned down a narrow overgrown dirt road until it ended in a clearing by a small bay on the ocean, where collapsed and rotting bunk houses with a wooden chapel stood in the center. The name "Camp Ais" was visible on the crossbeam of the entrance to what appeared to be an old, abandoned church camp.

"Come, my sweet, sit with me here awhile and listen to the waves."

CHAPTER NINETEEN

Living with the Ais

Though less aggressive than the Calusas, the Ais people had sway over the southeast coast of Florida and the neighboring tribes of the Jaega and the Surruque peoples. Ponce de León and his crew settled in a small, isolated village of the Ais. The only connection the small tribe had with the head cacique or chieftain in the main capital town was that they shared the same language and culture. They had to give tribute and fighting men when required, not too different from the feudal system of Europe.

Barely visible footpaths connected the Ais villages, making them largely isolated from their fellow tribal villages. Game and fish were so plentiful that they never took up agriculture. They could gather whatever else they wanted from the natural abundance of the land. Men and women wore loincloths of woven palm leaves and nothing else. When it was rarely cold, they wore shawls of the same material. They constructed their huts with a wooden frame covered by a roof and walls of palm leaves.

This was the hamlet of thirty-seven people, which Ponce de León and his men found when they made landfall, searching for a place to disappear after discovering the Fountain. The locals did not exactly welcome them, but nor did they attack. The Spaniards made a camp a little distance away to gain their trust. Ponce de León knew well that the best way to the untrusting was through their stomachs. After a few weeks of getting nowhere with them, he decided a feast was in order.

It took a week to prepare. They built wooden tables and benches so they did not need to sit on the ground, as was the local custom. Several fire pits were required for a grand meal of over seventy people. They used the same palmetto leaf plates as the Ais used. They hunted and fished until everything was prepared. Ponce de León then invited the headman and everyone in the hamlet to the feast.

They were still distrustful at first and not too sure about the Spaniards' idea of cuisine. That was until Ponce de León brought out the rum. Soon, everyone was long-lost best friends. Ponce de León's men sang sea shanties and danced jigs. The headman did not even wince when many of the women joined in. In turn, he and his people danced and sang according to their traditions. This went on until everyone joined in together, singing and dancing according to their want with the Ais trying to copy the Spanish dances and the Spaniards trying to mimic theirs.

Ponce de León had to stay somewhat sober as drinking parties often could turn violent. He did not intend to have a drunken party but to win over their neighbors. The Ais needed little rum to become inebriated. Many fell asleep under the tables. As for the headman, Ponce de León and three others of his men carried him back to his hut in the village. He sang and laughed the whole way. Before his first wife led him to bed, he grabbed Ponce de León's arm and, with words and gestures, indicated that he and his men were welcome to live with them as friends and fellow tribesmen.

The gamble paid off. Fortunately, the headman did remember what he told his host the night before, though he was somewhat upset about having a headache the next morning. Fortunately, Ponce de León had a special herb for that side effect of extreme jollity. This made the headman trust even more the strange interlopers who had all manner of bizarre and magical things to share.

The Ais built the same type of wooden huts beside the main village for them, just on the other side of a small stream. Ponce de

León and his men built a jetty at the deeper end of the bay to dock their ship only a ten-minute walk away. Fortunately, it was not visible to any passing ship sailing by. They wanted to keep their new home and themselves a secret from the outside world.

It was not too long until they stored their European clothes on the ship and wore the same palm leaf loincloths as the locals. It perfectly suited the hot and humid climate. They were permanently brown from decades as sailors in the Caribbean. They did not need protection from the sun. The women were free with their affection and the men were free with their comradery. Life was good.

Over time, they learned the Ais language and their ways, their religion, and their traditions. Occasionally, when life became too boring, Ponce de León and his men would sail out for a few weeks on their stolen Cuban caravel and go pirating. He would always bring back gifts for the headmen and his wives. The headman would share them among his people, not believing in keeping everything for himself like his European equivalent would do. Sometimes there would be metal tools and knives. Other times there would be glass beads and colored linen the women could make shawls from. But there would always be rum for their once-a-month merry feasts.

Without fail, once a year, the entire group of Spaniards would disappear for a month. The trek to the Fountain took about twelve days through trackless scrubland, forests, and hills. They went a slightly different way every time, as they had no intention of leaving a path to their special secret. Ponce de León explained to the headman that they had to pay homage to their gods. These gods were a jealous lot and would become furious if any non-believer tried to follow them. The headman promised that his people would ignore their annual pilgrimages and leave them in peace.

Years passed in the routine of village life, an annual trip to the Fountain, and monthly pirate raids. The raids were more for distraction than wealth. The excitement of chasing down a merchantman, forcing it to surrender, then boarding it to take whatever was of value was a fine distraction. But in the end, they would always let the merchant ship continue unharmed, though somewhat lighter.

They considered themselves lucky if they found a cargo of Cuban or, even better, Puerto Rican rum. That would fuel many parties throughout the year with their kind hosts. Other times it was a cargo of grain, which they could sell at any port for a sack of coins. They could use the little money gained to refit their ship and enjoy some European culture. These gentle pirates always remembered to bring back something special for their Ais chief and his tribesmen. There was no sense in being greedy and burying treasure in the sandy beaches of an uninhabited island. Life gave them all that they could want.

All that they could want until the day they captured the Santo Simeón. As countless times before, they threw grappling hooks to grab hold of the surrendered prize and pull the ship closer to board. Just as the crew was boarding, their captain ordered his outnumbered and outgunned men to shoot their crossbows at point-blank.

Seeing some of his men being shot, Ponce de León lost his temper. After the captured crew and captain were subdued, he fired a lead ball into the captain's head. Then he locked the crew in the hold, surrounded by their precious cargo of grain, so precious to risk their lives to protect.

He yelled through the still open cargo hatch. "You have enraged me such that I haven't been for many long years. You shall cower around your precious sacks of grain, while I personally set fire to the ship. We shall watch it burn and then sink, ignoring the cries of you damned. Any last words?"

This brought desperate cries of despair from below. As the hatch was closing, their First Mate managed to cry out, "Please, sir! We beg you to have mercy! We were only following the orders of our captain. What would you think of your men if they disobeyed your commands? We are but poor sailors with families waiting for us at port."

Ponce de León locked the hatch, but then stormed up and down the deck, muttering and cursing at the winds. He stopped and stared out to sea. He saw a small islet in the short distance. Slowly, he reconsidered his decision as his anger subsided. Pitiful moans and cries rose from below deck.

"Bring them up." He ordered.

Falling on their knees, they gathered before him with their hands clasped in supplication.

"Do you see that little island over there? Swim to it and you can wait for a passing ship to rescue you."

"Oh, thank you for your mercy! May the Lord our God reward you for your Christian charity."

"If you mention 'Christian charity' once more, back into the hold you go."

"No, no Christian charity. But may our Heavenly Father reward you just the same. But please sir, most of us can't swim."

"Can't swim and you work on the sea that would gladly pull you down, holding you close in its deadly bosom? I require all my crew to be able to swim."

"Quite right you are, sir, to require it. But be it as it may, our captain never required it." He glanced furtively over his shoulder to the crumpled captain's body lying in a puddle of blood.

Ponce de León fumed some more but realized that it was too late to take back the mercy he had given. "Very well, you pathetic pack of scurvy dogs. My men will row you there. But don't think we will leave the lifeboats there. After that, you're on your own and at the mercy of the gods."

His men loaded the captured crew on the lifeboats and prepared to row the captives to the islet. Ponce de León threw casks of water and rations into the two lifeboats.

"That should keep you for a week or more, if you control yourselves and remember how to catch fish and seagulls. This is a busy sea lane. Another ship should pass by here in time. If not, then it's the gods to blame."

He scuttled the cursed merchantman and returned to their native refuge in silence. It took nearly a week for Martin and Alejandro to die, all the time in agony. The crew's surgeon could do nothing for the infection growing within their chests. The two men, who possessed the key to immortality, were buried at sea a day's journey from home.

Ponce de León was distraught for weeks later. He vowed that there would be no more pirate raids. Those days were over. They would be content with their simple, but peaceful life among the palm trees of southeastern Florida, forever if necessary. Some of his men did not agree with his decision. They grumbled that after some time, they would all be so bored with the simple life. They would prefer some life-threatening excitement to endless years of heavenly peace.

He answered their grumbling. "Oh, you want some excitement, do you? Then this is what we will do. We shall explore this entire region and map it. We probably will meet hostile tribes and aggressive beasts along the way. If any of you don't make it, I hope that will provide enough excitement for the rest of you. Do you agree?"

They agreed, and over a few years, they explored all of southern Florida. Through Ponce de León's culinary diplomacy, mastering of the native languages, and generally keeping his wits about him, everyone returned home safely. But home was changing slowly with their every return.

Thirty-five years had passed since they first arrived. The headman was growing older and frailer. He groomed his eldest son to take over. His son and his friends did not consider the hairy pale interlopers with the same generosity as his father, especially since the gifts of the pirate raids had stopped for many years already. The son considered these to be tribute from an inferior dependent vassal rather than honorary fellow tribesman. He also resented 'their' women fraternizing with the strange men.

The shaman sensed this. He resented deeply the powerful influence that the leader of their close neighbors had on their headman. Over time, their headman relied more on the strange explanations of the foreigners rather than his own. Their logic was so opposite of his own that the shaman was often at a loss for words when their chief challenged him.

After a baby's life was saved by using the methods of the foreigners, while his own were ineffective, many of his fellow tribesmen drifted away from the shaman as well. This was the last straw. Were the gods of these foreigners so much stronger than theirs, who had been with them since the first day of their creation?

The shaman decided to manipulate the son to turn against them. Hopefully, the son would expel them. As the headman was growing weaker every day and giving more responsibility to his son, the shaman started his plan. The next time he was with the headman in the presence of Ponce de León, he raised suspicion with the tribesmen.

"Chieftain Kinhagee, may I point out something which is obvious to many of us? These pale men from the sea follow unknown gods and thus we know very little about them. Are they even men or are they spirits? Look at them! As we all grow older, weaker, and even prepare to join our great Mother, have they changed in the slightest? They look exactly like they did when they first arrived nearly 150 seasons ago.

"Also, how is it that they have laid with our women for so many seasons and have not produced one child the whole time? Like many of our men, we never liked the idea. But we thought that if they could increase our people's numbers, it would be fine in the end. They enjoy our women's generosity but give nothing in return. They used to give us tribute, but even that has stopped. What about those strange trips they make every year to pay homage to their strange gods? Where are they exactly? I want to meet them on their next trip to see for myself."

"Stop you fool! They are our brothers and our friends. Away from my presence!" The shaman slowly retreated in shame but was secretly happy to hear the murmuring in agreement of many of the tribesmen. He had successfully planted the seed of doubt. Shortly after that, the women stopped visiting. The son stopped the monthly feasts and even prevented Ponce de León from visiting his old and dying father.

Chieftain Kinhagee finally passed into the land of shades. His son, the new chief, forbade his father's white friends from participating in the mourning rituals. Slowly, though living so close for so long, Ponce de León and his men were now excluded from most contact with their erstwhile brothers and sisters. Tribal spies followed them when they made their annual trip to the Fountain. Ponce de León's men had to beat unconscious the followers, allowing them enough time to continue in secret.

The son was enraged when he learned what happened. He expelled Ponce de León and his men, threatening them with death. The son made sure that all Ais people knew of the evil white spirits and not give them any hospitality. With great sadness, they boarded the old ship and sailed away. But where to? They could not sail to any Spanish port with their pirate ship. So, they sailed to the Bahama islands to find another friendly tribe or even just an uninhabited lush island of their own.

As fate would have it, they found the small French outpost of Abaco on one of the northern Bahama islands. There, they learned of the new Spanish town of Saint Augustine. The French did not welcome such a large number of Spaniards in their midst. They allowed them to rest and refit, but then sent them on their way. Most of Ponce de León's men clamored to live among Europeans again, preferably Spanish speaking.

So, they decided to sail for the new colony, which happened to be not too far from their all-important Fountain. A few days' sailing from their destination, two Spanish anti-piracy caracks became interested in them. Ponce de León could not risk being caught. Summary hanging was the usual end for captured pirates. He could not take that risk.

He sailed in the opposite direction, but his caravel was no match for the larger caracks, designed for war. Fortunately, nightfall was coming with dark clouds of a pending storm. They sailed into the inland waterway that runs along the east coast of Florida. They hid among the many small islands in much shallower water than the caracks could manage.

Ponce de León waited until morning before sailing away. But morning came and their pursuers were still there. The caracks maneuvered as close as they could get and started firing their cannon. Their shot was falling short, but clearly, Ponce de León and his crew could not stay there. Even if they could evade their pursuers, Saint Augustine would be alerted, and they would still end up hanging from a yardarm.

He ordered the ship to sail as close to the beach on the mainland as possible and scuttle it. They took whatever they could carry and waded to the beach. Not having any telescopes, their pursuers could not see clearly what Ponce de León and his men were doing, but they could make out that their prey was half sunk, tilting at a 45-degree angle. With this knowledge, they sailed away.

It took a week for Ponce de León and his crew to reach Saint Augustine on foot. They could not miss the town as all they had to do was trek along the beach northwards. Upon arrival, the colony master asked them about their origins. Europeans just did not appear out of the wilds like that. Were they the pirate crew that escaped?

Ponce de León explained that they were private explorers sent by the governor of Cuba to explore and map southern Florida and its eastern coast. Luckily, he had the maps as evidence. He presented the maps as a gift to the colony master. Maps were extremely valuable and considered as top state secrets. Fortunately, Ponce de León had made copies.

The colony master was pleased and let them stay. Besides, such a large number of new colonists arriving at once was a great boon. It ordinarily might take many years for the colony to attract so many new strong hands to build and expand the roughly hewn hamlet into a town. In fact, these strange explorers looking for a home would more than double the hamlet's population. The colony master told them there was not enough space for them to build homes within the stockade, but that they could choose anywhere they wanted outside, and he would immediately deed the land to them.

Saint Augustine was nothing but a small harbor, a wooden stockade surrounding two muddy streets of a dozen squalid huts, and a chapel with its small spire not quite standing straight to the skies. There were no women and no taverns. Just a handful of soldiers with their pikes and simple armor stood guard. The rest were farmers with a single priest to aid in the expansion of the Church. They were all simple men with simple minds.

Ponce de León was happy to live apart from them. He and his men chose the best farmland and built their houses, all of them helping the others in the constructing and the laying out of the land. After the month or two that this took, they next requested from the colony master to acquire the monopoly to sell strong drink. This was happily granted for twenty-five years, and Saint Augustine's first tavern was built. They had found their home.

CHAPTER TWENTY

Meeting the Parents

Six months later, Isabel finished her PhD dissertation. She compared the use of pagan allusions in the works of Luís Camões of Portugal and Miguel de Cervantes Saavedra of Spain. Despite writing during the depths of the Inquisition, they both got away with the many references to pagan gods, myths, and worlds. Besides being able to read, their writing required a Renaissance education from their readers to understand the allegories and allusions.

She had to defend her thesis in front of five professors, all experts in her field. She practiced with Juan, the only one she knew who could understand what she was trying to demonstrate. He knew if an allusion came from the Iliad, the Odyssey, or the Aeneid. He knew all the references to the obscure minor nymphs and demigods. More importantly, he knew their significance in the writings of those two luminaries of the Iberian Peninsula.

If Juan could not follow a certain line of thought in her dissertation, she knew she had to rewrite that section. Sometimes he would suggest a better example to strengthen her logic. He proved to be an invaluable resource for her preparation. After nearly a month of either confirming or picking apart her thesis, she felt she was ready. She informed the Chair of her department it was time.

The Chair arranged for her thesis defense six weeks later. Besides himself, there would be four other professors eager to pounce on her work of five years. During these six weeks, Isabel was growing anxious, as if she was preparing for a sports championship. She managed to not panic, as she had the best coach and trainer she could possibly have found. Juan both calmed her and challenged her in the right ways.

He accompanied her to the event of mental gymnastics on the south side of Chicago. It took all day. Juan sat outside on a bench in the hallway the whole time. During breaks, they would walk within the gothic quadrangle of the University with gargoyles staring down from their perches. Her anxiety flowed out of her heart as she held Juan's hand tightly in her own. After a tight hug and light kiss, she was ready to dive back into the fray.

It was 1600 when the interrogation was finally over. The professors would discuss her thesis for another hour and decide if they would allow her to join their ranks as a Doctor of Philosophy. She would return to learn their decision after an hour. During this time, they walked around Hyde Park. Her silence and fidgeting revealed her nervousness. Juan gave up trying to distract her with conversation. The best she could do would be to point out the many landmarks surrounding one of the greatest universities in the world.

Isabel returned at the appointed hour. She stood in front of them as they sat behind a long table. They pointed out many flaws in her thesis, the illogical conclusions, and the weak evidence of her presentation. They held off informing her of their decision like the hosts of the Oscars, delaying the results of Best Actor or Best Film. But in the end, they approved her dissertation and the granting of her degree. She literally jumped in the air and shouted with joy. One professor even suggested that she publish it.

She was floating on air as she left the room. She ran to Juan and leaped into his arms. Her tears of relief wetted his hair. She cried with joy. It was a major accomplishment. She had no idea what she would do with it, nor even cared. She was now free to shake off the shackles of academia and experience whatever Juan would show her. She wanted to share as much of life as he would with her, whether that would be only months, years, or hopefully decades.

Juan told her to not think of anything and let her mind rest. He would take care of everything else, starting with a celebration. They still had a few hours before dinner. Juan flagged a taxi, and they went to the iconic bar, the Berghoff in the Loop. There he had their signature Berghoff bourbon, and she had one of their self-brewed ales. They both had a perfect, warm, soft pretzel to stop their stomachs from growling. They sat at the long bar, noticing what a fine couple they made in the reflection of the equally long mirror covering the wall in front of them.

Another taxi took them to the Michelin-starred Boka for their dinner. The maître d' showed them to their private table in the glass-enclosed terrace. A waiter from the bar accompanied them. He suggested perhaps one of their famous cocktails. Juan ordered a bottle of NV Egly-Ouriet "Les Crayeres Blanc Noirs Grand Cru Brut" Vielle Vigne, instead. With a name like that, price clearly was no object with him.

To further the point, he ordered the eight-course tasting menu with the addition of a whole roasted dry-aged duck. They washed it down with the suggested reserve wine pairing, though Juan could have easily created one himself from their magnificent wine list. They lingered with the grand finale of a bottle of sixty-two-year-old port wine. The feast more than made up for their meagre lunch.

It was almost midnight when Isabel placed her hand on his thigh, leaned her head on his shoulder, and whispered that they had been eating and drinking for six hours in the most wonderful way imaginable. Still, it had been a long day for her and perhaps he could ask for the bill.

They walked a bit wobbly out to the waiting taxi; she more than him. It was the middle of November. The bracing icy wind blowing off Lake Michigan hit them full in the face, sobering them to a degree. The taxi drove down Lake Shore Drive and returned them to their hotel, the Sophy-Hyde Park on East 53rd Street.

They slept until noon. After a room service lunch, they discussed ideas of what to do next. She offered to show him her Chicago. He accepted, but only in the late Spring of the next year when the weather was more hospitable. This pleased her immensely, as it meant that he planned on being with her for at least the next six months. Besides, she was not feeling energetic enough after the night before to do much of anything.

The next day, they flew back to Saint Augustine and packed away their winter clothes. They had breakfast in shorts, slippers, and light bathrobes on the terrace overlooking the gently lapping waves of the ocean. The seagulls flitting above shrieked, 'welcome home'. They made plans to return to Chicago in a month for her graduation ceremony. That would be cause for another major celebration. Juan was pleased to have another occasion to give her a very memorable experience.

They flew back to Chicago two days before the graduation ceremony. Juan hated flying. As they were approaching O'Hara airport to land, he tried to dispel his nervousness and asked Isabel, "Did you know that the O'Hara's of Ireland are one of the lost tribes of Japan?"

Isabel looked at his serious face and wondered for a moment. "Lost tribes of Japan? What?"

"Like I just said." Then he smiled.

After a moment, she laughed, "Oh, I get it. Ohara is a common Japanese surname. Now, Juan, that's silly. Sometimes I can't tell if you're joking or telling me another arcane fact unknown to everyone but you."

She appreciated his one-of-a-kind sense of humor. There was always a twist that appealed to the intellect in a bizarre sort of way. She was terrible at telling jokes; so, she never tried. Good humor required a kind of logic that challenged reality in unexpected ways. Her logic was always expected. People just shook their heads and smiled politely at her attempts at funny stories.

They had to stay at The Peninsula Hotel on the Magnificent Mile on the Near North Side, as all the hotels in Hyde Park were booked by friends and family coming to see the convocation of their loved ones. It was even colder than their visit a month before.

"How do people live here in this clearly inhospitable climate?"

"Just like they do in Moscow and other northern cities."

"My Latin blood will never be used to it."

"Just don't think about it. Let's go pick up my cap and gown."

They took a taxi to Hyde Park and returned to the hotel suite. Juan had no interest in stepping outside even to eat. He stood by the wide window of their room overlooking Lake Michigan. The furious wind blew clouds of powdery snow like a sandstorm in a desert. Even the double-paned glass could not keep out the sound of the angry, howling winter wind. They still had a wonderful dinner in the hotel.

As they sat back with their typical after-dinner Portuguese port wine, Juan was warm inside and ready to share another life experience.

"You know, Isabel, I stayed at the Peninsula Hotel in Hong Kong, their flagship hotel. It sits on the southern edge of Kowloon Peninsula, across from the old brick clock tower. That's where the regularly scheduled train from London a hundred years ago would finally run out of track.

"I stayed there about twenty years ago. I remembered an African potentate took over an entire floor of the most expensive hotel in Hong Kong, with about fifty court denizens and other camp followers. They came for a week's shopping trip. I remembered how they all wore their very colorful robes and took the hotel's Rolls Royces about the city, stopping traffic to buy the brand-name luxury items.

"I preferred to take the passenger ferries across the harbor to Hong Kong Island, a one-minute walk from the hotel. Didn't need a Rolls Royce or a Bentley to get to the other side. The hotel had a wonderful Swiss restaurant on the ground floor. I don't know what's there now. I can tell you there's much more to their cuisine than fondue. Had a great wine collection, too."

"Juan, I must admit that nothing else besides fondue comes to mind. You'll just need to add that to the long list of things you need to teach me."

"Fine, but you're the one that's keeping the list. There must be a real Swiss restaurant somewhere in the entire state of Florida. Let me find one." Juan reached for his cell phone and did a search for Swiss restaurants in Florida.

After ten minutes of frustration, he put his phone down. "Nothing but fondue, German, or French restaurants. Swiss cuisine is not German or French. I don't even know what that means, French cuisine or German cuisine. Is it the cuisine of Gascony or of Languedoc? Is it the cuisine of Bavaria or of the Rhineland? Will have to do a proper search after we get back."

They walked up the stairs to their room and went to sleep early. The next day would be a long one. They had a quick breakfast. Isabel could not sit still. She paced about, her heart fluttering with the excitement of finally finishing the too long chapter in her life of being a student. It was time to live with the best teacher of life she could imagine.

Ponce de León muttered to himself as he rushed from the hotel's front door to the taxi, waiting to hold the door for Isabel to enter before getting in and shutting out the winter wind. "How can it be colder than yesterday?"

Crowds were already milling around the entrance to Rockefeller Chapel where the University holds all graduation ceremonies. It is called a 'chapel' but it really is as grand and huge as any gothic cathedral. Isabel changed into her gown and joined the other PhD's to-be. The BA's and the MA's, with their simple black gowns and black paper board square hats, overwhelmed the smaller group of PhD's with their maroon gowns and soft black caps. Isabel only recognized a few others. She had not been in a classroom for four years already, having done all her research online.

Isabel looked frantically for her parents, but they were not to be seen. She took her place in the procession of the robed, preparing to march into the Chapel. Juan found a seat as close to the front as he could. The graduates marched in and took their places, waiting for their names to be called. The President of the University gave a stirring and spirited convocation address about future citizens of the world and lifetime learning.

Each student's name was called. That student solemnly walked up and received his diploma. Juan was shocked that the PhD in front of Isabel was wearing sneakers. The tacky sneakers extinguished the solemnity of the occasion. He shook his head at the youth of the day.

Finally, it was Isabel's turn. As she approached to receive her diploma, a great commotion broke out. Her mother rushed up with her winter coat still on, pulled out a camera, and interrupted everything. Two ushers pulled her away, telling her that the official photographer was taking professional photos, which would be available after the convocation. Clearly, they could not have every parent and grandparent stopping the ceremony to take photos.

All Isabel could do was roll her eyes, shake the President's hand, and accept her hard-won diploma. She could do nothing about her face turning red. Looking down at her shoes, she quickly exited the stage. Juan felt bad for her. No one can choose their parents. He knew that they would have dinner together later that evening. He would have to be at his most charming.

After all the fresh graduates processed down the center aisle and out the door, everything was over but the celebration. Isabel pushed her way back in and found Juan standing by his seat. He gave her a great hug and kiss. "I'm so proud of you. You were wonderful."

"Why, Juan? Why? Why must she ruin everything I do? She delights in embarrassing me whenever possible." Tears rolled down her face.

"Now, don't even think that. I'm sure she doesn't mean anything bad."

"Juan, please don't. I know her all too well. Look, why don't you go back to the hotel. I'll meet you there in a few hours. I need to meet old friends and my parents, too, everyone taking many photos. We'll have dinner tonight as planned. You made the reservations, right?"

"Yes, of course. Fine, I'll meet you back at the hotel."

It was past 1600 when a frazzled and exhausted Isabel entered their room. She dropped everything on a chair and collapsed on the bed. She awoke two hours later, just in time to prepare for dinner with her parents and Juan.

They arrived on time at the Alinea in Lincoln Park. Isabel's parents had arrived a half an hour earlier and were waiting in the cocktail lounge. Isabel's mother ran up to them and gave Isabel a great tipsy hug.

"Oh, my dear, you look so beautiful! You gave a great performance today. This must be your new man. So glad to meet you. Isabel has told me a lot about you. She likes you very much.

"I must say, Isabel, he doesn't look bad for a man his age. I just can't understand why you choose men so much older than you. The last one had children as old as you and, it must be said, was married. What you saw in him was beyond me. At least Juan here has money. It's old money, if I understand correctly."

"Mom! Will you stop! Please, at least try to behave yourself. You know, you really don't need to embarrass me every chance you get."

"Embarrassing you? How's that?"

The maitre'd interrupted. "Your table is waiting for you this way. You can bring your drinks with you."

They followed the maitre'd to a private room with the lights along the Lake sparkling in the distance. Juan offered his arm to Isabel's mother, who took it with a great beaming smile and fluttering heart. The maitre'd pulled a chair out for Isabel's mother to sit. Then did the same for Isabel. The maitre'd placed the menus on the table and told them their waiter would be with them soon.

Juan shook the hand of Isabel's father, who clearly was the shy one of the couple. "How do you like Chicago, Mr. Silva de Santos? Do you come here often?"

"Call me Miguel. No, I've just been a few times on business. I like it except for the wind. It's not called the 'Windy City' for nothing." A nervous chuckle trailed his banal statement.

They settled into their seats and gave the orders to the waiter. Juan chose an appropriate wine, and the evening began.

"Juan! This place is expensive! I looked it up. It's a Michelin starred restaurant. Are you sure this was a good choice?"

"Now, don't you worry about a thing, Mrs. Silva de Santos. It has all been taken care of. The Alinea is the only three-starred Michelin restaurant in Chicago. It's easier to make choices when others have decided who's the best. Besides, it's not every day we can celebrate such a wonderful and talented young woman as your incredible daughter."

"Oh, Juan, please call me Sophia." She would have purred if she could.

"Sophia, a beautiful name that means divine wisdom in Greek."

Sophia did most of the talking. She grilled Juan, digging into every detail of his life. Juan rose to the occasion and answered her questions without actually answering them. Yet he carried on with such charm that Sophia was pleased, no matter how he answered.

Isabel and her father were practically silent the whole time. Near the end of the evening, Sophia leaned on Juan's shoulder and whispered loudly into his ear, audible to everyone else at the table,

"Let me tell you, buster. If I was twenty years younger, you wouldn't have a chance."

Unfazed, Juan thanked her for being so kind and generous with her compliments. He offered cocktails at a new and hot rooftop bar in the Loop. Miguel came to the rescue and politely declined as Sophia appeared to be suddenly drowsy.

The two couples found their separate taxis and parted ways. Isabel leaned her head on his shoulder. "Thank you for all that. You really are the most charming man who knows exactly how to handle women of a certain age. Any other man would have cracked under the pressure. Let's just go back to the hotel. It's been a long day already. Besides, I have just enough energy to thank you the best way I know how."

CHAPTER TWENTY-ONE

After the PhD, Now What?

It was late January when the topic came up. They had just finished breakfast and were discussing Isabel's future. She had an advanced degree in something that was really best used in academia, like being a professor in comparative literature or the like. That, of course, was the furthest from her mind. She was through with classrooms and stuffy academic departments where the culture of publish or perish thrived. No, it was time to live.

"So, my precious, you have finished your degree, and we are past the holidays. The new year is well underway. What would you like to do now? You know I will do anything I can to make you happy in whatever you choose to do."

"My adoring man, the answer is simple. I want to be with you. Whatever you choose to do, I want to be by your side. I love you with every fiber of my being."

"As I love you, too. But you're too young to spend your days watching the waves. Give me some ideas and we'll do it."

"OK, fine. I want you to teach me how to live. Show me everything I have been missing all my life so far. Educate me in the ways of the world."

"Educate you in the ways of the world? In that case, I guess we should start by seeing the world. How about if we start with your roots? Let's go to the Azores and then on to Portugal. We'll continue east until we return full circle. Since we are in no rush, let's sail around the world. Sailing's my favorite way to travel. Let me get a map of the world and we can plan our route." Juan was clearly becoming excited about the idea.

"That's a great idea! I'd love to."

Juan returned with a world map and spread it out on the table.

"How long would you like to sail? One year, two, five, more?" As soon as he said that he silently considered that he would have to leave her at some friendly port while he and his crew flew back to Florida for their annual ritual. That probably would be a very long flight. It was doable, but not preferable. Isabel came to the rescue.

"I would love to see the world, but I'm not sure about years. Let's see how we feel after six months. But my dearest, I've never been on a cruise before, but I doubt I could take all that I have read about them for so long. The endless buffets, the horde of people, the short times visiting ports, etc."

"Precious Isabel, I said 'sail around the world'. That's exactly what I meant. We'll sail my yacht, stopping where we want for as long as we want."

"Sail your yacht? I don't know how to sail at all. Aren't sailboats kind of small for long cruises?"

"I'll show you mine this afternoon. It's not so small. As for sailing it, I'll bring some of my best friends along. They can be the crew who does the actual sailing."

"Really? When I think of sailing boats, I think of twenty-foot boats for two couples going out for an afternoon. There's more space in an RV." Isabel was doubtful that would be a good idea.

"Twenty feet? I would not go out of sight of land in the Atlantic with that. Do you know the difference between a 'boat' and a 'ship'?" Isabel shook her head.

"Imagine this: a 'boat' can go on a ship, but a 'ship' cannot go on a boat. Mine is more of a ship than a boat. It's 184 feet long. Mine is a ketch, which means it has two masts and three sails. It also has two diesel engines; in case we enter the doldrums. But we never enter the doldrums. I know where they all are. So, we just sail."

Ponce de León always thought it was way over the top. It was two and a half times larger than the caravels they sailed together in the beginning. His mates insisted and bought it themselves as a present about twenty years before. That was after a hurricane smashed the previous one to pieces, which sank still tied to the dock.

"184 feet? How many people do you need to sail that?"

"For ocean sailing, I generally take ten crew members plus me. I'm the Captain. I could also have fourteen guests, but I think it would be better if it's just us."

"How big are the bedrooms? How many sleep to a room?"

"In most yachts of this size, the captain puts the crewmen two to a room. But my crew are my closest friends. Everyone has his own room. We'll stay in the captain's quarters. It's bigger than most hotel rooms. We'll bring Jorge along, so we'll eat well, too."

"What if the crew members get tired of sailing? I wouldn't want any mutinies on board."

"Mutinies? Impossible! We're all the closest of friends. These men are all very experienced sailors, having spent many months at sea without stepping foot on land. For us, we'll spend only a few weeks at sea at a time. In any case, I have many more sailor friends. Anyone who gets tired can fly back and another would come to replace him."

"No women sailors?"

"Women sailors? What do you mean?"

"You know, sailors who happen to be women."

"Sailors who are women?" Juan considered the idea for a moment. "No. Not a good idea. It might cause conflict among the sailors and that's the last thing we need. Conflicts like that could cause a mutiny. And mutinies are no joke."

"Really? But what about me?"

"You? You'd be a guest. You'd be my guest and treated with the utmost respect."

"Hmm… I admit the idea is intriguing. I trust you completely. Oh, why not? Live a little, Isabel." Isabel grew excited about this never-before considered idea.

"Wonderful! It would be my greatest pleasure to show you the world. We'll start our voyage in May after the winter storms and before the hurricane season. That will give us time to prepare. It just so happens that the Azores are on the way for those sailing to Europe. I named our ship The Odyssey."

"How would we go? Would we just sail in a straight line?"

"A straight line? No. We wouldn't do that even if we were on a steamship. No, from here we will head to the Caribbean islands. We'll catch the southern Trade Winds somewhere east of Puerto Rico and sail northeast to the Azores. From there, it would be an almost straight line to Lisboa. We want to avoid the low-pressure systems as they are what cause the storms. For your first voyage, we'll keep it as calm as possible.

"From Lisboa, we'll head south through the Mediterranean, out the Suez Canal and on to Asia. We'll cross the Pacific, pass through the Panama Canal, and return home. We'll save the rest of the world for future voyages."

"And Spain. We must visit your homeland."

"Spain? That was not part of my plan."

"Why not? I want to understand your roots and everything about you. You simply must show me your hometown, your family, and this wonderful uncle you've spoken so much about."

"My family? My uncle? Ah, no, that's not possible. They have all passed on to the next realm."

"Everyone, Juan? I can't believe that."

"Everyone. No one is left. I'm the only one left alive. Maybe it's better we don't go after all." The smile left Juan's face, and he fell into silence.

Isabel panicked. What mistake did she make? What is wrong with meeting his family? She still had much to understand about her strange lover. What could she say to correct the situation? She rose from her chair and hugged him closely against her bosom.

"Oh, come now, my precious Juan. What's with the face? How about you show me exactly what you want and nothing more? If you don't think it's important, then it's not important to me either. Forget I asked about it."

"No. Your question is normal. But my situation is anything but normal. All of my family and childhood friends have died or otherwise disappeared. Going back to my village would just cause me great pain. That is all behind me now and has no bearing on my life today. It was close to Madrid. We can visit the rest of Spain and the sights, if you like. No problem."

Juan was still not his cheerful self. Isabel understood he must loath his homeland. She thought of a solution, as she very much wanted to visit the land of Cervantes.

"Look, Juan, this is what we'll do. After we've seen Portugal, I'll go to Spain on my own for a week or two and meet you back in Lisboa afterwards."

That idea cheered Juan up. "Well, that might be an excellent idea. Let's decide after we've arrived in Lisboa."

They chatted about traveling and possible destinations. What should she pack and what planning did they need to do? Then the subject slowly changed to other things and finally to silence. Isabel clearly had something on her mind and was preparing Juan to introduce it. Then she asked the question.

"Juan, we have been together for almost a year, ten months exactly. Yet, I know I already love you with all my heart, mind, and body. Now that we have this wonderful plan, I want to ask you something." She went silent.

"Of course, dearest. You know I love you the same, if not more. What is it?"

"Juan, I've been thinking lately... I've been thinking how wonderful it would be if we lived together. I already have decided you are my man, my man for the rest of my life. I can't even imagine life without you. What do you think of the idea?"

Now it was Juan's turn to fall silent.

Sensing his discomfort, she sputtered, "Of course, if it's still too early, I understand completely. Forget I even asked the question."

"No, no, Isabel. It's a wonderful idea. It's just that I would feel much better about it if we married."

"Married?! We don't need to do that. Really. I have no problem living with a man being unmarried. You should know that despite my being quite naïve about many things in life, I'm still a modern girl and such traditions as marriage are simply unnecessary. I don't want any legal claim on you. A claim of love is much better. A legal claim without love is just not part of my mental makeup."

"I would much prefer if we were married before living together. Call me old-world old fashioned. It's a form of respect and commitment of two people for each other."

This extremely traditional way of thinking threw Isabel aback. She was not expecting that. Of course, many young women would love to have a legal claim to the Ponce de León estate. Would gladly sign any prenuptial agreement. But that just was not her. Was this the end, then? She tried another tack.

"Look, Juan. First, I don't know in what century you were raised. As we can easily see around us, marriage has nothing to do with commitment or respect. It's just a legal contract. Nothing more. We don't even need to be married to have children. Any children we have will carry your name.

"Second, even if I did want to get married, I would never marry a man I haven't lived with for quite some time. Sleeping with him a few nights a week is not the same. If you want me to even consider marriage, we need to see if we can survive being together all day, every day. If you insist, I can see we might have an irreconcilable difference in our ideas about life. Oh, dear! I wasn't expecting this."

Now it was Juan's turn to panic. After all, he really did love this odd young woman greatly.

"OK, OK, my precious Isabel. Let's not talk about the subject now. We can think about it after we return from our voyage. Who knows? Maybe after a few weeks at sea, we'll stop talking to each other."

"Oh, I highly doubt that, my adorable man. Let's get dressed. Show me this incredible yacht of yours. I can't wait to start our odyssey on The Odyssey!"

Juan quickly responded, "I hope it will not be an 'odyssey', but smooth sailing with everything going to plan, not at all like Odysseus' arduous trip home from the Trojan War. You didn't grievously offend Poseidon by blinding his son, the Cyclops, did you? If so, we better call the whole thing off."

CHAPTER TWENTY-TWO

Onboard the Odyssey

Three weeks later, they were all aboard the Odyssey, leaving the marina for the open seas of the Atlantic Ocean. Antón was at the helm. The wind was behind them, and the sun was just rising ahead.

Isabel was standing at the bow with the sea breeze blowing her long cinnamon-colored hair all about her face. She was thrilled as she had never been before. This was the start of her first glorious adventure. She held the railing to steady herself while her feet were dancing. A brilliant smile lit up her face.

Juan came up behind her and pulled her tight against his chest. "How is my beautiful adventuress?"

"Absolutely wonderful! I'm completely thrilled by it all. We seem to be going so fast. How fast are we going?"

"Last I checked, we're sailing at eighteen knots."

"Knots? What does that mean?"

"A knot is one nautical mile or, putting it another way, one minute of latitude. Do you remember your high school geometry class? The equator is a circle and a circle has 360 degrees, right? A degree is too large on a global scale for navigators. So, each degree is equal to one hour or sixty minutes. This equates to a nautical mile being 1.15 times longer than a land mile, which was defined long before ocean navigating. We use nautical miles because it's much easier for navigation. We're going about twenty miles an hour, which is quite fast for sailing."

"Twenty miles an hour? Only? That seems very slow."

"Yes. Sorry, my dear. We're not driving down Interstate 95. Even the modern cargo ships go no more than thirty miles an hour. I hope this isn't a disappointment."

"No! Not at all. I'm just surprised."

"The great explorers of 500 years ago sailed around the world in caravels that had a top speed of nine miles per hour, but usually sailed at five or six miles per hour. Don't worry. Even as slow as we're going by your modern standards, we'll still reach the Azores in about three weeks."

"OK, so tell me where we're going exactly. I don't need to know because I'd follow you anywhere without question. I haven't asked any detailed questions until now, already several hours from land. There's no turning back and I wouldn't want to, anyway. I'm just curious. Apparently, we have a lot of time for good conversation."

"That we do, my precious. Fine, let me explain. First, we'll sail to Bermuda. That will take about a week. From there, we'll head to the Azores. That will take another two weeks. From there to Lisboa will take another week. So, we have about a month before we arrive in Europe, depending on how many days we spend stopping at Bermuda and the Azores."

"Bermuda? Hmm… Never thought about visiting there before."

"It's a quaint British island, far from anywhere else. They say it was the inspiration for Shakespeare's play, the Tempest."

"The Tempest? That's my favorite play of his. Well, that's reason enough."

"Ah! Great minds think alike. It's mine, too. 'What's past is prologue'."

Isabel recited another line. "We are such stuff as dreams are made on, and our little life is rounded with a sleep."

"Allow me, my dear:

Our revels now are ended. These our actors,

As I foretold you, were all spirits and
Are melted into air, into thin air:
And, like the baseless fabric of this vision,
The cloud-capp'd towers, the gorgeous palaces,
The solemn temples, the great globe itself,
Yea, all which it inherits, shall dissolve
And, like this insubstantial pageant faded,
Leave not a rack behind. We are such stuff
As dreams are made on, and our little life
Is rounded with a sleep."

Isabel's passion was intensifying. She wrapped her arms around his neck and pulled his ear to her lips. She nibbled his earlobe and whispered,

"I am your wife if you will marry me.
If not, I'll die your maid. To be your fellow
You may deny me, but I'll be your servant Whether you will or no."

Juan lifted her in his arms, kissed her warm neck, and replied,

"I would not wish Any companion in the world but you, Nor can imagination form a shape, Besides yourself, to like of."

"Oh, my dearest, most precious Juan. I feel the same. Let's discuss this after we return from our grand voyage. Right now, what I really want to do is to take you to our cabin, the Captain's Cabin, and try out that comfy looking bed there. Would that be an appropriate thing to do onboard an ocean-going yacht?"

"It is the most appropriate thing of all." And he led her below deck.

They resurfaced in time for lunch, roasted turkey legs and grilled eggplant served in the galley by chef Jorge. Everyone enjoyed lunch as if nothing had happened earlier in the Captain's Cabin. The crew present discussed details of the wind and current, while the others continued manning the rigging and lines (ropes).

A few of the crew were sleeping as they would do the sailing through the night. After all, they could not rest at anchor in the middle of the ocean. The anchor would just hang uselessly far above the ocean bottom. In this way, though they only sailed at an average of fifteen knots per hour, they still could sail 360 nautical miles a day.

For the rest of the afternoon, the two lovers relaxed in the shallow cocktail pool with chilled white wine and their current favorite novel. Isabel took care not to let her kindle get wet while Juan did not really care if some water splashed on his hardback novel. She was reading Homer's The Odyssey for the third time. Juan was reading Henry Miller's Tropic of Capricorn for the second time.

Dinner was always a magnificent gourmet experience. Tales both long and short were shared, both hilarious and tragic. Slowly, as the voyage progressed, Isabel came to know the mates of her man. Each was as fascinating as the next.

Isabel asked Antón one day, "Say, Antón. Why does your name have an accent mark over the 'o'?"

"Ah, Juan, you found yourself a thinking one. Well, dearie pips, I never thought about it. I guess you know the rules of Spanish spelling. Normally, the accent of a word falls on the second to last syllable. Unless,…"

"Unless it ends in a consonant, in which case it falls on the last syllable. So, you don't need an accent mark."

"You're a sharp one, Isabel. As I was saying, unless it's short for António, which is always spelled with an accent over the first 'o'. At least, that's how my mother explained it to me. Otherwise, just call me by my Russian name, Anton, which has no accent mark." He broke off into a loud laugh.

They spoke English in her presence, but broke into their native archaic Castilian, accented by whatever region they grew up in, whenever they spoke to each other. Isabel could barely recognize it as even Spanish. She could understand nothing. She just shrugged her shoulders and listened to it as she would to classical baroque music.

And so, the days passed, and they arrived at Bermuda, the magical home of Shakespeare's Ariel and Prospero. They docked at the tiny town of Hamilton that served as the capital. Tiny because the entire population is about 800.

As they approached the marina, Juan introduced the crown colony to Isabel. "They named Bermuda after the Spanish navigator Juan de Bermúdez, who discovered it in 1505." Juan stopped and chuckled to himself. "Oh, he was such a rogue, yet had the funniest jokes, especially after some pints of ale.

Isabel was learning to ignore Juan's sometimes bizarre comments.

"Anyway, it took until 1612 before the English established a permanent colony here. There are over 180 islands and islets that form this archipelago. There are about 60,000 people living here, many of whom are originally of Portuguese descent. We are about parallel to North Carolina about 650 miles that way." He concluded by pointing to the west.

"That's enough to start, my love. I'll just have to discover the rest." She said as she took his arm in hers.

They only spent one night docked at Bermuda. Two weeks of smooth sailing landed them at the small marina at Praia de Vitoria on the island of Terceira, one of the nine islands of the Azores. Isabel was buzzing with excitement to finally step foot on the homeland of her beloved grandparents.

"OK, Captain, tell me about this place."

"Alright. There are nine islands in the Azores. This one, Terceira, is where the US airbase is that also serves as the island's airport. There is basically only a small squadron of transport or communications planes here now.

"All of these islands are the tops of volcanoes. Several are slumbering and steaming. About every two hundred years, there are major earthquakes and eruptions. That's why you won't see anything built before 1841. The disaster before that was in 1614. I guess we're due for one any time now, though I doubt during the time we'll be here.

"If you want to lie on the beach, you're out of luck. The land is full of black volcanic rock right to the water's edge. The best thing these islands produce, besides its people and their descendants," he kissed her lightly on her forehead, "are dairy products. Their cheese and butter are some of the best in the world. Unfortunately, their wine is not the best example of what Portugal can offer. I'd prefer to show you the rest rather than tell you about it."

The crew headed to the Quinta de Açores and filled the veranda overlooking the Isle of Brazil (no relation to the country). They spent the rest of the day eating Azorean beef washed down with the local craft beer.

Juan found a taxi and started the tour of the island for Isabel. Juan had no trouble communicating with the local taxi driver. Isabel learned 'proper' continental Portuguese growing up and could barely understand anything he said.

"How do you understand him so well?"

"It's the Portuguese I learned, my sweet. Why? You don't?"

"It sounds like what my grandparents spoke when speaking to each other. But they made sure I learned what I guess you would call proper Portuguese."

"You know that any "proper" language is a very modern thing. "Proper" French, "proper" English", "proper" Spanish", etc. are all less than 100 years old. That all came about through universal public education. Even now, there are strong regional differences. For example, I don't speak "proper" Spanish or even "proper" English, for that matter."

They left the port town and drove across cobbled country lanes to the top of an apparently dead volcano to a magnificent lookout point called Miradouro da Serra do Cume. From there they could see far below them a panorama of rolling fields with dairy farms, the blue ocean, and other volcanic hilltops. One was even slowly letting off steam.

Isabel hugged him tightly. "Ah, this is incredible. Did I forget to tell you this morning how much I love you?"

"No, my precious, you did not forget. I clearly remember every time you tell me."

They drove back down and along the coast, through little villages where the front doors of the houses were only two steps from the road. Within forty minutes, they arrived at a larger village. It was Biscoitos, the hometown of Isabel's grandparents.

"This is it, my love. This is where your grandparents came from."

The taxi stopped at a small café on the main road and waited for them. Juan took her hand and showed her what there was to see. He showed her the simple wine museum that used to be a working winery. Walking carefully along the narrow space by the side of the road, he pointed out how very tidy and clean the houses and streets were.

They walked down to the ocean side where they had something to eat at the small restaurant. They sat outside on the deck by the rocky coast where the ocean had carved out natural swimming pools. Beside them were a few wooden kiosks selling local produce.

"The wine's not very good here. So, I recommend the local liqueur made from honey, called appropriately 'Abelhinha', which means little bee. The typical bread of the islands is made from sweet potato flour. Let's order that with some of their cheese."

They leisurely drove around the island along the coast. Several times, they had to stop and wait for a herd of dairy cows to move aside or let a large farm tractor pass. They returned to the yacht in time to clean up for dinner. The rest of the crew was already there.

They walked the short distance to the restaurant Sabores do Chef, which offered fine Portuguese dining for those who arrive by yacht and not by plane. They had the local seafood with decent white wine from the nearby island of Pico. The next day they set sail again, continuing to continental Portugal.

Eight days later, they docked at the Cascais Marina, a wonderful example of a well-to-do traditional Iberian cobblestoned town, about forty minutes by light rail to the center of Lisboa. Juan hired a car and driver to show them the important sights of Lisboa, one of the most beautiful capitals in the world. He let the driver do most of the talking, which was just as well.

Juan had not been there since before the disastrous earthquake and tsunami of 1755 that destroyed most everything around Lisboa (nine on the Richter scale). Cascais was just a sleepy fishing village the last time he was there and not the bustling rich tourist town it had become.

The driver was friendly. Speaking Portuguese, he asked, "Senhora, I think I can hear an American accent. Is that where you are from?"

"Yes. My grandparents were Portuguese."

"Ah, wonderful. And you, senhor, I can guess you are from Terceira?"

"That's exactly correct. In fact, we just came from Terceira now."

"I thought so. I can hear your accent. I'm from São Miguel myself."

"Really? The Azorean homeland of João de Melo."

"Yes, but I never read anything by him. I'm not much of a reader, I'm afraid."

"I only read 'O Meu Mondo não É deste Reino' (My World Is not of this Realm). I found it to be very heavy reading, though I learned a lot about agricultural village life of seventy-five years ago on an Azorean island. That was the time when this young woman's grandparents were growing up on Terceira."

They chatted about various things between stopping at the many tourist sites for Isabel to take it all in. This was her first

European city, and she loved every minute, every detail, every sound and smell. They spent a week in and around Lisboa.

For another four weeks, they drove north through the center of the country, stopping at places like the old university town of Coimbra, the Douro River wine valley, and Guimaraes, where the nation of Portugal started. Once they reached the northwest border with Spain's Galicia, they followed the coast all the way to the Spanish border at Andalucía in the southeast, passing places like Portugal's second city, Porto, Sines, the hometown of Vasco de Gama, and windy Sagres, the site Prince Henry (Henrique) established as his center of navigation from where the Portuguese explorers set sail to discover the rest of the world.

They drove back through the heart of Alentejo, where over half the world's supply of cork comes from, enjoying that region's wonderful cuisine and wine along the way. After resting in Cascais for a few days, Isabel was ready for Spain.

"Are you sure you don't want to come with me, my love?"

"Yes, I'm sure. I have too many terrible memories of my homeland. I would not be good company. Take your time. Rather than wait for you here, we will meet you at the marina in Barcelona. Call me when you're ready. I'll take you to the airport. Your flight leaves in less than three hours."

She cried as he waved her off at Lisboa's airport. Juan was sad himself, missing her already. Once she disappeared into the security line, he turned and left. On the way back to the Odyssey, he pondered why he did not go with her. He really did not have any aversion to Spain. What was it?

After staring at the passing highway for some time in the taxi returning to Cascais, the answer came to him. It was obvious. He had a secret to keep. Even if no one would ever believe it, they would think he was crazy. She would insist on him showing her his home village where no one would know him, despite his small but excellent museum being there.

She would want to meet his uncle's family. His uncle died 500 years ago. How could he explain any of that? How could it be that literally no one in Spain knows him? Any explanation he would try would not be believable. He would become a fraud in her eyes. No, best to avoid all that. He already loved her too much to lose her. Unbearable pain would grip his heart to see doubt grow in her eyes and extinguish her love for him. The very thought caused his heart to race.

CHAPTER TWENTY-THREE

Memories of the Conquest of Granada

After Ponce de León returned from the airport, he gathered his friends at the half subterranean Pato brew pub off a pedestrian-only side street in downtown Cascais. A Canadian woman started the pub and brewery about ten years before. She usually had over a dozen beers on tap.

They filled the place, empty despite it being late afternoon. Ponce de León preferred the Belgian Trappist-style ales, being stronger and more flavorful. The pub was playing American rock and roll from the 1970's and 1980's. His mates cheered him up. They preferred their captain alone, without the complicating presence of a woman.

After a few pints, their archaic Castilian Spanish spilled out into the street. A few more pints brought on gutsy singing of sea shanties and drinking songs from their caravel sailing days. More than a few eyebrows were raised by passers-by. A few hours later, hunger started settling in. It was dark and time for dinner. Ponce de León paid the bill and herded his mates out to the street.

About halfway back to the marina, they stopped at the five-star Hotel Pestana Cidadela in the old city fort for dinner. They filled the back room of the restaurant in the converted old cistern, complete with rough-hewn rock walls and floors with heavy wooden beams holding the ceiling. They ate the hearty and flavorful

Portuguese cuisine with excellent examples of Douro and Alentejo wines. Fortunately, they were only a ten-minute walk to their cabins.

Ponce de León stood up and raised his glass. "My dear shipmates and friends, I thank you for joining me and my dear Isabel on this around the world adventure. Now that we have stepped foot back in the old country, what should we do?

"It's only a three-day sail to Barcelona. We have about two weeks to do it. We could stay in this wonderful hospitable Cascais eating, drinking, and being merry. We could do the same in Barcelona. Or we could stop at various port towns along the way. Any ideas?"

There was never a shortage of ideas with them. After an hour of boisterous discussion fueled with more wine, they decided to set sail after the next morning's breakfast and see if any port interested them as they sailed along the coast.

They embarked after a local breakfast at one of the marina cafes the next morning. These were all men of the seas. They always felt more at peace, more philosophical when being rocked by the Great Mother Ocean, either gently or fiercely, as the mood struck her. They sailed south, always with the coast just barely in sight, passing Setúbal, Sines, Sagras, Lagos, and Faro. Soon they entered Spanish waters. Everyone became pensive and silent, each lost in the thought of returning to their homeland.

It was already dark when they approached Cadiz. Without thinking, Ponce de León suddenly called out, "Let's spend the night at Cadiz. Any objections?"

There were none. Antón docked an hour later. When they stood on the dock, it was just about 2200, Spanish dinner time. They found an excellent tapas bar a short walk away and enjoyed themselves until early morning.

The next day, Ponce de León decided to walk the old city alone. This was where he embarked on the fateful second voyage of Columbus to the New World. Memories flooded back. He could hear and smell the same sensations when he first walked the streets of the major port city of Spain's exploring caravels and the treasure galleons returning with plundered Incan and Aztec silver and gold.

More importantly, Ponce de León remembered how excited he was when he boarded the Colina, one of Columbus' caravels. He was full of hope and excitement that he would at last find his destiny. If he did not find it, he would create it himself. He was confident that he would do so or die trying.

Lost in the revelry of his memories, he walked straight into the back of a young woman.

"Oh, I'm so sorry. ...Isabel?! Is that you?" His heart was racing at the coincidence.

She turned around and replied in Spanish. "I'm not Isabel. You're mistaking me for someone else." She walked hurriedly away from the strange man.

Ponce de León sat down on a nearby park bench to gather his thoughts. He closed his eyes. What's wrong with me? I'm mixing my past and my present. I'm confusing strangers with Isabel. Need to stay clear.

He had enough of Cadiz. He quickly returned to the Odyssey, gathered his mates, and set sail for the Mediterranean. They passed Gibraltar, a piece of little England attached to the underbelly of Iberia, and turned north along Spain's eastern coast full of tourist-laden beaches and over-built sea resorts.

By the end of the afternoon, Ponce de León recovered enough to suggest they spend the night at Málaga. This was met with general acclaim. They docked at the port marina two hours later. They filled the closest tapas bar and soon ordered enough tapa plates to cover the table. Many of the men were glad to be back in their homeland. Ponce de León was not, even without the burden of fending off Isabel's queries of his personal life.

He was quiet, sitting at the end of the table, sipping his wine and sampling a few of the tapas. His mates knew when he was in a pensive mood, it was best to leave him alone. Blocking out thoughts of Isabel, he asked himself why he wanted to stop at Málaga.

Of course! He was last here at the siege of the only remaining port of the Nasrid Moors of Spain in 1487. It was during the last war to drive the Moors finally out of the Iberian Peninsula and make Granada a part of Spain. He commanded a squadron of Knights of the Order of Calatrava. The Grand Master died at the earlier siege of Lopez. King Ferdinand took that opportunity to bring the Order to heel. This campaign would be the last gasp of glory for the old, once illustrious Order of Calatrava.

****

Granada was the sole remaining Muslim state on the Iberian Peninsula. The ascendant Christian kingdoms of Portugal and Castile had already absorbed the others. Granada was already a vassal state of Castile, meaning that it made annual tribute payments to stay independent. Giving tribute to one's neighbors does not indicate a relationship between equals.

Granada was weak and in near constant low-level civil war. Taxes were three times higher than in Castile. Everything was in decline and Grenada was friendless in the world. The rising Ottoman Turks were threatening the other Muslim nations of the Mediterranean and they needed the help of Spain.

Emir Abu-l-Hasan Ali of Grenada did not help matters. He took a Christian slave as his second wife. Though she dutifully converted to Islam, his first wife, their children, and the people were all offended by this. This would have consequences from the start of hostilities.

There often were border raids from both sides for decades. They were too minor for Castile to worry about. They had a much greater threat from their powerful Iberian neighbor of Aragon. Once the War of the Castilian Succession was over in 1479, when Ponce de León had his first experience of war, Isabela and Ferdinand joined their two kingdoms of Castile and Aragon, respectively. This allowed Castile to concentrate on absorbing Granada into its realm.

Such a border conflict occurred in December 1481. This time, Castile decided to finally end any Muslim governance in Iberia. By April 1482, King Ferdinand arrived and took command of Castilian forces himself. He pushed the Moors back and advanced into Granada proper.

Abu Abdallah, the son of Emir Abu-l-Hasan Ali's first wife, rebelled and styled himself as Emir Muhammad XII. At the battle of Lucena, he was captured. Ferdinand understood that this ambitious son of his enemy could be helpful in conquering Granada and released him in 1483 with a title of Duke of whatever cities he could capture.

In 1485, Abu Abdallah was defeated by Emir Abu-l-Hasan Ali's half-brother, Al-Zagal, and was forced to surrender to the protection of Ferdinand again. Al-Zagal, who was the one doing all the fighting, overthrew his ailing half-brother, the Emir, and occupied the throne himself. Ferdinand released Abu Abdallah again to continue causing mischief with their common enemy.

Meanwhile, Spanish forces were pushing deep into Granada from the west, approaching Málaga. Al-Zagal could not march to meet the Spanish army for fear of Abu Abdallah taking the capital city of Grenada. Indeed, on April 27, 1487, Abu Abdallah's army actively helped Fernando capture Vélez-Málaga, the gateway to Málaga itself.

Ponce de León and his squadron of Knights accompanied the Spanish army from the start. Since there were no pitched battles and only boring sieges, he and his knights saw very little military action. But they were certainly witnesses to the conduct of the entire war. It was May 7, 1487, and the army completed the encircling of Málaga. The Aragon navy was blockading the city by sea. The siege began.

The biggest difference between Ferdinand's army of the War of the Spanish Succession, which ended in 1479, and the current one, only eight years later, was the much greater quantity of cannons he had available. The sieges of the former war would go on interminably due to the lack of artillery. King Ferdinand bought cannon and bombards from whatever source he could find them, including Flanders, Burgundy, France, and elsewhere. The bombards were most effective against castle walls. They fired a large iron ball at a high angle, like a modern howitzer.

At twenty-seven years old, Ponce de León found himself with his knights patrolling the periphery against any smugglers trying to bring supplies into the city, or bandits trying to steal from their supply wagons. During the whole time, the roar of the bombards and the loud crunch as they hammered the city walls echoed throughout the land. Fires broke out in the city and lit up the night sky.

Despite all of this, Málaga held out until August 18. Ferdinand offered lenient terms of surrender to the besieged twice, but they refused. The commander with his North African soldiers and the local Spanish who converted to Islam to serve in the Emir's army had too much to fear by surrendering. When the besieged were finally defeated, it was too late for mercy.

In the end, their worst fears were realized. The commander killed himself. The North Africans were simply beheaded. The so-called 'renegade' Christian converts to Islam were burned at the stake. The Jewish population would have been sold into slavery but for the Jews of Castile paying their ransom. The remaining civilian population was enslaved.

Al-Zagal lost much prestige from the fall of Málaga, as it was the last port of the emirate and thus his last window to the world. Abu Abdallah took advantage of the situation. His army occupied Granada, the capital city, in late 1487. Al-Zagal and his remaining army fled to Baza.

Meanwhile, Ferdinand took nearly two years to consolidate what he had already conquered before he laid siege to Baza in the middle of 1489. The castle built high on a craig made bombards ineffective. They either had to starve the defenders or assault by force. Ferdinand knew that time was on his side. So, he waited.

Despite being so close to final victory, the morale of his army was sinking. Winter was approaching and normally campaigning ended until the next Spring. Yet they still found themselves below the undamaged walls. It took a personal visit from their Queen Isabella to motivate them to continue.

It was the first and only time Ponce de León saw her in person. This was the lady he and so many tens of thousands of others were fighting for in two wars. She was only eight years older than him, but she already looked aged. He could tell she was never beautiful, even in the blush of youth, when she married Ferdinand at age seventeen. Her over pious face did not help matters. She was always seen with a rosary and a prayer book in her hands. In short, she was nothing like the idealized Queen he had pictured, risking his life for her and her dynasty's success.

Ponce de León had never been much for piety. He could easily see the hypocrisy behind the mask. He would see so much more of the same by the 'Vicars of Christ' and their representatives in power. Emir Al-Zagal accepted Ferdinand's generous peace terms, knowing full well further resistance was hopeless. No one was burned at the stake or enslaved. Al-Zagal was pensioned off and never heard from again.

Isabella and Ferdinand had conquered the Emirate of Granada. Their friendly vassal Abu Abdallah occupied the city of Granada and the surrounding area. The conquered land was divided and given to various Spanish nobility in the best feudal fashion. The Spanish monarchs returned to Madrid, leaving the nobles to sort out local affairs. This included taking land that Abu Abdallah understood was to be his. Incredibly, he revolted in 1491.

Once again, Ponce de León marched with Ferdinand and his army south to lay siege to Granada. The siege began in April and would last for eight months. Once during this time, King Ferdinand invited Ponce de León for dinner in his tent. The King asked the young Ponce de León his advice on numerous subjects, including the possibility of being able to sail west to Asia (Ponce de León had no opinion on that), military matters (build roads through the mountains to help supply), what to do with Abu Abdallah after he was defeated (clearly he could not be trusted), how to treat the Muslims after the war (treat them as any other Spanish subject), and many other things.

Ponce de León gave the best advice his life experience and common sense would allow. At the end of dinner, the King gave him some advice of his own. There was no point in ignoring the obvious. The Order of the Knights of Calatrava was created as crusaders to drive the Moors out of Iberia. Their goal was nearly obtained. But their use as a nearly independent monastic military order was over. After the war, the Order would be brought under control of the Spanish crown and exist mainly as a symbolic tip of the hat to the Order's centuries of service.

King Ferdinand liked Ponce de León and was impressed by his ideas and his long service campaigning with the King's army during two wars. He advised him to leave the Order and find his destiny in the King's service instead. The King was considering the offers of several explorers and their ideas of discovery of lands beyond the oceans. He loathed the idea that his old enemy, the Portuguese, would acquire all the fruits the unknown world had to offer.

Ponce de León replied with all due respect that he had taken monastic vows that he could not so lightly break. He was not even sure how he could do it. It would probably need a special dispensation from the Pope himself. Ferdinand assured him that would not be a problem. Nonetheless, Ponce de León needed to think about it. For his part, King Ferdinand would remember Ponce de León for the rest of his life, eventually becoming his mentor and protector.

Once the siege and the war were over, Ferdinand followed Ponce de León's advice and guaranteed the respect and freedom of religion for the large numbers of new Muslim subjects. The King gave Abu Abdallah a small county (land ruled by a Count) in the

Alpujarra Mountains, which would have been hard to pacify in any case. The impulsively restless Abu Abdallah fled to Morocco two years later, where he lived out his remaining forty years of life.

As for the new Muslim and Jewish subjects, it did not take long for the initial agreement of tolerance to end. The bishops and clergy sent to Granada quickly made life unbearable for them. Finally, unconverted Jews and Muslims, usually the best educated, the most able administrators, and the most successful merchants, were expelled from Iberia in 1492 (Portugal followed this ridiculous policy a year later).

Those who did convert were highly suspected of practicing their original faith in secret and were called 'crypto-Jews' and 'crypto-Muslims'. Isabella agreed with the Church that they needed to be rooted out. The Inquisition started their long, murderous, and barbaric history of torture to uncover any 'false' Christians in Iberia. No one asked what Jesus would have done.

This so disgusted Ponce de León that he decided he needed to break his monastic vows to the Church that was perpetuating these crimes. He saw the power of the Church growing all around him as the 'Catholic Monarchs' consolidated their power and needed the support of the Pope and his minions. Ponce de León decided he needed to get away and join the voyages of discovery. He took the advice of Ferdinand.

He wrote to his mentor and king, humbly requesting his intervention to allow him to break the monastic vows that were meant to be lifelong. He could have simply left for the new colonies without breaking them. But out of respect for his late uncle and to avoid any potential future trouble with the Church, he decided to wait. For example, without officially breaking his vows, the Church could annul any marriage he had made, instantly bastardizing his children and making his wife a fornicating whore. He could be fired from any position he may have gained. No, it was better to wait.

The royal letter arrived six months later. The brief note from Ferdinand was simply to wish that his path would be successful, to bring glory to Christ's name and the royal family of united Spain. It also contained a letter of release from the Cardinal of Madrid and personal spiritual advisor to the king. That is exactly what he needed. Ponce de León hurried to Cadiz in 1493 and joined Columbus' second voyage to the newly discovered lands across the western sea.

CHAPTER TWENTY-FOUR

What Was it about Him?

The Odyssey set sail for Barcelona the next day. Ponce de León decided he had enough of Spain, as all the terrible memories flooded his mind, reminding him why he left and never came back. Spain of five centuries before clearly differed completely from the modern age. His memories growing up in the too long era stuck between feudalism and absolute monarchy, between the proverbial rock and a hard place, clouded his attitude to his birthplace.

Life was nasty, brutish, and short in his youth. For 90% of the population, there was no opportunity to do anything but what their grandfathers and fathers did. Practically, no education was available. Even the Bible was forbidden to read in case anyone came up with a different interpretation than what the Church preached. Minor diseases of modern times would carry off entire villages. There was practically no law available to most everyone. Capricious lords and bishops took and did as they pleased. Most everyone was dirt poor, except for the master class of Church and Thrown weighing heavily like a crown of thorns on the peasants' bleeding heads.

Ponce de León's mind was thinking dark thoughts as he stared out to sea late in the evening before they would arrive in Barcelona. The stars covering the night sky and the bright full moon reflecting on the gentle waves could not cheer him up. But then, one of his crewmen and mates passed by, saying: "Capitán, you'll soon meet your lovely Isabel. That must make you happy."

This jolted Ponce de León out of his mental funk. Ah, so there is a reason to look forward to Barcelona and more of Spain! I so miss my dear woman. His mind shifted gears from a long reverse to a high gear moving forward. He asked himself what was it about her that had such a power over him, making him do what all common sense would indicate to avoid? None of his mates had any long-term relations with anyone. They accepted that as the price of immortality.

No! He refused to make such a deal. He wanted it all. He wanted love and life, though it always ended in tragedy. It was easy for them to drift off into the eternal sleep. It was much harder for those kneeling by the bedside, holding their love's hand, feeling the pulse of life slipping away. Yet, he persisted in creating great pain for himself.

Perhaps it was as simple as a life without love is not worth living? Because love was what it was all about. There was the challenge of creating a relationship and instilling a passionate love in the heart of a new woman. But what about after that? Why would he marry them and love them until death took them away?

Yes, he and his mates often asked himself why marry at all? There was no reason to continue such folly in the modern world, especially since there would never be any children involved. Every marriage he had was a happy one with no divorces or even regrets. All he could reply was that there was something instilled in him 500 years before, that it was the right thing to do. Clearly, the answer had no logic and even made no sense. It was simply who he was.

As for a long-term relationship, that was a lot easier to explain. There was nothing quite like a woman who understands him and his moods, whose gentle touch can bring a brilliant sun to dark and threatening skies. The sound of her voice calling for him, the scent of her hair as it splashes across his face, her words "I love you" embracing his heart like a warm shelter in a violent winter storm, these and much more passed through his mind one after the other. Clearly, a good woman was crucial to a wonderful life. But now for the next question: what was it about Isabel in particular?

Ah, Isabel. Where to start? It was the first time he actually thought about her in the abstract. They had been together for over a year, and he never considered her beyond the warm fuzzy feeling that filled his heart whenever she entered his conscience. Since he already mentioned marriage to her, he thought he should at least go through the mental exercise.

As a woman, she had all the things that wonderful gender can offer. But what about her as Isabel? Of course, her attractive cinnamon beauty was a great start. No, no, Juan! As a person! What about her as a person? He chided himself.

She was very intelligent, with an excellent world-class education. She knew so much about so many things, yet nearly nothing about the world and life itself. She was like a medieval nun living in her cloister, copying by hand all the knowledge that books contained. Yet, she would put down her quill occasionally and stare out the window, wondering what life was really like.

Isabel was at once exceedingly knowledgeable and completely naïve. She had placed her heart and mind into his hands, begging him to show her the world and how wonderful life could be. That was exactly the kind of challenge that inspired him. Of all the possibilities under the sun, which were more important than others to grasp the meaning and the joys of life? He gladly took on the role of teacher and guide.

Even so, their relationship was one of equals. Isabel had the innate wisdom of Woman that could care for her man-child, a wisdom that began before the first campfire. Sometimes a man just needs to be hugged in that primordial embrace, as the warmth of the fire with its hypnotic flames dancing before his eyes, entrancing him with a peace that man has known since before time. Most modern women have forgotten this, but somehow Isabel's unconscious memory tugs at her heart strings, allowing to always say and do the right thing at exactly the right time.

Oh, how he wanted so badly to arrive in Barcelona! Hopefully, she will not take so long to meet him there. But what if she changed her mind? Or maybe she simply grew tired of him and was ready for something new. Maybe a young man said the right thing at exactly the right time and swept her off her feet? What if she never called him? How long would he stay in Barcelona's marina waiting for her? His good cheer suddenly turned to panic. Clearly, he needed her, and he needed her now.

****

Tears blurred Isabel's eyes before and during the flight to Madrid. Many people asked if she was all right. She answered that she was, but no one believed her. After twenty minutes of staring out the airplane window and seeing nothing, she was sorry she did not think to bring more than one handkerchief with her. A flight attendant brought her a pack of tissues.

She tried to get a grip. Just why was she crying like it was her first day at school? What was it about that man that had such a hold on her heart and mind? Clearly, he was a man, in the full meaning of that word. All the equivalating that occupied her generation, about how men and women are the same, clearly did not match the reality that was causing so much turmoil in her.

Isabel only really knew two other men in her life. Both were much older yet were more needy than her. They were emotional, crying at minor pretexts, clinging to her like drowning men grasping for a life preserver. She had no problem with men crying and revealing their inner feelings. It was healthy to not live with inner repressed pain. But both would cry when they misunderstood her answer to a loaded question.

A typical example would be: "Do you love me?" "Of course, I do." "I hear your words, but somehow your eyes don't show it."

"My eyes?" "Yes, your eyes. And your voice is lacking in warmth and feeling." "Oh, give me a break! Why do you imagine such things?" "See? That's exactly what I mean. Now you're accusing me of imagining things." "You really are insecure, aren't you? I would think a man of your age would be more mature about life." "A man of my age? What's that supposed to mean?" Etc.

Of course, she knew she could only blame herself for choosing such pathetic examples of men. She was in her early twenties. They were in their mid-forties, married with children nearly her age. Why would she even choose men of another generation? Perhaps she hoped to learn something from their much longer experience with life. Yet all she experienced with them was one year of adult experience twenty-five times.

Many of her university classmates in her undergraduate years experimented with playing lesbian. It was the cool thing to do. Many eager, zealous twenty-year-old women tried to open her mind and teach her that men are unnecessary. Only a fellow woman could really understand her needs and desires. All Isabel could see was the same manipulation, petty jealousies, and even worse hissy fits than she saw in her hetero friends and their relationships with boys of the same age.

'Boys of the same age'. That was probably why she preferred older men, but when they proved to be men-boys, too, with nothing to bring to the relationship despite having twenty more years of life than her, she felt a tremendous disappointment. Even so, she continued searching for a mate worthy of the name, a man. She had to disappoint her lesbian classmates. There was nothing a woman could offer that was better than a man.

It was not just a man's body that attracted her, which it did mightily. It was the way a man conducted himself with his fellows, the way he walked and talked. His self-confidence that he could take on the gods themselves and emerge the winner. Those are the things that impressed her and hoped to find. She certainly could not and would not find them in the men of academia, the world that she freely agreed to enter.

Ah, but she found him now. Of course, Juan was in his forties, too. But that is where the similarity ended. He had the life experience of a man much older than that. He was sure of himself, self-confident to a fault. Full of gravitas, he was a natural leader of men. He always said and did exactly what the situation required. There was a hardness, a toughness about him. Everything about him exuded life experience and wisdom that was rare in even old men.

Extremely well educated, he could discuss things she had studied for ten years, even revealing entirely unknown facts and insights that eluded her PhD research. He knew everything worth knowing. His money meant nothing to her, except that he was not enslaved to some corporation. He had all the time to spend with her. The lack of money that limited life in so many ways simply did not exist. Those were good things, yet he was the opposite of born-to-wealth playboys. He came to his wealth after a hard life of squeezing a living from the unforgiving sea.

That was all very wonderful. But there was something else that was hard to even put into words. He was gentle in a way that only the very self-confident can be. He was a gentleman, always gracious and chivalrous to everyone. It was always important to her how a man not just treated her, but complete strangers, too. Yes, she acknowledged she used the archaic word 'gentleman'. But there was no better word for him.

Then it struck her. The sudden realization surfaced like a buoy that a submarine released deep under the ocean that steadily floats to the surface through a thousand fathoms. It was her dearly beloved Portuguese grandfather. Juan had all his good points and none of the bad. Her grandfather had the old-world charm and savior faire. He had the sense of what it meant to be a man, in the sense that died generations ago. He was as reliable as a great rock that could take whatever storms life could throw at him.

He always knew what the right thing to do was, and he invariably did it. He was stable and reliable to friends and family alike. He thought nothing of himself, only of others. Not only did he have sympathy, he also had empathy for others. He was a warm and loving man with always a kind word and a wonderful laugh that came from deep within. Indeed, he could see the humor and the irony of life.

Yet, he was infuriating, too. Her grandfather had a closed mind about many things. He had a machismo that had no place in modern society. His curiosity never extended to education nor even to knowledge of the world at large. She never saw him read a book. He could recite scores and names of the world of European football (soccer) from fifty years earlier, but he could not name the capital of Canada, nor cared to even know it. His mind was simply very limited.

Isabel was startled to consider that Juan was simply the perfect version of her grandfather. It would explain her attraction to older men. She had nearly given up, deciding to live happily unattached for over six years, until that fateful flight of the beach frisbee a year and more before. Even after all that time, her heart still felt an electric buzz every time she thought of him. She felt it even then, as the plane landed in Madrid.

Her tears had long ceased. The excitement of exploring Spain and discovering the land of Cervantes gripped her mind. It was too bad that Juan chose not to accompany her. He certainly had a strange side to him. There were certain things that he believed in and would not budge. Fortunately, he always had well thought-out reasons. There was nothing knee jerk about him. If his aversion to his homeland was the only strange thing about him, that would be fine with her.

After a day of catching her bearings, she leaped right into her journey to understand Cervantes and his Spain. The very next day, she flew south to visit Córdoba in Andalusia, where the brilliant author's father was born and raised his family. Little did she know she was less than a two-hour drive to Málaga, where her beloved was lost in thought regarding his distant past.

She visited Seville, another important city of Cervantes' early life. She returned to Madrid by train. Next on her itinerary was Alcalá de Henares, the suburb of Madrid where the great man was born. She stayed for a few days in Toledo, where she rented a car to explore La Mancha, the land of Don Quixote.

After a week of Cervantes, she chose to look at another side of Spain. She visited all the faded imperial glory of Madrid. Two glorious days passed in the museums of the Prado Museum with its great paintings of Goya, Velasquez, El Greco and many others and the Thyssen Bornemisza Museum, which had a cross section of the greatest painters of all time, including one of the largest collections of US paintings in the world.

Ten days had passed, and she still had not arrived in Barcelona. She traveled by the high-speed train that only took two and a half hours, quicker than flying if considering security lines and the boarding process at the airport. Traveling by train was her favorite way to go.

Isabel missed his arm around her, his hand lightly holding hers, his warm accented voice. She decided to call him, but there was no answer. She thought nothing of it, as he was probably sailing too far from cell phone coverage.

She took in the sights of Barcelona, a very different world from the capital. This was a modern, energetic city whose ancient past had long disappeared under the overpowering imperial weight of Madrid. It was a city of grand and wide boulevards. A long beach sweeping around the warm waters of the Mediterranean. It was a city that took itself seriously yet allowed the highly eccentric Gaudi to leave his unmistakable mark of great flights of fancy throughout.

The time between her calls to her beloved shortened until she was calling every twenty minutes. She could not sleep, panicking that perhaps he changed his mind about her and sailed away. That would be the greatest sorrow of her life. No, even if he did change his mind, he would not simply disappear without even a fare thee well. Would he? Why would he not answer his phone?

It had already been two weeks, and she was beside herself. Finally, Isabel had enough. She went to the main city marina for large yachts and see if he was docked there. If not, she would start to pick up the pieces of her broken heart. She took a taxi and asked the harbormaster's office if the large Odyssey was docked there. Much to her joy, they showed her where it was on their marina map.

She ran to the location, anxious that it might be a different Odyssey. But no! It was the same. She sprinted to it. She had to stop and rest with her hands on her knees, trying to catch her breath. Finally, she cried out: "Juan! Where are you?"

Within seconds, he appeared, leaping down to the dock, and hugging her tightly. After a moment, she pushed him away, her voice full of anger. "Why? Why didn't you answer my calls?"

"What calls, my precious? My phone has been in my pocket the whole time."

"Give it to me! ...Oh, you have no signal! How can that be? Ah, you never changed it to the GPS band they use in Europe. Your phone should have changed it for you automatically."

"You know I don't use my phone much. I'm not clear on the ins and outs of using cell phones in foreign countries. You'll have to teach me."

She ran back into his arms. "Oh, you silly, silly man. At least there is something I can teach you. But right now, it's all about hugging you." All was well in her world again.

CHAPTER TWENTY-FIVE

In a Sea of Troubles

Moments after their tight embrace, Juan asked, "So, what would you like to do? Shall we visit the sights of Barcelona?"

She whispered in his ear, "I've seen enough of Barcelona. What I really want to do now is for you to show me your special sights in the Captain's Cabin."

"Right this way, my lady."

Hours later, they resurfaced. Sipping cool Conde Vimioso Reserva Branco that Ponce de León brought from Portugal, they basked in the wading pool under the late afternoon sun. Once the sun's golden glow disappeared behind the city, they took a taxi to retrieve Isabel's luggage from her hotel. They returned and dressed in their evening finest. Ponce de León wanted to take Isabel on a special romantic date, just the two of them.

"Jorge recommended the restaurant Lasarte. It supposedly has excellent cuisine and, even better, they have an extensive selection of Portuguese wines. Oh, he tells me they also have three Michelin stars. That must mean something besides small quantities on large plates. Shall we give it a try?"

She had no better idea and so they had an excellent dinner until early in the morning. The next day, they set sail, continuing their journey toward the rising sun. They docked at the port of a city that Ponce de León thought Isabel should be acquainted with. They would use that as their base to visit the surrounding region.

First, they docked at Nice and visited the Riviera, as well as Arles, Aix-en-Provence, and Montpellier for a week. Next, they docked at Livorno in Italy and for two weeks visited Florence, Siena, Pisa, Roma, and Venice. They continued down the coast of Italy, through the Messina straits, around the Italian boot to Greece.

As they sailed close by Ithaca, he pointed out the homeland of Odysseus, one of the greatest heroes of the Occident. Homer's epic tale of Odysseus' journey home after the Trojan War in the face of every possible obstacle thrown at him by the gods is the source of Western literature. The story of an individual man who battles the gods and wins by using his wits and single-minded courage forms the basis of Western literature to this day.

In stark contrast to Homer's other famous epic tale, the Iliad, where mankind is the plaything of petty and jealous gods, the Odyssey takes a deeper look into the nature of mankind versus the gods. The gods have something which we will never have: immortality. Mankind, however, has something the gods covet: freedom of choice. The gods are what they are and can change nothing about themselves. The god of war could never be peaceful. The god of peace could never make war. They are what they are until the end of time or until the last believer forgets them. But we can be anything we want. We can change as necessary and control our own destiny.

In the curious case of Ponce de León and his crew, they had both immortality and control over their destiny. They certainly never considered themselves as gods. They did indeed live life to the fullest, but in a low-key, unobtrusive way. In short, they had the best of both worlds. Nonetheless, they still were men with all the conflicts between heart and mind, the sorrows of losing loved ones, the normal doubts and fears, the challenges of dealing with whatever life threw at them. Another name for the vagaries of life might be the whims of the gods of old. And so, the age-old story continues.

They docked at Piraeus, the ancient port of Athens, where they visited the Parthenon, spread across a flat hill majestically dominating the city that inspired the world with its art, philosophy, theater, and early example of democracy. Later, they sailed through the Aegean, stopping at the islands of Santorini, Crete, and Rhodes.

They sailed up the Turkish coast to one of the great cities of the world: Istanbul. They soaked up the fragrances of great spice bazaars, covered their heads while entering the majestic mosques, and took in the greatness of the Ottoman empire and the Byzantines that form its foundations. The people were very European in their sophisticated outlook and style of life.

What impressed Isabel greatly was it being a city of cat lovers. The street cats were part of a great family of fifteen million Turkish residents. Everyone fed and cared for them. Even the street dogs were calm and friendly. None of them were feral. They were free to come and go as they pleased. Every open door and window offered shelter and food; even medical care as needed.

After visiting the Topkapi Palace, they stood in a garden, taking in what they just experienced. About fifty feet away, such a street cat perused Juan, considering him for a few minutes. Suddenly, she ran to him, climbed up his pant leg and shirt sleeve to perch on his shoulder. She settled in and purred loudly.

Juan always loved cats but losing them to the next realm caused him grief. So, he stopped having them. He would only take a cat if she clearly chose him by entering his house to stay or in some other unmistakable way. Isabel was enthralled by what happened and took a photo of her purring on his shoulder.

Juan started walking to the exit, thinking that she would grow tired and leap away. But she just clung to his collar tightly. Finally, he put the cat down. But she followed them to the street. He hailed a taxi and while waiting, she rubbed up against his legs, still purring all the while. The taxi came and as they entered the back seat, she jumped in with them. Isabel clearly saw a fellow traveler and put her on her lap. Juan reached to toss her out.

"Looks like we have a new voyager on our journey, Juan. Please don't say no. She obviously wants to be a part of your life like I do. You would not so cruelly push me away, would you?"

That is how Penelope entered their lives, named after the long-suffering wife of Odysseus. Fortunately, unlike the original homebody wife, this Penelope loved the ship and the sea. She would sit at the bow above the undulating waves with the wind blowing her long furry ruff and whiskers without a care in the world. If she was not there, she would be close to Ponce de León, following him everywhere like a little satellite.

The next port of call was Tel Aviv. There, Juan showed her the White City, the UNESCO site of thousands of buildings from the 1930's, built in the Bauhaus and Art Deco styles. They enjoyed the modern Western city populated by people who clearly love their city.

They drove about forty-five minutes east and about a thousand years into the past to Jerusalem. Isabel enjoyed wandering through the old city, visiting such places as the Wailing Wall and the Church of the Holy Sepulcher. There was a long line of tourist pilgrims to see the tomb where Jesus is claimed to have been buried. Juan dissuaded Isabel from getting in the hours long line, telling her it is just an empty hole (at least it better be).

Sailing south, they passed through the Suez Canal. Juan explained their itinerary.

"We will not stop until we reach Goa in India. We will sail for eight days straight. Why, you may ask? I'll explain. To the right of us is a country with a serious terrorism problem directed at foreign tourists. That would be us. To the left, we must be married to check into a hotel and where there is no wine to be had. Further on to the right, another country is in turmoil with coup and counter coup with the hapless people in the streets. Further to our left is a country in a terrible civil war with the humanitarian crisis of starvation. Next to our right is another country in a terrible civil war. The next country on the right has been in a civil war for forty years or more and, to make matters worse, is the source of a serious pirate problem."

"Pirates? I don't know if I should be excited or scared."

"Fortunately, we're prepared. So, you can be somewhere in between those two extremes. I know all about pirates and how they think. They are bullies preying on the weak. If the weak turns around and punches them in the nose, they'll run yelping with their tail between their legs. So, don't worry about it."

Ponce de León had his own pirate phase, doing it out of boredom, the worst reason to do anything. He was not exaggerating in his explanation to Isabel. Isabel scanned the sea with binoculars for high-speed pirate raiders approaching. He explained to her they would only attack at night. But it gave her something to do.

It was 0400 one night as they were sailing through the Gulf of Aden between Yemen and Somalia's Horn of Africa (Puntland) when a frantic knocking on their cabin door awoke them. Pirates were coming, four large and fast skiffs were approaching with about twenty heavily armed men on board. They would arrive in about twenty minutes.

Ponce de León leaped out of bed. The night crew were already mounting four M260 machine guns on the railings, both port and starboard. Juan helped Isabel to put on a flak jacket with helmet before he did the same. He told her to stay in the locked cabin with Penelope and handed her a pistol, briefly explaining how to use it. He joined the rest of the crew on deck, each armed with an assault rifle.

Just as the four skiffs approached, a crewman turned on the spotlight, blinding the pirates. The machine guns opened up and almost immediately shot to pieces two skiffs, leaving ten of the pirates suddenly swimming in the ocean. Two pirates of the remaining two skiffs raised their RPG's and fired their grenades at the Odyssey. Between the blinding spotlight and the skiff bouncing on the waves, they both missed. The M260's sank them, too. Antón had already turned the engines on and had them at full throttle.

Once the pirates bobbing in the ocean were out of sight, the crew put away their weapons and their protective gear. Ponce de León called to Isabel through the locked cabin door, telling her to put the safety on and place the pistol on the floor. It was safe to open the door. She did so and ran into his arms.

"Are we safe now?"

"Yes, my love. It's all over. Let's get you out of this flak jacket."

"Where are the pirates?"

"They're floating in the sea far behind us."

"Floating in the sea? How far are we from land?"

"Oh, I'd say we're about sixty miles."

"They'll drown!"

"If they did, that would teach them not to attack innocent ships again to rob and kidnap the crew for ransom."

"How terrible!"

"Not to worry, my dear Isabel. Those skiffs could not come so far from the coast. They would have some kind of mother ship nearby, like a fishing ship or some other trawler captured from an earlier raid, which would pick them up. It's so sweet that you have such concern for the well-being of those who would have raped you and, if no ransom came, would have sold you into slavery or simply killed you."

Her face went pale, and she sank to the bed, trembling.

He sat down beside her and gently rocked her in his arms, caressing her head with his lips. "Now, now, everything is fine. There is no danger now and because we were well-prepared, there never was any danger."

Even so, she stayed in the cabin for the next three days. When they reached Goa's port city of Panaji, she resurfaced, happy to be on dry land again. But the chaos of a typical Indian city was too much for her, even with over 450 years of Portuguese imperial history to tempt her. She asked Juan if they could continue their voyage. He immediately agreed, seeing the effect of the noise, smells, sights of extreme poverty, and leprous beggars missing important parts of their bodies approaching her.

As they were rounding the southern tip of India, he asked her if she would prefer to sail to Australia and New Zealand or through Southeast and Northeast Asia. Though he was not worried, another encounter with pirates on the way through the Malacca and Singapore Straits might be too much for her.

"Is all Asia like what I saw in India?"

"Not to the extreme of India, which I never considered as a part of Asia. It is its own subcontinent. But it is a matter of degree. Jakarta, Bangkok, Manila, etc. would be similar without the beggars."

"In that case, I'd prefer Australia and New Zealand."

"Are you sure? Asia, and India for that matter, are full of great cultures and history. India and China both have cultures and histories much older than Europe. Australia and New Zealand would be similar to the USA of fifty years ago. Like the US, they have great natural beauty but not much else. Nothing like a Forbidden City or a Taj Mahal. Are you sure?"

"Yes, my dear man. I'd be happy to sail calmly by, sipping white wine in the pool, and trying to rock this ship from the bed in the Captain's Cabin."

"That would be fine with me. I've already visited these foreign lands before. We'll return when you feel like it. Jorge will still want us to dock somewhere about every few days to restock his kitchen with fresh food. That reminds me. I'm getting hungry. How about you? Let's go see what he's preparing."

They stopped at Perth for a day and then at Melbourne, Juan's favorite city in Australia. He told his crew to meet them at Sydney. He could sense that Isabel wanted some quality time with him out of earshot of everyone else. They rented a car and drove along the coast, dodging the occasional kangaroo bounding across the road, visiting the capital Canberra, and the wonderful wineries with the world's best Shiraz wines along the way. They rejoined the

Odyssey after enjoying what Sydney had to offer, including its iconic opera house.

They then sailed to Wellington (Windy Wellie) at the southern tip of the North Island of New Zealand. He told Antón to continue sailing to Auckland, the largest city in New Zealand at the northern end of the island, where they would meet after another winery trip. This time they drove through the wineries of the world's best Sauvignon Blanc. 'Savvy sav' as the natives call it.

Isabel loved particularly New Zealand and would not mind living there. Juan agreed, but that it was just too far away from anywhere for his tastes. They island hopped through the south Pacific at about a week's sailing distance from each other.

They peacefully passed for several weeks through the idyllic tropical atolls. Isabel had forgotten already her close encounters with pirates and lepers. Juan was always the perfect companion. He was always calm and attentive to her needs, even before she knew them herself. She accepted that she really could spend the rest of her life with him.

But danger reared its ugly head again. They were two days out from Christmas Island, with only one more day to Honolulu. Suddenly the Odyssey hit something big like a car hitting a speed bump too fast, knocking everyone off their feet. What could they have hit in the middle of the ocean, far from any rocks or reefs? Or perhaps something hit them?

The hull was damaged, and they were taking on water. The keel was probably damaged, too, though they could not see it below the water. Ponce de León ordered the metal bulkhead doors to be sealed tight, isolating the damaged bow from the rest of the ship. Everyone put on a life preserver, and the debate began over what happened.

There were only three possibilities: either a whale surfaced below them, or they hit a half-sunken ship's hull or a shipping container that fell off a freighter that was floating just below the surface of the water. Reported collisions with whales are about two per year. Ponce de León believed they hit a semi-submerged hull of a sunken ship like the pilgrim ship did in Joseph Conrad's Lord Jim. Antón believed it was a whale.

What mattered was getting to a port as soon as possible. The closest port was Honolulu, which, without being damaged, was still a day away. With a damaged hull, they would have to sail even slower than normal to not put pressure on the hull and keel. Maybe it would take two days. Isabel sensed the nervousness of Juan, though he did his best to hide it from her.

The ship was slowed even more by the damaged front section filling with water, further weighing it down. The water line of the bow went from sixteen feet to nine feet from the deck to the sea. As the ocean's surface slowly rose and the bow was tipping into the sea, Isabel's heart sank at her impending doom. She wanted to panic but did not want to show such weakness to Juan. Even if she did panic, it would change nothing in the slightest. He showed nothing but calm confidence.

He called the Coast Guard and informed them what had happened. They were on their way but would need about twenty hours to arrive. All Juan's crew could do was continue at about seven knots and hope the damage did not spread.

Isabel did not panic, but she sulked in their cabin. Juan entered and sat beside her on the bed to calm her.

"Oh, Juan! What a stupid idea to go on this voyage! We could have just taken a plane, instead of …"

Juan pressed his fingers to her lips. "Don't say another word. Don't say anything you might regret. I told you I would show you the world and life. And life is not always idyllic. Maturity and wisdom come from meeting danger and hardship, then overcoming them makes us a stronger person. We will not meet our end here.

"We have lifeboats, and the Coast Guard knows where we are. You might not believe me, but I have been in much worse situations than this. Besides, you're with me and I will let nothing happen to you. I value your life even greater than my own. As

Captain, I may go down with the ship, but you will always have a place on the lifeboat."

Isabel turned and hugged him tightly and replied with a wan giggle, "I thought it was the cook who went down with the ship."

He laughed, dispelling the gloom. "No one is going down with the ship, not even Penelope. Odysseus loves her too much. And I love you even more."

The Odyssey did not sink. The Coast Guard arrived and transferred everyone to their cutter. They towed the damaged ship to port. Back on dry land, joy and relief replaced Isabel's regrets and fears. She was relieved that Juan had the wisdom to stop her from continuing her escalating rant and damaging their relationship. He proved, again, that he was exactly the kind of man she wanted in any emergency. He remained calm, cool, and collected at all times, even when pirates were attacking or when their ship was sinking.

They put the ship in dry dock. The keel in the front was separated from the hull and the gash above it was big enough that Isabel could have crawled through it. They told Juan that it would take at least three or four months to repair, maybe even six. The ship was going nowhere until it was repaired.

Antón took Ponce de León aside. "Juan, we have already been seven months at sea. We left three months after our annual meeting. It would have taken a month to sail back home without this. Our original plan was for us to be home with only a month to spare for our next annual meeting. We clearly cannot wait until our ship is repaired. We have to fly back. I know how you hate flying, but we have no other choice."

"Yes, you're right about me hating to fly. Maybe we can catch a cruise ship going to Miami."

"Juan! No more ships for a while. It's time for you to enter the late twentieth century! You flew to Chicago twice before we took this trip. You survived intact."

"Yes, but that was only three hours. How long would it be from here to home?"

"It would probably be about eleven hours."

"Eleven hours on a plane!"

"Tell you what. You can fly to Los Angeles and take a train the rest of the way. That flight would probably be about five and a half hours."

"I'll look into the next cruise ship to Miami."

"Look, do what you want, but you better be there on the designated day. Don't make me come look for you."

"OK, fine. I'll tell the crew to go home as they like, but they must all take separate flights. I don't want every one of us to go down at one go. I know the sea and I know ships. I don't really understand planes and wouldn't have a clue how to abandon a plane in mid-flight."

"That would be called parachutes."

"I don't recall those ever being issued to us. I just remember them telling us there were inflatable life vests under our seats, as if that would somehow comfort me flying over the Appalachian Mountains."

They all checked into a hotel and planned their return. As it turned out, there were no cruises to the US West Coast for about a month and as they make stops along the way, it would take another two to three weeks to arrive. That would be too late for his rendezvous with the Fountain. Juan also considered the additional risk of catching some airborne disease along the way and, besides, he had no idea of the qualifications of the captain. In the end, he booked a flight for Isabel and him after a few days of much needed R&R in Oahu.

CHAPTER TWENTY-SIX

The Meaning of Life for the Immortal

As expected, they arrived at LAX with no problems. They took a taxi to Union Station where Juan inquired about trains to Saint Augustine at the ticket window.

"Two tickets for the next train to Saint Augustine, please."

"Sir, there are no trains for Saint Augustine, Florida. The closest station would be Jacksonville. How would that be?"

"That would be fine. How long would it take?"

"The next train would take 105 hours and require changing trains in Chicago and Washington, DC. There are no direct trains. The train after that would take 85 hours. That would be the shortest time possible."

"What? That's over three and a half days!"

"The other option is to take the train to Lafayette, Louisiana, and then Greyhound buses the rest of the way. That would just be over three days, but you would have to change buses several times."

Juan was exasperated. "Whatever happened to rail transportation in this country?"

"Sir, you clearly have not taken a train in many years. No one takes the train for long-distance transportation anymore. They are for tourists who want to see this glorious land of ours. Everyone flies to get somewhere these days."

Juan was fuming with frustration. Isabel held his hand. "Juan, dearest, we could have checked all this with our cell phones at the airport. We'll either have to fly or drive. Driving would take longer and be much more tiring, not to mention much more dangerous than flying. Let's just fly back. Come on, gentle Juan. Let's go."

He let her lead him out to the taxi stand and return to the airport. Juan loosened up at the United Executive Lounge before the flight. With the help of the excellent Californian old vine Lodi Zinfandel in First Class, he managed to relax enough to get through the flight. Sleeping for half the time helped, too.

He arrived back home with just a few weeks to spare before his annual reunion with all his crewmates in their special grotto of glowing blue water. On the drive there, he pondered what it would mean to miss the life-giving water after the 365-day mark. Would it stop working forever or would it work anyway, just a day later? Or worse, would they immediately become their actual age and disappear into 500-year-old dust as the clock struck midnight? Who would want to test that question and risk losing their special gift?

He pondered that question, staring vacantly at the passing coastal towns and landscape. As they pulled off the highway and made their way by the dirt roads and grass paths to their rocky hidden house, his thoughts turned philosophical. He was silent the rest of the time before their banquet.

They arranged themselves at their traditional places around the heavy wooden table. As usual, Ponce de León rose with a glass of wine in one hand and a cigar in the other, with a light stream of smoke rising above. Everyone fell silent as he started his annual state of life speech.

"My friends, mates, and comrades, we gather yet again to celebrate this wonderful life we have found together. Please indulge me as recent events have made me somewhat philosophical. We have passed the 500-year mark of our incredible discovery. We have what mankind has dreamed of since we first were sentient beings. We have eternal youth. However, we are not indestructible like we imagine the gods to be. Accidents and other means can kill us like anyone else. We only need to survive until we can sip our strange blue ambrosia once a year.

"That means we still need to take care of ourselves as anyone else would. Everyone here now knows of our experience during our sea voyage around the world. We had a dangerous encounter with pirates. That was a bit of bad luck, but of course, we were sailing a very conspicuous luxury yacht through the worst pirate-infested waters on the planet. We were prepared.

"Then we hit or were hit by something large lurking unseen just below the waves. What are the odds of that happening? Again, we were prepared with lifeboats and vests. The Coast Guard would have saved us, anyway. Fortunately, we were not in the middle of a typhoon.

"Of course, a truck in India could have crushed us riding in a taxi. A truck could even crush us here in Florida. So, what's my point? My point is the value of life is much greater for us, as we have much more to lose if we die in whatever way that could happen during the year. As far as we know, we could live until the end of time. We have a gift that the entire world would want. Yet, we still lost eleven of us over the years for various stupid reasons.

"What to do? We could let fear run our lives and never leave our fortified bunkers. But we don't. We would have never taken that voyage if that's how we thought. Maybe that's why I always want a special woman friend in my life. They force me to come out of my shell and engage life in all its dangers and excitements. They make me feel alive.

"That brings me to my next point. Some of you tempt fate. Some of you do nothing but eat and drink all year, enjoying life that way, then arrive here forty-five pounds (twenty kilos) fatter. Your doctor and the gods only know what your organs look like. The waters return you to a fully healthy young man again. But what if one year you're hit with a sudden heart attack or stroke and die in your bed? Or you're so drunk you fall down the stairs? You know of whom I speak. Fifty years ago, we lost João as he pushed his heroin habit just a bit too far.

"Some of you ride motorcycles so fast on winding roads, pushing your luck with every turn by the edge of a cliff or passing a car into the front of an oncoming truck. That's exactly what happened to Pedro some years ago. Some of you bring different, unknown women into your bed every week. You don't know if one day a drug-addled prostitute goes off her nut and kills you when you least expect it. Again, I won't name names here.

"I could go on, but my point is, why do we do these things? My conclusion is that we are bored and want to feel alive again. For some of us, we feel alive by living dangerously. For me, I find life through love. Because of our solemn secret, I am always living a lie, knowing that I will lose the loved one, as they slowly age and die in front of my eyes.

"Hate to say it, but for many of you others, you have chosen to become numb like animals, who stay alive for no other reason than that is the one imperative that drives them. At least animals can procreate. We can't even do that.

"Anyone else outside our circle would ask, how is it possible that we have everything: wealth, health, youth; yet we somehow still feel empty. Something is missing that those things cannot give. It's not simply boredom. We have the entire wonderful world and the accumulated knowledge of mankind in front of us. We merely just need the will to pursue new experiences and learning.

"Everyone else would think we are living in a near-paradise. That is the problem. They think that because they aren't living in anything that even closely resembles a paradise. That is exactly why they yearn for a heaven that is not here but will come after life. They imagine heaven to be a place where nothing bad ever happens: no death, no disease, no political chaos, no want, no violence, etc. Heaven is a lack of all bad things.

"But they don't realize what the conclusion of that would be. I'm reminded of a line in that old Talking Heads' song, 'Heaven'.

'Heaven is a place where nothing ever happens.' The Church Fathers would have us believe we would do nothing in heaven but chant praises to God with our harps wearing our white robes for all eternity. For such a heaven, they would need to give every soul who enters a lobotomy.

"Our Muslim brethren at least believe that we would spend eternity in air-conditioned gardens that always play our favorite songs, with our favorite fruit always within reach. We would enjoy the company of very desirable young girls with fountains of wine that never give us a hangover. That sounds like a perfect place for someone who is a perpetual teenage boy. But I think the great enemy of heaven, boredom, would set in fairly quickly. And then what? That's my point. There's nothing else.

"Others believe we are reincarnated back into this world of mortal misery to try again until we get it right. What happens when we finally 'get it right'? Well, then the speck of light of our souls joins the splendid light of the Great Spirit in the cosmos, and we're annihilated as individuals. Others believe nothing happens at all, and we molder in wooden boxes in the earth until we become of the earth again. At least in that theory, we would be doing something useful.

"Many of you are probably thinking 'yes, yes, Capitán, get to the point'. What's my conclusion? It's simply that we must not let boredom and ennui creep into our hearts, making us either dare devils tempting the gods or as primitive numb animals living day to day with no other point than to see the sun rise one more day.

"Do something meaningful. We have the greatest gift mankind yearns for. We have time with health and wealth to do something great that might even take hundreds of years to accomplish. That's my advice. I don't have answers to every question, though having lived so long, one would think I do. We must live every day to the fullest, as if it were our last day, but we must plan as if we were to live forever. So, live life while undertaking a grand project that can improve our world in some way, great or small. Who's with me on this?"

Everyone leaped to their feet, cheering and toasting their wise Capitán Juan Ponce de León. They cheered because they agreed with him and were excited about changing the world in some great way. Or more likely, they cheered because his solemn lecture was over, and they could get to the festivities that the rest of the night would bring. Most important, above all, they would descend into the caverns to drink their youth giving water.

As for Ponce de León, he sat down, sinking into a pensive silence. It was a wonderful speech with deep sentiment and wisdom. He asked himself whether he was following his own advice. Yes, he had started a new relationship with a woman that was bringing him alive more than he could possibly hope for. Besides that, and supporting various worthy causes with his wealth, was that the best he could do?

He was so lost in thought that he did not hear the enthusiastic celebration going on all around him. His best friend, Antón, noticed him brooding alone. He was always concerned about Juan when he saw him thus. The sacred waters could heal all things physical but do nothing for the state of mind. Sinking into madness was his own greatest fear. His next greatest fear was to see his dear friend descending into the black pit of insanity. For if Juan did, Antón would put him out of his misery and end his life.

Hours passed. Everyone had already taken the rejuvenating waters from below, except Ponce de León. Silently brooding at the end of the table, he took another drink of wine. Antón leaned over and gripped his arm. Ponce de León opened his eyes with a shudder.

"It's time, my friend. We have all been downstairs. It's your turn to take your drink."

"But I am drinking, Antón, I am. Pass me that bottle."

"No, I mean, it's time to drink the waters from downstairs. It's why we're here."

Ponce de León focused on all the worried faces looking at him from down the table. They all had a tinge of blue radiating from them.

"Hey! Why're you all so blue? Be happy! Happy, I say! And that's an order!" He reached for the bottle of wine and filled his glass.

"Juan, please. I've been watching. You've had three bottles of wine on your own tonight. You never drink like this. What's the matter?"

"Why, nothing's the matter, Antón. I feel fine, mighty fine, in fact. Maybe I'm just getting tired, that's all. I'm getting tired of everything. So tired. So tired and sleepy, too." His eyes closed like shutters and his head sunk against the high wooden back of his chair.

Antón motioned to the crew's doctor and priest sitting across from him. "Hey, help me. We need to get him downstairs quickly before he passes out."

The three of them lifted their nearly incapacitated leader to his feet. Two of them took him under the shoulders and guided him down into the cavern. Slowly, but carefully, they took him to the Fountain. All the while, their captain was shouting, "No, no, no! I don't want to go. I need to rest, need to sleep. Where are you taking me? What is this place?"

Fortunately, he was in no condition to stop them. He let them take him forward and down the rock steps. Presently, they reached the blue glowing Fountain. Antón filled the chalice, while the other two held him up.

"What is this you're giving me? Wine! Bring me more wine!"

"Here. Drink this wine."

"Wine, you say? Doesn't smell like it. Where did we find such wine?"

"It's not important. Just drink it. It'll make you feel even better."

He did as directed. Immediately, the effects of three bottles of wine dropped like a wet towel to the floor. "Hey, friends. What are you doing down here with me? Have you drunk from the chalice yet?"

"Yes, we all have. We just wanted to make sure you didn't fall. You know, we really should put in better lighting before next year."

"Hmm, this was never a problem before. Let's discuss it tomorrow. It's getting late."

The four blue-hued men hastened back to the dining room. When their comrades saw their captain striding in, as blue as the rest of them, they all rose and broke into relieved cheers.

"Jeez, friends, what's with the cheering? What has gotten into you? If everyone has had their share of the chalice, I suggest we all go to sleep. What time is it, anyway?"

CHAPTER TWENTY-SEVEN

He Popped the Question

A few months later, Isabel and Juan were having breakfast on the seaside veranda after an unusually passionate late night. The morning sun was already high in the sky. Isabel was holding his hand, playing with his fingers.

"You know, Juan, I've been thinking. I only spend just a few nights every month at my apartment in town. The rest of the time I spend here with you. When I'm not with you, I think about you all the time. Silly things like it's hot today. I hope you're out of the sun. It's raining, I hope you brought an umbrella with you. It's lunch time. I hope you're eating well.

"I know we talk many times throughout the day. I don't want to interrupt you by calling you every ten minutes. It's not the lack of talking. It's the lack of being with you all the time."

She paused for a minute before she abruptly continued. "What I'm trying to say is: how do you feel about me moving in with you? If you prefer the way things are, I have no problem with that and would not change an iota of how I feel about you. I know you like to be alone on Sunday afternoons. And that's completely fine with me. I would just sit quietly waiting for you to return, whether it was hours, days, or an eternity. Juan, don't say 'no' right away. At least consider the possibility at some time in the future, maybe we ..."

Isabel was working herself into accepting the inevitable rejection. Juan interrupted her. "My precious, I would like nothing more than to have you by my side always. Do you remember what I asked you at the beginning of our voyage?"

"Yes, dearest. I remember. You asked me about marriage. I was not suggesting that."

"We survived what turned out to be a stressful, dangerous trip. I didn't want to bring this up, not wanting to risk you being angry with me for putting you through all that."

"Oh, Juan, it was a wonderful adventure. What would an adventure be without a little danger? I learned a lot about you as you faced down every crisis with calm and confidence. I learned a lot about myself, especially that I lack so much that you have. Even though I was always at a borderline full panic whenever we met danger, I thank you again for such an experience. So, I guess this is the time I need to answer your question."

"Isabel, you don't need to answer anything. If you are not ready to marry or are simply against the idea..." He paused, considering that possibility.

"Well?"

"Well, since you brought up the idea of living together, I see a connection. Call me old-fashioned, which I know I am. But I would feel much better if we lived together as husband and wife. It would break my heart if you refuse, but I would get over it and we would still be ..."

"Friends? Friends?! Oh, my gentle Juan, we'll always be friends; friends until the end of our days. I want us to be so much more than that. The very idea drives my entire being into panic! Please don't say that. Don't even think it. Yes! Yes! I agree. Let's do get married. I will never meet another man like you. It would be the biggest regret of my life to lose you. So, 'yes' is my answer." With tears of joy rolling down her cheeks, she leaped into Juan's arms, burying his face tightly in her breasts.

"Really? Oh, that's wonderful!" His muffled words were barely audible. He hugged her tightly against him. She was busy kissing his head, her heart rapidly beating against his cheek. She finally got up, dried her tears, and started pacing around the veranda. Her mind wrapping around the idea that her heart so quickly agreed to.

"My adorada (adored), actually I wasn't going to say 'friends'. I was going to say 'lovers', as in continuing to be a couple. I hope that doesn't change anything."

"No, Juan, it doesn't change a thing. Don't try to wiggle out of it now that you have me hooked." She smiled, shaking her finger at him. She continued excitedly pacing about. "I'll go get a pen and some paper. We have so much to plan. So many details to consider." She skipped like a little girl up to the house.

Juan watched her skipping up the steps two at a time, while thinking, God, I love that woman!

They discussed their wedding plans for the rest of the day. Juan would plan the church service and Isabel the reception. They would marry in their private chapel, presided by Padre Pedro, in the traditional Spanish way, as Juan had done from the first. Isabel wanted to have the reception on the beach, but not on any beach. She wanted it to be at the very white stretch of sand spreading before them.

Juan agreed and proposed that they wed in April when the orange blossoms fill the air with their delicious fragrance. He would choose a date when the tide was at its highest, so the dry part would be on their private beach. There was no sense in making it a public spectacle. April was in six months. They had time to prepare and also time to change their minds.

A few days later, after a wonderful dinner, he led Isabel to the grand sofa in the living room. He put on Debussy and lit a fire in the fireplace. Isabel curled up beside him. "You know, Juan, I have never been drunk before. I'm curious what it's like. I mean, I've had enough to make me drowsy and fall asleep. What I mean is to get really drunk so that I'm hung over the next day. It's an experience that I think is worth doing at least once, just to understand what's the attraction to so many people. There is no one else I would rather do it with than you. Would you do this for me?"

"Isabel, that's ridiculous. I'd really rather you didn't. There are some experiences not worth doing."

"Please, Juan, please just this once? If you don't agree, then I guess I could go back to my apartment and do it alone. But I'd feel so much better and safer with you. Please, my dearest."

"If you insist, but only this once. Jorge! Bring us some old port. Ah… Bring two bottles of the Kopke 1941 with two glasses. Pick a good cheese to go with it."

Turning back to Isabel, "If you really want to do this, better do it with quality. And I promise you, no matter how you'll feel tomorrow, you will never forget how you got there. We'll also have to change the music to something much more appropriate. John Coltrane's Complete Village Vanguard recordings from 1961 will be an excellent start. If you last longer than the three hours that will take, you'll most likely be ready for some Pharoah Sanders."

"I have no idea about any of those names you just said, but I'll follow your lead. Let's start with the first mystery. Do I take it to mean that Kopke is a kind of port wine?"

"Indeed, one of the best."

"Fine, but what does the '41' mean?"

"That's the year it was bottled."

"1941! Older than my parents? Why would we drink something so rare and precious? No, Juan, we don't need to do that."

"Well, it is old and precious, but they are not the only two bottles like it in the world. In my wine cellar, I have port wine from the 1500's. Trust me, my sweet, we're not overdoing it with port from 1941. Even if you would drink a thousand bottles of port in your lifetime, it's not worth even one of them to be nothing but excellent."

The port came and Jorge poured out two small glasses and handed them to his charges. He lit the many candles all about and dimmed the lights. Juan changed the music and raised the volume. They clinked glasses and settled in for many hours of great jazz and port wine.

"Before we start, I would like us to follow the custom of the ancient Persian kings. In a few days, I will announce our engagement party to our family and friends. Before we do so, I'd like us to be as sure as we can be.

When the ancient Persian kings had to make an important decision, they and their advisors would discuss it while drunk after dinner, then make a decision. Later, they would discuss the same thing when they were stone sober. If the decisions were the same, they would proceed. If not, then they had to arrive at a different decision, starting the same process again."

"My sweetest, loveliest man, my decision will not change, even under torture."

"Wonderful. I'll ask you again tomorrow when you first wake up."

He switched to old Bourbon and let Isabel drink most of the Kopke '41 for the next three hours, until Isabel's eyes rolled into her head and fell into his arms while dancing nude to Pharoah Sanders' Message from Home. The flickering flames of the fireplace had accompanied her beautiful dancing body while her clothes, discarded one by one, were strewn across the floor.

Juan was only somewhat inebriated and jolly. After all, someone had to be the adult in the room. He carried her up to bed. The next morning, Isabel was not feeling well. Juan got up and let her sleep. As he opened the door, he heard the muffled words, "Juan, my decision is still the same. Is yours?"

"Yes, my most precious woman. Yes, it is." She fell back asleep with a pounding headache and a smile.

Juan organized an engagement party for three weeks later to make the formal announcement. She invited her friends and family, twenty-four in total. He invited his crew mates, holding steady at twenty-six. They had no family and no serious women friends. After five centuries, none of them had made close friends outside of their inner group.

The excitement of Isabel's family and friends bordered on ecstatic. They knew how much Isabel loved him and all they had been through on that strange voyage around the world. Isabel's mother understood a good catch when she saw one.

As for Juan's crew mates, they were less than excited. They had seen it too many times before. Every time it happened again, they all felt concerned that it would be the time when their friend would snap into madness at the inevitable loss. Juan had long ago stopped asking for their advice on the matter. He simply did not care. They clearly could not understand the matters of the heart like he could.

He clearly understood better than they how it would end in great grief again. He just could not help himself. The months or even years of sorrow were worth the many decades of blissful peace, being in a relationship based on love and kindness. Caring for each other, through every point of pain and stumble, made it all worth it. They were already living it. He knew the formality of marriage was unnecessary and even silly in the modern age, especially with no possibility of children. Yet somehow it put a golden glow around their relationship, uniting them into one.

CHAPTER TWENTY-EIGHT

The Big Day

The eighteenth of April was a good day for a wedding. The sun god smiled upon the proceedings without excessive heat and humidity. Isabel and Juan had not talked or seen each other since the beginning of the month just to be sure of their feelings for each other. The silence of their voices only caused the yearning in their hearts to grow.

Juan's mates arrived at their private chapel early, all dressed in their black suits with matching blue ties and black shoes. They sat on the left side, leaving the right side for the bride's family and friends. Padre Pedro was standing at the altar in flowing white robes, preparing things. Juan and Antón sat in a separate room, waiting for the ceremony to begin.

Juan, not having a mother or any other woman worthy of the role in his circle, had no padrina. So, Antón served that role, yet again, as he had done for 500 years. The bride's father was the padrino, so he had to be the padrina. Fortunately, he had the imagination to accept being the masculine padrina. Padre Pedro had no choice but to accept this slight gender-bending fact for his marriage ceremonies. No one else in the Church hierarchy would ever need to know.

"OK, Juan, I'm your mother for today. Tradition dictates that I need to ask: are you sure about this?"

"Yes, mother dearest, you know I am. I also know what every one of you is thinking. 'Why is he doing it again?' My answer is the same as it's always been. The love of a woman is vital to my life. I know marriage has nothing to do with commitment and love. But something deep down inside causes me anxiety at the idea of living together without being married."

"Living in sin, as Padre Pedro would say?"

"You know I don't believe in sin, nor in anything else the Church teaches. Unlike the rest of you, I was raised 550 years ago in a nobleman's family. For better or worse, the mores of my time were instilled deep within me, though I have successfully rid myself of most of the more ridiculous ones. I could go on, but my dear mother knows perfectly well that this conversation has nothing to do with marriage."

"Yes, my son, you are correct. The rest of your family and I are concerned about what being a widower again will do to your state of mind. You always become so distraught, and the grief nearly breaks you every time. One day, you may not be able to put the pieces back together."

"Of course, that's what this is all about. I have done so twenty-six times. Why do you think I couldn't do it again?"

"Because every time it's worse and takes longer for you to recover. You are our Capitán, our best friend, our leader, our big brother, our brave Apollo. We hate to see you go through the suffering. You must stay strong and lead us, lead us through eternity. Only you have the wisdom of keeping it all together, carrying us through the serious challenges of a changing world. We would be lost without you."

"You know very well that I'll always be with you."

"Will you?"

"The answer, as always, is 'yes'."

"Did you at least get the prenuptial signed?"

"Yes! Don't worry. Once again, I had to overcome my great distaste for these things. Every one of my marriages has been nothing but love and happiness. Not one ended in divorce. I guess I know how to pick them."

"I'd say you're just lucky. The more modern women get, the more I worry."

"What are you worried about? It's my money. Let's drop this extremely unpleasant subject. Shall we? Oh, good! They've arrived. Let's go." They were interrupted by the bride's entourage arriving.

Isabel was stunning in her long black silk dress, holding a bouquet of white flowers that covered her from chin to waist. A black veil covered her face and flowed to the ground behind her. Juan could just make out through the veil the radiant face of his beautiful love and soon to be wife.

It took some time to convince her to wear black, but that is how traditional Spanish weddings are, and he would have it no other way. The black represented that she would be his wife, even as his widow. This unusual tradition always caused a pang in his chest, for he knew he would be the one wearing black at her funeral.

He admitted in some ways he was a slave to tradition. One day he may rebel. Isabel had trouble accepting any of it, but knew he had to have his way. Their arrangement was that she had unquestioned reign over the reception details, and he had the same over the wedding details.

Padre Pedro met them at the entrance to the chapel. Everyone else entered to find their places in their allotted pews, except her father, serving as her padrino. Juan and Antón strolled over to join them. He squeezed Isabel's hand with a beaming warm smile, then he greeted and shook her father Miguel's hand.

Once they confirmed they were ready, Padre Pedro led the small procession towards the altar. He slowly walked with deliberate steps, arrived, and turned around. He motioned for Juan and Antón to approach. Antón dispensed with holding Juan's arm like a mother would have done. They stepped up to the front and turned to watch Isabel approach, holding the arm of her father. They each took their positions on either side of the Padre. Everything was done in silence.

Juan always detested Church music, considering it ponderous and unsingable.

The air was heavy with the fragrance of the orange blossoms outside the open windows. The sound of chirping birds was the best music for any occasion. Both enhanced the day's magic for Isabel. Despite initial reservations, she came to fully embrace the idea of being Mrs. Ponce de León.

The service started. Miguel returned to sit next to his wife and Antón to his fellow mates. The Padre opened with a prayer and then read the entire Sermon on the Mount, from Mathew 5:1 to 8:1. It was the only part in the entire Bible that made any sense to Ponce de León. The Padre continued with a short sermon of his own, mainly on the subject of maintaining their love through all manner of life's challenges. Ponce de León could only indulge the Padre a short sermon, as he did not think that a man who never married could really give good advice on the subject.

Antón stepped up and pulled out the gold ring for Isabel and handed it to the Padre to bless, who then handed it to Ponce de León. The groom gently took his bride's hand and placed the ring on the ring finger of her right hand. Antón handed Juan's ring to the Padre, and the process was reversed.

Next Antón handed a small silver casket that contained thirteen gold doubloons, minted by the Royal Mint of Castille 500 years before with the profile of King Charles I of Spain, better known as the Holy Roman Emperor Charles V, ruler of the German states, the Netherlands, Austria, and much of Italy. His beard made his long, pointed face even longer.

The Padre blessed the coins, called Arras, and placed them in Ponce de León's hands, who then handed them to Isabel. Isabel held them for a few seconds and then returned them to Juan. Each of the thirteen coins represents the thirteen qualities needed for a long-lasting, happy marriage: love, trust, commitment, respect, joy, happiness, harmony, wisdom, wholeness, nurturing, caring, cooperation, and peace. The number thirteen is an auspicious number, symbolizing Jesus and the twelve apostles. Juan placed them back in their casket and handed it to Antón.

The wedding continued with the Liturgy and Mass. Ponce de León made sure the Mass was open to anyone who wanted to take part. He considered himself almost a pagan, though he highly respected Jesus and His message of love to the world. As far as what happened after Him, Ponce de León had simply seen too much at first hand the workings of the Church. Quoting Nietzsche, he would often say, "The last Christian died on the cross".

He chose an excellent port wine for the Mass to symbolize the union of the two families as the Douro/Duero River unites the two countries of Portugal and Spain. It was the river that flowed near his hometown of Santervás de Campos and continued west to enter the sea at Porto, the second city of Portugal. The port wine grapes came from the Douro River valley. Besides, every important step in life after the first one should follow a sip of excellent wine.

Ponce de León made the Communion bread himself, a good dense and crusty loaf as his mother made. The normal wafers always seemed to him like eating a piece of paper. Everyone filed up to the railing and received Communion. Padre Pedro concluded with a final blessing and the married couple, holding hands, followed their Padre down the aisle and out the door. Everyone threw rose petals as they passed.

The entourage returned to Juan's home, where Jorge's hired crew of gourmet caterers had prepared a wonderful feast under a large tent on the beach. It was early afternoon when the cars filled the space in front of the house. Everyone filed through the front door, through the living room, out the sliding glass back door, past the veranda to the tent below.

Each place had an engraved name card, indicating where everyone was to sit. The head table in the front was on a raised platform. That was where Juan, Isabel, her parents, the Padre, and Antón sat. Each table had six places ready. A jazz band played in the corner. They had the honor of playing the entire sessions of

Miles Davis' In a Silent Way album, all three hours of it. By that time, the dance band would replace them and play until the last ones dancing would collapse. Isabel let Juan choose the music.

Paella and various seafood dishes made up the main course. Before dessert was served, Juan and Isabel went to each table. Juan gave Cohiba cigars to the men. Isabel gave garnet rose pins to the women. Juan could not accept the idea that a woman might want to smoke a cigar, too. He did not know any man who would have preferred a rose pin for his lapel. Tradition was maintained.

After dessert, Antón took off Juan's tie and cut it up into small pieces. Juan did the same with Isabel's garter. Her upper thighs were exclusively his domain. Antón distributed a piece to each guest: the tie to the men, and the garter to the women. Ordinarily, these pieces would be sold to the guests to raise money for the couple's new home. Juan had no need for their money, but thought the ancient custom was worth it for sentimental reasons.

Juan rose and led Isabel by the hand to the large empty space in front of their table. Antón began strumming a traditional acoustic guitar. His mates joined in by clapping out the rhythm. Antón, with his strong and sonorous voice filling the tent, began to sing the traditional Spanish wedding dance of the Sequidillas Manchegas. Juan and Isabel faced each other and started the dance, according to how he taught her, spinning and swaying to the lively music. Her skirt swirled. He lifted her high into the air. Everyone joined in the rhythmic clapping.

They returned to their seats. The dance band replaced the jazz band and the festivities continued at a faster pace. Wine flowed. Guests crowded the open bar. All sorts of food, both dainty and hearty, covered the side tables. Isabel and Juan had to pace themselves. The party would continue until dawn. They had to be the last ones standing.

CHAPTER TWENTY-NINE

A Tropical Honeymoon

Everyone more or less recovered within a day or two after the celebration. Isabel and Juan were alone again. Isabel liked Juan's idea for their honeymoon. They would sail in a large clockwise circle through the West Indies, the northern coast of South America, the eastern coast of Central America and Mexico, along the Caribbean coast of the US, before returning to their home port.

This time Juan would sail the Luna Bella (Beautiful Moon), a much smaller Mariner 36 sailing yacht with a 36-foot length with no crew. It would just be the two of them. They could take all the time they wanted. That size was about as big as one sailor could comfortably handle. Even so, he had an assistant who was eager to learn the ancient art of sailing.

He had timed their love voyage for just after his annual date with the Fountain, so they had nearly a year before the next one. A crew of his mates had flown to Hawaii to sail back their repaired Odyssey with a reinforced bow and keel. But Juan wanted a honeymoon with no one else near them. If they wanted to make love under the moonlight, while anchored in a lonely Caribbean cove, they could do so and so they would.

Juan had their contact send him a new passport. It used to be a fairly simple procedure to forge a US passport, but they all had computer chips in them by then. This just made the process more complicated. The contact would find a US Latino citizen who needed a good dose of cash and looked like Juan. This person would apply for and receive his passport, which he then sold to Juan's contact. When entering the US, Juan had to remember his name and birthdate. Problem solved. Driving licenses, fortunately, were a lot easier. It was relatively easy for a 550-year-old man to live normally in society with some creativity and good contacts.

It was a fine early Spring morning in early May when they cast off from Saint Augustine. The sun was rising from the eastern ocean and a light breeze promised smooth sailing. Juan had their route planned so that they would never be more than fifty miles from land. Sailing time from one island to the next would be a leisurely afternoon with plenty of time to have an island rum drink before dinner.

Juan could not care less about the distance between points of land, having sailed across unknown oceans. But considering Isabel's rather stressful experience on their last voyage, he had to think of her. Though she said nothing, she was visibly relieved when Juan explained their sailing plans.

They sailed south along the Florida coast. Fifteen hours later, they arrived at Palm Beach. It was already nightfall, but not late enough to have a relatively early dinner by Spanish standards. They slept that night and every night of their voyage on their yacht. The cabin was quite spacious, with a full bath and a wide bay window to view the blue world beyond. The dining and living areas were more than sufficient for a couple to explore their love for each other.

The next day, a leisurely lunch followed a late breakfast. It took only five hours sailing directly east to reach Freeport on the island of Grand Bahama. From there, they island hopped through the many Bahama islands, sometimes less than an hour sailing from one to the next. They came across many deserted islands with a dense forest and an expansive white sandy beach just begging them to visit.

Often, Juan would anchor close enough to the beach that a short swim could reach. If they wanted to bring a picnic, Juan would ready the rubber Zodiac to carry everything. Sometimes they dined on a secluded beach with wine and lobster. Later, they would make love in the lapping waves like in that old movie, except with the pale light of the moon embracing their bodies tightly wound.

The morning sun would find them sleeping on a blanket spread across the soft white sand in the shade of palm trees. Seagulls would awake them with their urgent cries. Breakfast, a swim, another dalliance in the quiet waves, and they would return to the Luna Bella. There, they would avail themselves of a shower and rich coffee before pulling up the anchor to start the next quick jaunt to another beautiful experience.

The Turks and Caicos Islands marked the end of the Lucayan Archipelago. From there, they continued south to the Greater Antilles. They sailed along the northern coasts of the Dominican Republic and Puerto Rico. During this part of their trip, they had to confine their trysts to the Luna Bella's cabin.

As in the Bahamas, Juan would often stare at the island coasts for hours in silence. Isabel knew him well enough to know there were times when it was best to leave him in his silent thoughts. She would not even ask him about what he was thinking. In those mental states, he would not even hear her until he returned to the present. Just how far in the past his memories of those coasts and islands reached, she would never know.

When he relived those memories of the distant past, he was actually there. He relived the times of the old colonial ports with their rum taverns and the busy docks full of small caravels groaning at the ropes holding them fast. There, he rescued the stranded crew of his rival. At that clearing on the coast, he and his fellow crewmen of Columbus' second voyage landed to find fresh water and coconuts. And there, that was where they built the first colony in the Dominican Republic. Oh, and Puerto Rico, where he was the first governor.

The memories would flood in, crowding out any thought of the present. Hours would pass until he pulled himself back and noticed his radiant new wife. He would apologize to Isabel, but she always answered there was no need and, besides, there was beauty in the silence. Words are often unnecessary and can sometimes only distract from the higher truths.

As they approached San Juan on the north coast of Puerto Rico, Juan became more agitated. Finally, he blurted out, "I wasn't planning on it, but let's stop and visit San Juan. They have a statue of my ancestor and his tomb there. He was the first governor of the Puerto Rico colony. I'm his namesake. I haven't been in a long time. It's now a big modern city, but please indulge me with this."

"Juan, my precious man, I'd indulge you in anything."

They docked by the bridge to the mainland and walked the two miles and a bit through old San Juan to the point where it all started. Occasionally, Juan would stop and stare at a seemingly unimportant house or square, lost in thought. Isabel thought it strange but said nothing. This unplanned stop was clearly something much more than a tourist visit.

They passed grand government buildings, plazas with fountains, forts with old cannon facing out to sea, and serenely imposing churches. They arrived at one of these impressive churches, a cathedral in fact, the Catedral Basilica Menor de San Juan Bautista. Juan pointed out that it was the second oldest cathedral in the Americas.

Juan motioned for her to enter.

"Juan, I never took you for a religious man. Have you come to pray?"

"I don't go to churches to pray. I only go to remember. Come. I want to show you something."

They entered the dark, cool cathedral. He led her along the north wall to a room painted a cheerful yellow. Between two windows stood a tall marble statue of a woman holding a sword in one hand, a flag in the other, while kissing a small casket.

"This is it. This is the tomb of my illustrious ancestor. What do you think?"

"Looks baroque, medieval, even. But I would expect that for what I guess you could call 'funerary art'."

"I don't like it at all. To start, why a woman? It looks like she's kissing her jewelry box. They could have put a statue of the great old man himself, making a grand gesture like pointing to Florida or something."

"I admit I have no explanation."

"Some say he's not really buried here at all."

"Then where would he be?"

"What if he was never buried? What if he really did discover that Fountain of Youth and is hiding among us today, hiding in plain sight even?"

"If you say so."

"Well, I don't say so. I was just asking a rhetorical question. All I know is that his blood runs through my veins. Come. I have something else to show you."

They walked two blocks north to the Plaza de San José where the Church of the same name forms the northern side of a park. Rows of tall trees flanked the other three sides. There in the center, standing on a fifteen foot high pedestal, was a statue of the heroic leader himself.

Standing in a self-confident pose, quite debonair with a feather in his hat, stood the bronze man, pointing into the distance.

"He was cast in New York in 1882 from British cannons captured after a failed attempt to invade the city in 1797. It is identical to the statue of him in Saint Augustine. They were made at the same time. Tell me, is there any family resemblance?"

"Can't tell, really. The beard looks similar, but I can't see the eyes. It couldn't be really as it was cast 350 years later."

"Later?"

"Yes, later from the date on the tomb."

"Ah, the date on the tomb."

"Since you know almost everything about almost anything, smarty, where is he pointing to?"

226

"They say he's pointing to the original settlement of San Juan. But that can't be, because the first settlement was actually further to the right of where he's pointing. No. I'd say he's pointing to his next adventure, somewhere over the horizon."

"Hm, I prefer your explanation. It's far more romantic."

"Yeah, he was always the romantic. Let's sit here for a while."

Again, Juan closed his eyes and transported himself back to the early days of his governorship. Isabel thought of the adventures they had in the relatively short time together. She also considered the strange man who was now her husband. The strangeness was what made him interesting in her eyes. He clearly was a man of great depth, always having a well-thought intelligent opinion. If he had not considered something in depth, he would offer no opinion on it.

After an hour next to her silent man, she closed her eyes and fell asleep. It was late afternoon when she awoke to Juan nibbling on her ear lobe. He whispered, "Let's go. This is no place for sleeping. Let's head back to our yacht and sleep there."

Isabel yawned her reply, "Sleep? Nah, but I'm sure we can find something else to do there."

The next morning, they continued their voyage, island hopping through the Lesser Antilles to Trinidad and Tobago. From there, they turned west and followed the coasts of Venezuela, Columbia, Central America to Mexico. They stopped at the ports along the way, visiting whatever interested them.

At Cancun, for example, Juan hired a local guide to show them the many magnificent Mayan ruins spread throughout the Yucatan. While at Chichen Itza, their guide pointed out a Mayan stone carving that had a few figures that looked like Roman centurions. "See? Here is proof that the Romans were the first Europeans to land here."

Juan would not let that pass. "Now, this is an example of how a guide loses his tip. I know for a fact that the first European to sail here was a Spaniard with a family name of Alaminos in 1517. What do they teach you in school?"

The worried guide replied, "It's just a legend, sir. Pay it no heed. Yes, of course, I learned about the great navigator, Antón de Alaminos. Forget I said anything so absurd as Romans sailing here. It was a bad joke."

Later, Isabel asked Juan if their Antón de Alaminos was related to the famous navigator. Juan explained that, indeed, he was. Latinos like to name their children after any relative with even a touch of fame. The idea was that maybe their children would attain wealth and fame, too.

They returned to their yacht and continued following the great coastal crescent past Texas, Mississippi, Alabama, and finally back to Saint Augustine, Florida. It was ten and a half months since they set sail. It was a wonderful honeymoon voyage. But it sure felt good to be home again.

CHAPTER THIRTY
Communing with the Dead

On Sunday afternoon, Ponce de León went to the silent, lonely chapel on the wooded hill facing the ocean. The Padre had stopped offering Mass centuries ago after no one would come. None of them believed anything he preached, anyway. The chapel was available if anyone felt the need to be alone and contemplate the higher truths.

When Ponce de León had these urges, he would do as the tribal shamans did. He would sit on the beach from when the moon rose until the rising sun took its place, listening to the words of the waves. The silence between the waves was where the Spirit whispered to him as It embraced his heart. When he rose in the morning, his Inner Light was warmer and brighter.

Other times, he preferred to commune with the Spirit by laying with his woman before breakfast. Together they moved like the waves of the primordial sea from where all life came. As he came close to consummating their timeless ritual, he would close his eyes and fly towards the sun, ever brighter, ever warmer.

The sun would pull him unrelentingly in to its fiery embrace until its power overwhelmed him. Then he would explode into oblivion and become as one with the Spirit, joining his small flame to the great cosmic one.

Every Sunday afternoon when he was not traveling, he would spend time at the chapel and the family crypt. He would first sit in the quiet dark chapel with his eyes closed, centering himself, emptying the typical flotsam that fills our minds all our days. Then the Spirit would fill his peaceful heart. Having sanctified himself, he would enter the crypt. This was one of those Sundays.

He rose from the hard wooden pew and entered the cemetery through a side door of the chapel. The main gate was solidly locked and only opened once every forty or fifty years when a new inhabitant of the family crypt would arrive.

Passing by the rows of crooked head stones covered in moss and weeds of long-since forgotten people who once roamed the earth, he stopped in front of the imposing gothic marble crypt, the last home he could offer his ever-growing American family. He considered the significance of the words 'Ponce de León' carved into the rock arch above the cold heavy iron door. Before entering, he busied himself cutting away any vines and weeds that were, trying to pull the dark, windowless marble structure down into oblivion.

He did nothing about the moss and lichen covering the walls and roof. It might take a thousand years for them to break down the structure. Ponce de León just shrugged at the idea. He would just rebuild it. He had to build a new one anyway in about a hundred years, as the current one was almost deep enough to hit the water level.

Mixed melancholy thoughts filled his mind as he considered eventually having a dozen family crypts with hundreds of past loves entombed within. He would need a week to honor them properly. One day, he would need to live in the chapel like a monk and do nothing else. At least there would be no more wives to plan for.

He forced his mind empty and opened the somber door. Instead of the normal dank, moldy smell of a just-opened sepulcher, a perfumed fragrance greeted his nose. He left the hanging scented oil lamps burning always. He preferred their dim gloom to the garish electric lights they needed to carry a new casket down many stairs to its final resting place. They fit his state of mind perfectly.

After allowing for a few minutes for his eyes to adjust to the relative darkness, he moved deeper within. His first wife and their four children occupied the ground floor. Each casket nestled snugly in its place within the walls. He dropped down on a marble bench in the corner. He closed his eyes and remembered.

Leonora was a cross between a perpetual child and a wild woodland creature. She followed her instincts more than her ration. She had an insatiable need for pleasure from any source, whether food, rum, or a man. She introduced him to the wonders of nature: rolling in the hay in the stables, the waves of a beach, the leaves of trees in the forest. She was the opposite of the women of his homeland, so full of guilt of enjoying what the gods gave them.

With such a woman, he should have known what would have happened during his long absences, exploring the new world, finding his destiny. He had four children with her, who all looked like him. Of that, he was confident. She had at least enough respect for him to not produce any physical evidence of satisfying her needs.

As for his children, he provided well for them and their mother. He provided for their every need. He had them well educated and set up for a good life, excellent marriages for his daughters and all his wealth to his son, making him a rich man from the start. They all died much too young, either in childbirth or by tropical diseases. Of course, it takes much more than meeting material needs. Before they were adults, they were complete strangers to him.

His thoughts returned to Leanora. She never learned to read, despite him trying to teach her. She just did not have a head for it. Proper Spanish grammar eluded her. But she so enjoyed when he read to her a story of King Author or a fable from the Bible. She would curl up with her head on his chest, looking at the meaningless words on the page but painting every detail of the story in her mind, better than any illustrator could.

She was a simple woman, a barmaid with the wisdom of the essence of life. They had a great time together. She was his first passion. He smiled. He loved her then; he loved her still.

He rose and descended to the next level down. There five more caskets nestled in their niches in the walls. He sank down on the cold corner bench and reminisced. He did not marry again until fifty-six years later, ten years after he settled in Saint Augustine. Marriable women were very rare in the beginning.

He had no shortage of women. He had enjoyed the affections of every woman below the age of fifty in the tribal village of southeast Florida. Even in early Saint Augustine, there were certain rooms in the village tavern that were occupied by past-their-prime professionals from the port cities of Spain, hoping to extend their careers by another decade or two.

What was it about marriage that made him different from all his mates, who were quite content once a week to drink their fill at the tavern and take their turn going up the stairs for some release? He felt a stability and a comfort in having a special woman create a home for him. He needed someone to love and think about as he went through the travails of the day.

If he wanted such a woman, he needed to marry her. Until about fifty years ago, it was a rare woman who would live with a man openly unmarried. Between culture and habit, being married was more important to him than it was to contemporary women.

There lies Maria José. She came from the brothels of Cádiz. But unlike her sisters, she came to the colonies to change careers and find a husband. She was right to think she would have much less competition in the predominantly male towns of the newer colonies. She took a job as a barmaid at one of the taverns of the growing town. She unwittingly played the same game with the mysterious handsome gentlemen who kept to himself in the corner.

Ponce de León fell for another barmaid. He did not care about her past. He just wanted a woman to love who would be reliable and faithful until the end. And she loved him, loved with total abandon. She had learned from an early age a Catholic loophole around the guilt. She would do whatever 'good girls' should never do and enjoyed it.

She would go to Confession every Sunday, contritely describing her carnal acts, and then do whatever penance the padre would prescribe. Sometimes she would say 500 Hail Mary's or Our Fathers, or fast for a day only wearing a burlap sack, or even circle the church on her knees. It did not matter, because by doing so, her moral slate was wiped clean of sin, freeing her for a new week of debauchery. Twenty-one years later, she died at the age of fifty-two from yellow fever.

The next one was Sara. She was brought to Saint Augustine against her will as a slave from Guinea. She was captured by the coastal tribes who did slave raids into the interior to sell to the Portuguese at the ports they built along the African coast. Ordinarily, Ponce de León avoided the town square when the slave auctions occurred. He knew slavery had existed for millennium in every culture around the world. Even so, the idea of owning another person, held in lower estimation than a good horse, offended him.

That day he was returning from an important meeting with the governor and had to pass by the auction square. There they were. Six women standing naked on the wooden platform, looking bewildered at the nasty turn of their once peaceful lives. Men were examining them, feeling their breasts and bottoms.

The second one from the left stood like an ebony statue with her head held high, looking stoically into the distance while they examined her like a cow. Her eyes lit on Ponce de León's as he strolled by, shaking his head, dismayed by the proceedings. He stopped as her eyes held his with a silent cry of 'help' burning into his brain.

When the bidding started, he did not even hear the prices offered. He just raised his hand at every bark of the auctioneer until she was his. He covered her with his cloak and brought her home. She was the daughter of her tribe's chief. She and her friends were unlucky to be captured while they were searching in the forest for an escaped pet lemur.

He freed her officially and taught her to speak Spanish. Once she was conversant enough, he had her baptized and then married her. The first time he laid with her, he was a little scared. She was as black as the depths of the abyss. Her tight, curly hair rose like the flames of a bonfire all around her head. It was his first time with such a strange but beautiful woman from the African continent. She gladly showed her appreciation to her kind and gentle hero.

She was ashamed of how they first met. He was ashamed of the way she was brought there. Despite everything, they came to love each other. Being the wife of one of the town's wealthiest citizens helped but did not shield her completely from the racism of her fellow citizens. She felt it in every subtle way it was given. She would come home and cry for hours. It would break his heart. He was helpless to do anything about it. She died forty-three years later from cholera.

He continued in that way for all twenty-six of his wives, remembering what made them special, how they fell in love, the joy they gave him, and finally how they died. He sat reminiscing for an hour on each floor. Finally, he stared down the stairs to the last floor. An icy hand gripped his heart. No, he did not want to descend to the empty bottom floor.

A morbid spirit compelled him down the stairs. His steps were leaden. With dread, he sat down and stared at the empty spaces hewed from the rock walls. One day, they, too, would be filled with the lifeless forms of future loves. He broke into a cold sweat, realizing that the first would be his precious Isabel.

One Sunday he would sit on that same bench remembering her, their life together, the joys and passion. Suddenly, his eyes closed, and his mind went blank. His thoughts all went dark. He was alone and could release his emotions into the open. He cried for his future grief, his future heartbreak. He yelled and screamed at the dark, damp, foreboding stone walls, beat them with his fists until they bled. Finally, sinking to his knees before the space meant for

Isabel, he silently sobbed into his arms resting on her future rough stone shelf.

Almost an hour later, after he had no more tears to cry, his knees loudly complaining, he rose from the floor. He forced himself out of that dark place in his mind and the darkness of the crypt. He slowly locked the iron door and returned to the chapel, collapsing exhausted on the front wooden pew. He looked up at the rough, plain wooden cross. What did it mean? What did it all mean? Where was the sense?

He was not a praying man. He only sought peace in his troubled mind. Surely that was not too much to ask. He closed his eyes and emptied his mind. He waited for the Great Spirit to enter and fan the dying embers within his heart back to life. An hour later, he felt the great peace he was yearning for. The flame was now warm and bright, filling his heart with a slight electrical buzzing. He slowly opened his eyes and returned to his car.

CHAPTER THIRTY-ONE
The Crisis Finally Bursts

Ponce de León came home several hours later than normal. Isabel was worried. When she heard his car enter the driveway, she hastened to open the front door. She stood in the doorway and was shocked to see the state he was in as he walked up the stairs.

"My god, Juan, what happened to you? You look like you saw a ghost or something. Your hands are swollen and bleeding. Did you get into a fight? What happened?"

He approached to hug her. She thought he wanted to enter the door and stepped backward. He thought she was avoiding his hug. That baleful thought rekindled his sorrow of the inevitable future of losing her. He quickly gripped her in a tight bear hug. His tears wetting her hair.

"Don't step away from me, my love! Don't step away! I don't want to lose you, my precious Isabel! By the gods, I don't want to lose you!" His voice choked up and he could not continue.

With her face tightly buried in his chest, Isabel could say nothing until he loosened his grip on her. She tried to gently push him away enough to speak. But this caused him to squeeze her even more. He tried to speak but instead broke into sobs. She managed to turn her face enough to cry out, "Juan! Stop! You're smothering me!"

At this, he loosened his grip. He let Isabel lead him like a lamb to the sofa. She pulled him down beside her. "Now tell me what's happened to you? You've made me anxious. This is nothing like you."

Juan regained enough composure to respond, "I just don't want to lose you, Isabel. You are the greatest love of my life. You have no idea how significant that means. I just don't want to lose you…" He lowered his head onto her breasts and more tears rolled down his cheeks.

"What are you talking about, silly man? You'll never lose me. I'm yours forever."

"Forever? Oh, please don't jest with me! I want you forever, too, but not like that. I don't mean floating together in the cotton white clouds, strumming a harp."

"Juan, you're making no sense. Will you just tell me what happened to you?"

"I know you won't leave me on your own, dearest. But one day you will, just the same and my heart will be broken in unbearable grief."

"Leave you? Do you mean dying?"

Juan shook his head with his eyes tightly closed.

"What's come over you suddenly? Why would that make such an impact? Who knows what the future has in store? Maybe I'll go first. Perhaps you will. Maybe we'll go together? In any case, that's a long time into the future. Let's just concentrate on the joy and love we have now." She hugged him tightly like a child who just discovered that death exists.

He let her hold and comfort him like the baby he was being for nearly a half an hour. She hummed an unknown tune as she gently rocked her damaged man against her bosom. Eventually, he regained some composure and realized what a spectacle he was making. Worse, he was upsetting her, too.

"Sorry, Isabel. I don't know what's come over me. I need to lie down. I think I'll go to bed early tonight. I'm sorry, my precious, you'll have to eat dinner alone tonight. I have no appetite at all. Jorge will make something nice for you." He gave her a wan smile and slowly climbed the stairs to bed.

Juan slept like the dead, awaking twelve hours later. Beside him Isabel was still sleeping. Her soft breathing gently flowed on to his cheek. He smiled and laid back, wondering what came over him the day before. That was the worst it had ever been in 500 years. He tried to analyze himself.

The grief and emotions he felt were all too real. He was not losing his mind. But what came over him? Clearly, it was the thought of one day losing Isabel like he did with all the others. Isabel was a very special woman, but did he really love the others any less at the time? Of course, it was very difficult to lose them, too. He always recovered after some time. He would do the same again. Love is a wonderful thing, but it is no reason to fall to pieces.

By rationalizing it, he could regain his old cool and collected self. He looked away from Isabel. He needed a shower and something to eat. Afterwards, he went on a long walk on the beach, alone.

Life returned to its normal loving tenderness. They did everything together as usual. Their days were filled with the joy they were used to. Isabel was relieved. She had considered if Juan needed professional help. He would have been too proud to accept it. But still…

Over the next months, Juan started to change. He had extreme mood swings. Sometimes he would love her with such passion as if it were the last time they would ever see each other. Other times, he would be distant, even a little cold to her. He did not seem to know how much this hurt her, though she kept her feelings well hidden. She did not ask him about it, just hoping he would snap out of it, whatever 'it' was.

Juan's subconscious was simply creating a defense mechanism. Perhaps if he did not love her so much, it would not be so painful when he would kneel beside her, holding her weakening hand, while she breathed her last. He would feel guilty and then swing the other way, revealing the intense love he really had for her. It was sapping his energy, though he did not notice it consciously.

One morning, they awoke early and had a simple breakfast. Isabel wanted to go on a long, thoughtful walk before anyone else would appear and distract. She had something serious to tell him. With not a little foreboding, Juan agreed, dreading if this was when she would tell him she was leaving him. How would he react to that?

After walking hand in hand for half an hour, Isabel stopped and turned to him. "Juan, something has changed in you. It's strange and I have no idea what it could be. I know you love me as much as I do you. Sometimes you are the most adorable lover, but sometimes you're cold and distant. You're having very extreme mood swings. Maybe you should see a doctor. You know, discuss your feelings with a professional."

"A professional? Discuss my feelings with a stranger? Isabel, I don't discuss my feelings with anyone."

"Yes, I know. But maybe that's exactly the problem. If you won't discuss them with a stranger, then how about me? What is going on inside you, my wonderful husband? I want to help you, help us."

"Us? Do we need help? I don't need help. No one can help whatever's bothering me, except me. As for us, what exactly do you mean? Am I hurting you? If so, tell me. That is the last thing I would ever do. The last thing." He repeated himself as his voice drifted to silence and he stared out to sea.

"Ok, ok, I knew that's how you would answer. My grandmother could do nothing with my moody grandfather, either. So, I have an idea. Let's have children. Let's start a family. That would pull us together again."

"But we ARE together, Isabel, together forever." His faced turned gray, and he continued walking down the beach.

Isabel hurried to catch up to him. "Juan, I'm in my mid-thirties. I want at least two children. We need to talk about it now. Just don't walk away."

Juan continued walking, quickening his pace. Isabel was struggling to keep up. Suddenly, he stopped and turned to her. "OK,

Isabel, it's time to talk. Look, we cannot have a family. We are our family. It's hard for me to say it, but I can't have children."

It was Isabel's turn to stare silently at the sun rising in the eastern horizon. She had not expected this. "Why, Juan, why didn't you tell me this earlier?"

"I was afraid that you'd lose interest in me. Break off our relationship. I'm sorry. You're right. We should have discussed this before we married." He stared at the sand by his feet.

She hugged him. "Oh, you silly man. This would not have changed in any way my love for you or my decision to marry you. OK, fine. No problem. Then we can adopt children."

After some silence, Juan replied. "I'm sorry. I just can't do that either. I won't raise another man's child. That's his responsibility. If this is so important to you, then as much as it would destroy me, I would understand if you would want to leave me and start your family with someone else. If we stay together, you need to accept that it would just be the two of us.

"Now, before you answer that, for my part, I promise you there will be no more mood swings. We will be as lovers from the first we met. I know what has come over me and I have expelled it from my mind. But if ever you have even an inkling of a mood swing, stop me right then and tell me. I doubt you will ever need to do so. Can you do that for me, for us?" He hugged her tightly, gently kissing her head.

Isabel relaxed in his arms. "Oh, my silly, silly, ridiculous man. Children are not so important to lose you. I hope to never experience coldness from you ever again. Yes, if I do, I'll tell you right away. We've always been open with each other in the past. I certainly have with you. I hope you will, too."

She sighed as a great weight was lifted from her heart. "I'm so glad we had this conversation. It's really cleared the air and my doubts have disappeared, such as they were. Come here, my man. Come unto me." She pulled him down onto the empty beach. The tension had turned into passion. Juan quickly laid beside her.

*****

Dear reader, at this point ask yourself if you are a realist, practical in the ways of the world and life. If you are, then proceed to the next chapter, Chapter Thirty-Two. If, instead, you are a dreamer and a romantic, always seeking the higher truths and meaning of life, please proceed to Chapter Thirty-Three.

CHAPTER THIRTY-TWO
Time Flows Serenely On

The time for their annual pilgrimage to the sacred Fountain had arrived. The trip was in the middle of a tropical storm. They drove slowly through dark sheets of rain. Flashes of jagged lightning lit up the dark sky, quickly followed by great booms of thunder. The wind blew the palm trees at unnatural angles.

They probably should have put off their trip until the weather cleared, but no one knew what the consequences would be for missing the exact anniversary. No one wanted to experiment and risk losing their special gift, either. Their native guide to the Fountain had made it clear to them it had to be the exact day.

As for Ponce de León, the weather matched the turmoil in his mind. For the first time in five centuries, he felt dread for the normal highlight of the year. It was always a grand festival feasting with all his mates and dear friends, catching up with each one separately and all together. He forced his mind under control as he stared into the stormy darkness outside. But soon his mind would return to its own inner storm with no specific train of thought, just random confusion.

Antón, sitting beside him in the car, sensed something was not right with his best friend. Something was clearly disturbing him and that equally disturbed Antón. Over the years, he became more worried about El Capitán. His mind was increasingly confused and was clearly becoming moodier. Antón decided he had to stay close to Juan all weekend, like a guardian angel. The previous year's experience was bad enough. What would this year's bring?

The trip took twice as long as usual. The small caravan finally arrived in their secret sanctuary and shelter. The rock walls shut out the storm and muffled the thunder to a mere whisper. After they parked their cars, everyone crowded around their friend and leader; so pleased to see him again. Their joyous welcome could not help but spread to Ponce de León, forcing him to smile. His mood lightened. He grabbed his bag and entered their lodge.

It was already late in the day when they sat down for their light supper. The grand banquet was the next day. But for now, it was just a friendly dinner with no agenda except to share their fellowship. Ponce de León listened and drank his wine without participating in the general conversation.

After Ponce de León had enough wine to help him fall asleep, he took his leave early. He did not want to have a heavy head for the next day. Once he left, the men looked at each other, puzzled by their friend's strange behavior. Antón exhorted everyone to continue their joviality with him the next day. Something was seriously bothering him. His friends could not fathom what it could be.

Antón knew what it was. It was Isabel. His latest love was affecting him, forcing him into gloomy self-reflection. At worst, the gloom would last at most a year after the inevitable funeral. But his friend would always find the strength to move on. Yet, this annoyed Antón. Everyone else on their crew had come to terms with their strange status and had calm, stable minds.

It had already been several years since the last funeral. Isabel was a very healthy young woman. What was wrong with Ponce de León this time? Even more, why was each new relationship affecting him worse than the previous one? With a heavy heart, Antón went to sleep early, too, not knowing what to expect during the next night's banquet.

Despite the wine, Ponce de León awoke at 0200 stone sober and completely wide awake. He looked out the small cloister window that pierced the thick stone wall and noticed the sky was clear, with a brilliant full moon illuminating the wet forest. He felt the forest's urge to commune with it, and the moonlight beckoned.

He dressed and left everyone else sleeping soundly, except for one person: Antón. Antón could not sleep either. When he heard Juan's door open across the hall from his room, he leaped up and quickly dressed. Hiding in the shadows, he silently followed his strange friend. Where was he going at this hour? Was he sleep-walking?

Ponce de León entered the trackless forest, stumbling and slipping over the wet branches and vines. Soon, a destination presented itself. There was a clearing ahead, with a small pond in the center. The moonlight was shining on the special space like a spotlight on a stage.

He sat on a rock and stared into the dark water with the moonlight sparkling on the surface. He could not rub two coherent thoughts together from when he climbed into the backseat of the car that brought him there to now. After an hour, the effect of the light on the water calmed the dark dread that filled his being. A strange peace pervaded him.

The shadows of the surrounding trees and the stones below the water formed strange images. Slowly a face formed, a face of a long-forgotten native, the spirit of the pond. Just below the surface of the water, the mouth of the spirit moved, forming silent words of an ancient lost language. It was speaking to him, but what was it saying?

He fell to his knees at the edge of the water. He placed his head close to the surface of the pond, trying to hear the words muffled by the water. Suddenly, a watery hand grabbed the back of his neck and pulled his head into the pond. The spirit kissed him, blowing air into his mouth so he could breathe. Then it spoke in an unknown ancient tongue, finally releasing him.

Ponce de León lifted his head out of the water. The sweet breath of the pond spirit still filled his senses like a wall of jasmine in full bloom. Whatever it said, the spirit's facial expression held the clue to its meaning. With a peaceful countenance and a smile, the spirit appeared to be giving him calming words to comfort him like a parent with a crying baby. Like a distressed child being gently rocked by his cooing mother, Ponce de León felt his turmoil fall away.

He raised his arms to the moon above and began chanting seemingly random syllables. Then he realized he was chanting a forgotten song in one of the native languages he had learned centuries before. He recognized it as the language of the long-gone Calusa whose territory included this exact forest. Within him, the peace of the local Forest Spirit joined the tranquility of the universal Moon Spirit. Still chanting, he rose and danced slowly but rhythmically around the pond.

Meanwhile, hidden in the forest shadows, Antón was observing his friend's strange behavior. Has he finally snapped? Antón was seriously worried, almost panicking. But the moonlight revealed a serene smile on his friend's face. Antón decided that whatever he was doing must be helping and let him continue uninterrupted.

Antón relaxed and leaned against a tree, noticing a face formed on the moon by the shadows of craters. This lunar smile slowly transfixed him, and a peaceful calm filled his heart. His mind went blank, but his feet moved him to the side of the pond and followed Ponce de León's ritualized dance. He, too, chanted in unison with words that had remained hidden in some dark recess of his mind, finally surfacing again in their native land.

Enraptured, Ponce de León did not notice Antón a few steps behind him. Two hours had passed, and the moon was sinking toward the treetops. An owl shrieked, freezing the two men in mid-step. The forest had spoken, telling them it was time to sleep.

Ponce de León focused his eyes and finally noticed that the moon shadow dancing with him was actually his best friend, Antón. Without a word, Ponce de León smiled and embraced his guardian angel, not at all surprised to find him there. He pointed to their lodge, and they walked back silently. Each slept soundly until mid-morning, when a knock on their doors signified breakfast was ready.

Over coffee, Ponce de León told Antón of his strange dream of the previous night. He described what happened, concluding with Antón joining him around the pond. Antón replied that he, too, had the same dream, but from his point of view, following Ponce de León into the forest. They marveled at how strange for them to have the same dream. Ponce de León posed the idea that perhaps it was real. He did notice that his shoes were strangely damp before he put them on that morning. They both fell silent at the thought that the strange experiences might have been real.

Eventually, Ponce de León shrugged his shoulders and stood up. He decided it was time to help the rest of the crew prepare for dinner. Antón felt a weight lift from his heart in relief that his friend seemed of much lighter spirits than the day before. Whatever happened the previous night seemed to have helped. He rose and joined in the preparations.

However, as the day drew on, Ponce de León increasingly withdrew into himself. By mid-afternoon, he had removed himself to the study. There, he lit a fire in the fireplace. He sat in the old leather chair before it and stared into the dancing flames. For hours, he relived all the significant points of his life. Fragments of random memories from 550 years flooded his mind.

Early evening arrived and a knock on the door roused Ponce de León from his reverie. Antón and the Padre entered and found Ponce de León somewhat dazed and confused. They always gathered for an hour before the banquet to share memories and common experiences from their long time together. This time, they were more concerned about Ponce de León's current state of mind.

Antón worriedly looked at the Padre before he asked, "Juan, are you alright? Something seems to be bothering you."

"Me? Oh, I guess so. I've just been thinking about my life. Where I came from and where I am going. I know the answer to the first but am confused about the second. Where am I going? Where are we going? Have you ever asked yourselves that question?"

"Friend, you know we aren't philosophers. We're simple sailors that Fate has brought together and given us an incredible gift. All our needs are met. We take life as it comes."

"Yes, but where are we going? Every year we meet here to give ourselves another year of youth and health. But to what end? We live like plants, like those old sequoias out west. They have been living for thousands of years, but always rooted to the same place with the same neighboring trees stretching their limbs to the same patch of sun above."

Pedro answered, "Juan, we're not plants. A few years ago, you sailed around the world. You cruised around the Caribbean for your honeymoon." As soon as he mentioned the honeymoon, he regretted saying it.

"Yes, Pedro, we can physically move about. If we had the hearts and minds of plants, we would be completely content if we can even use that word for them. But we don't. We used to have imagination, ambitions, plans. But we've lost them. For example, I've done everything that interests me. What's left?"

Pedro tried to sound excited. "We have the special ability to constantly renew ourselves, learn new things, take on new dreams and ambitions. Have plans that can stretch far into the future. Perhaps we can discuss this at dinner while we're all together. Let's come up with a plan that can re-spark our imagination. Yes, let's do that. A great idea!"

Ponce de León continued as if he had not heard what Pedro had just said. "You know what I miss, friends? I miss the ability to have the plan that every normal man has. I want a family with children. I want to plan for their upbringing and their future success. I want to plan for my old age with my precious woman. Like everyone else, I want love. All I can plan now is the next funeral for the woman I love." He fell back into silence.

Antón and Pedro looked at each other, trying to come up with a proper response. Antón's irritation broke the silence, "I knew that's what this is all about. Look, Juan, you have been through this so many times before. You always bounce back. Yes, Isabel is a wonderful woman, but so were all the others. And there will be many more. Just enjoy what you have and when the time comes, move on to the next adventure."

"You just don't get it, do you? They aren't "adventures" as you put it. They are women with hearts and minds, with hopes and dreams. They're loving creatures of beauty, both inner and outer. None of you have love in your hearts like I do. You've snuffed it out 500 years ago. I don't know whether that's a blessing or a curse. If it's a curse, I've been suffering from it for far too long. It's time to stop this suffering." His loud, angry voice fell to a near whisper.

Antón pleaded. "It's not a curse, Juan. What's a curse is growing old, slowly losing your ability to function, first as a man, then even as a human. You speak of dreams and plans, but all that exists is the ultimate end of the black abyss of death. What comes after that? Nothing. There is no heaven, no hell. We are extinguished. Plans go unfulfilled. The dying man looks back on his life with some smiles, but mostly frowns from lost opportunities, the might-have-beens and the could-have-beens. Is that what you want?"

He continued with a more logical tone of voice: "And love. What is it? It's nothing more than passion, which, because of our European Church-centered culture and our pseudo-morality, we expect it to last to our dying breath. After the passion dies, what's left but the self-delusion of an empty 'love' with a person we must spend the rest of our life with?"

"Ah, spoken like a philosopher or one of those nineteenth century German thinkers, like Nietzsche. Wait a minute. That was Nietzsche who wrote that. Well, Antón, clearly neither you nor he understand what love is. Nice try, but that line of logic fails with me. I'm sure our ever-faithful Padre would have a different explanation, which would equally fail for the same reason. Those who have never experienced love are in no position to have an opinion about it.

"Love can start from passion, or the passion could just be a temporary lust. Love can start from friendship or for many other reasons. Love can start from passion but then evolves over time as hormone levels drop across a wide spectrum to a deep caring for each other in decrepit old age.

"Look, you know you're my dearest friends and I love you both. But I am not like you, any of you. I am not a simple sailor, as you call yourselves. I never was. Life was always far more complex to me than to the rest of you. Now I'm lost at sea and none of you can help me. I'm on my own. The time has come for the banquet. Go! Leave me."

"Juan, please! You must come with us. Get a hold of yourself. You're our Capitán, our leader, our heart and mind. We need you!" Antón's pleading changed to begging.

Ponce de León silently stared at the fire while his two friends stood and watched. Finally, he answered with a weak and distant voice. "Go. I'll join you later."

All they could do was look at each other in shock, shrug their shoulders, and leave. They found everyone else already seated at the dining table, silently staring at them with questioning eyes. Antón told them that their Capitán was busy with something and would join them shortly. Dinner and wine would not be served until then. This brought low murmuring from around the table.

An hour later, Ponce de León appeared with the haggard face of a man struggling with despair. He gave everyone a weak smile and ordered the wine poured. He raised his glass to everyone and toasted to their good fortune and health. Sitting back down, he motioned for the banquet to start without his customary speech.

Dinner passed as normal as it could with such a great black cloud hanging over them. Dessert came and, one by one, each went down to the Fountain for their drink of reinvigoration. Ponce de León ate little and drank nothing. Antón, the last one to reappear from below, took his place beside Ponce de León. He gripped his struggling friend's forearm and said as sweetly as he could muster: "It's your turn, my dear friend."

Instead, Ponce de León rose and spoke clearly and calmly. He summarized the main points of the discussion he had with Antón and the Padre in the study. He elaborated:

"My dearest friends, you're my family. You probably know that I've been suffering for a long time. I should have reached out for help and advice. But we're proud ancient men from a proud ancient land. Even more, I am your strong leader who has safely and calmly led you through all manner of crisis. For many centuries, I've often not felt so strong inside. I entered my own crisis many years ago and have struggled to pull through, even now as I speak.

"Some of you might have noticed and said nothing, thinking I'll get over it. I knew things weren't right, yet I said nothing. But now I will tell you. My struggle has been dealing with the deaths of the loves who were so important to my life. I am locked in a cycle of falling in love and then slowly watching them die before me. It breaks my heart every time.

"You all know Isabel. She is the next in this cycle of love and death. She wants a normal husband and family with children. As much as I want to, if I continue as normal, I cannot give her these things. So, quite simply, my crisis is to carry on drinking from the Fountain of Youth or to stop and live a normal life."

He fell silent, gathering his thoughts. His friends sat silently, transfixed by the enormity of the words they just heard.

He continued. "It's clear to me I cannot continue like this. I must decide to not partake of our grand ritual and rejoin the ranks of normal men, finding happiness that only they can know. Or I must finally cast aside all doubts and continue to enjoy the wonderful gift of everlasting youth calmly and peacefully forever more.

"I must make that choice tonight. If I choose the first, I must leave you and create a new circle of normal mortal friends and family, sharing in the joys and sorrows of a life that will end one day. If I choose the second, I will banish from my head any more doubts and look upon every new woman as a temporary gift who will leave me one day. I will continue to love, but with reservations. Or perhaps I'll do like you do and call a temporary woman to comfort me as I feel the need. That would be the simplest of all.

"As I mentioned earlier how we are different, none of you have faced the same dilemma as I have. I consider our gift either a blessing or a curse. You clearly believe it's a blessing. As you know, I tend to always overthink everything. My mind doesn't give me inner peace like yours do. Nothing is simple with me. So, I must decide now. What will it be?"

He stood in silence, looking at each of the frightened faces staring back at him, afraid that they may finally lose the great man that has been the center of their lives, their benefactor, for five centuries. Ponce de León seemed almost as if he was expecting an answer to his plight from them. Even Antón and the Padre were speechless.

"Before I answer that, let me describe a dream I had last night. Sometimes answers in personal crisis come to us through dreams. Antón was there with me." Ponce de León described the details of his experience from the night before.

"The spirits of the pond and moon spoke to me silently. They gave my feverish mind a peace. They didn't give me an obvious answer to my dilemma. But they did open a door for me to consider entering or not. They inspired me to make a decision that I still struggled with all day. But I have stopped struggling. I will struggle no more."

Ponce de León closed his eyes in silence. Everyone was on the edge of their chairs, spellbound, waiting for his decision. Antón whispered, "What is it, Juan? For the love of the gods, what's your decision?"

Opening his eyes, Ponce de León spoke in a loud sonorous voice: "Well dear mates, I have looked into the face of death and seen what the ravishes of time do. We do, indeed, have a magnificent gift which the ancient gods have blessed us with. It would be a shame to throw it all away from a weakness of mind. There are so many things yet to do in this precious life we have been given. You're the best family any man can hope for. I have made up my mind."

Ponce de León smiled as a great weight had lifted from his heart and peace replaced the angst. He turned and walked slowly but resolutely to the stairway leading down to the Fountain of Youth.

The End

CHAPTER THIRTY-THREE
Time Has Come Today

The time for their annual pilgrimage to the sacred Fountain had arrived. The trip was in the middle of a tropical storm. They drove slowly through dark sheets of rain. Flashes of jagged lightning lit up the dark sky, quickly followed by great booms of thunder. The wind blew the palm trees at unnatural angles.

They probably should have put off their trip until the weather cleared, but no one knew what the consequences would be for missing the exact anniversary. No one wanted to experiment and risk losing their special gift, either. Their native guide to the Fountain had made it clear to them it had to be the exact day.

As for Ponce de León, the weather matched the turmoil in his mind. For the first time in five centuries, he felt dread for the normal highlight of the year. It was always a grand festival feasting with all his mates and dear friends, catching up with each one separately and all together. He forced his mind under control as he stared into the stormy darkness outside. But soon his mind would return to its own inner storm with no specific train of thought, just random confusion.

Antón, sitting beside him in the car, sensed something was not right with his best friend. Something was clearly disturbing him and that equally disturbed Antón. Over the years, he became more worried about El Capitán. His mind was increasingly confused and was clearly becoming moodier. Antón decided he had to stay close to Juan all weekend, like a guardian angel. The previous year's experience was bad enough. What would this year's bring?

The trip took twice as long as usual. The small caravan finally arrived in their secret sanctuary and shelter. The rock walls shut out the storm and muffled the thunder to a mere whisper. After they parked their cars, everyone crowded around their friend and leader; so pleased to see him again. Their joyous welcome could not help but spread to Ponce de León, forcing him to smile. His mood lightened. He grabbed his bag and entered their lodge.

It was already late in the day when they sat down for their light supper. The grand banquet was the next day. But for now, it was just a friendly dinner with no agenda except to share their fellowship. Ponce de León listened and drank his wine without participating in the general conversation.

After Ponce de León had enough wine to help him fall asleep, he took his leave early. He did not want to have a heavy head for the next day. Once he left, the men looked at each other, puzzled by their friend's strange behavior. Antón exhorted everyone to continue their joviality with him the next day. Something was seriously bothering him. His friends could not fathom what it could be.

Antón knew what it was. It was Isabel. His latest love was affecting him, forcing him into gloomy self-reflection. At worst, the gloom would last at most a year after the inevitable funeral. But his friend would always find the strength to move on. Yet, this annoyed Antón. Everyone else on their crew had come to terms with their strange status and had calm, stable minds.

It had already been several years since the last funeral. Isabel was a very healthy young woman. What was wrong with Ponce de León this time? Even more, why was each new relationship affecting him worse than the previous one? With a heavy heart, Antón went to sleep early, too, not knowing what to expect during the next night's banquet.

Despite the wine, Ponce de León awoke at 0200 stone sober and completely wide awake. He looked out the small cloister window that pierced the thick stone wall and noticed the sky was clear, with a brilliant full moon illuminating the wet forest. He felt the forest's urge to commune with it, and the moonlight beckoned.

He dressed and left everyone else sleeping soundly, except for one person: Antón. Antón could not sleep either. When he heard Juan's door open across the hall from his room, he leaped up and quickly dressed. Hiding in the shadows, he silently followed his strange friend. Where was he going at this hour? Was he sleep-walking?

Ponce de León entered the trackless forest, stumbling and slipping over the wet branches and vines. Soon, a destination presented itself. There was a clearing ahead, with a small pond in the center. The moonlight was shining on the special space like a spotlight on a stage.

He sat on a rock and stared into the dark water with the moonlight sparkling on the surface. He could not rub two coherent thoughts together from when he climbed into the backseat of the car that brought him there to now. After an hour, the effect of the light on the water calmed the dark dread that filled his being. A strange peace pervaded him.

The shadows of the surrounding trees and the stones below the water formed strange images. Slowly a face formed, a face of a long-forgotten native, the spirit of the pond. Just below the surface of the water, the mouth of the spirit moved, forming silent words of an ancient lost language. It was speaking to him, but what was it saying?

He fell to his knees at the edge of the water. He placed his head close to the surface of the pond, trying to hear the words muffled by the water. Suddenly, a watery hand grabbed the back of his neck and pulled his head into the pond. The spirit kissed him, blowing air into his mouth so he could breathe. Then it spoke in an unknown ancient tongue, finally releasing him.

Ponce de León lifted his head out of the water. The sweet breath of the pond spirit still filled his senses like a wall of jasmine in full bloom. Whatever it said, the spirit's facial expression held the clue to its meaning. With a peaceful countenance and a smile, the spirit appeared to be giving him calming words to comfort him like a parent with a crying baby. Like a distressed child being gently rocked by his cooing mother, Ponce de León felt his turmoil fall away.

He raised his arms to the moon above and began chanting seemingly random syllables. Then he realized he was chanting a forgotten song in one of the native languages he had learned centuries before. He recognized it as the language of the long-gone Calusa whose territory included this exact forest. Within him, the peace of the local Forest Spirit joined the tranquility of the universal Moon Spirit. Still chanting, he rose and danced slowly but rhythmically around the pond.

Meanwhile, hidden in the forest shadows, Antón was observing his friend's strange behavior. Has he finally snapped? Antón was seriously worried, almost panicking. But the moonlight revealed a serene smile on his friend's face. Antón decided that whatever he was doing must be helping and let him continue uninterrupted.

Antón relaxed and leaned against a tree, noticing a face formed on the moon by the shadows of craters. This lunar smile slowly transfixed him, and a peaceful calm filled his heart. His mind went blank, but his feet moved him to the side of the pond and followed Ponce de León's ritualized dance. He, too, chanted in unison with words that had remained hidden in some dark recess of his mind, finally surfacing again in their native land.

Enraptured, Ponce de León did not notice Antón a few steps behind him. Two hours had passed, and the moon was sinking toward the treetops. An owl shrieked, freezing the two men in mid-step. The forest had spoken, telling them it was time to sleep.

Ponce de León focused his eyes and finally noticed that the moon shadow dancing with him was actually his best friend, Antón. Without a word, Ponce de León smiled and embraced his guardian angel, not at all surprised to find him there. He pointed to their lodge, and they walked back silently. Each slept soundly until mid-morning, when a knock on their doors signified breakfast was ready.

Over coffee, Ponce de León told Antón of his strange dream of the previous night. He described what happened, concluding with Antón joining him around the pond. Antón replied that he, too, had the same dream, but from his point of view, following Ponce de León into the forest. They marveled at how strange for them to have the same dream. Ponce de León posed the idea that perhaps it was real. He did notice that his shoes were strangely damp before he put them on that morning. They both fell silent at the thought that the strange experiences might have been real.

Eventually, Ponce de León shrugged his shoulders and stood up. He decided it was time to help the rest of the crew prepare for dinner. Antón felt a weight lift from his heart in relief that his friend seemed of much lighter spirits than the day before. Whatever happened the previous night seemed to have helped. He rose and joined in the preparations.

However, as the day drew on, Ponce de León increasingly withdrew into himself. By mid-afternoon, he had removed himself to the study. There, he lit a fire in the fireplace. He sat in the old leather chair before it and stared into the dancing flames. For hours, he relived all the significant points of his life. Fragments of random memories from 550 years flooded his mind.

Early evening arrived and a knock on the door roused Ponce de León from his reverie. Antón and the Padre entered and found Ponce de León somewhat dazed and confused. They always gathered for an hour before the banquet to share memories and common experiences from their long time together. This time, they were more concerned about Ponce de León's current state of mind.

Antón worriedly looked at the Padre before he asked, "Juan, are you alright? Something seems to be bothering you."

"Me? Oh, I guess so. I've just been thinking about my life. Where I came from and where I am going. I know the answer to the first but am confused about the second. Where am I going? Where are we going? Have you ever asked yourselves that question?"

"Friend, you know we aren't philosophers. We're simple sailors that Fate has brought together and given us an incredible gift. All our needs are met. We take life as it comes."

"Yes, but where are we going? Every year we meet here to give ourselves another year of youth and health. But to what end? We live like plants, like those old sequoias out west. They have been living for thousands of years, but always rooted to the same place with the same neighboring trees stretching their limbs to the same patch of sun above."

Pedro answered, "Juan, we're not plants. A few years ago, you sailed around the world. You cruised around the Caribbean for your honeymoon." As soon as he mentioned the honeymoon, he regretted saying it.

"Yes, Pedro, we can physically move about. If we had the hearts and minds of plants, we would be completely content if we can even use that word for them. But we don't. We used to have imagination, ambitions, plans. But we've lost them. For example, I've done everything that interests me. What's left?"

Pedro tried to sound excited. "We have the special ability to constantly renew ourselves, learn new things, take on new dreams and ambitions. Have plans that can stretch far into the future. Perhaps we can discuss this at dinner while we're all together. Let's come up with a plan that can re-spark our imagination. Yes, let's do that. A great idea!"

Ponce de León continued as if he had not heard what Pedro had just said. "You know what I miss, friends? I miss the ability to have the plan that every normal man has. I want a family with children. I want to plan for their upbringing and their future success. I want to plan for my old age with my precious woman. Like everyone else, I want love. All I can plan now is the next funeral for the woman I love." He fell back into silence.

Antón and Pedro looked at each other, trying to come up with a proper response. Antón's irritation broke the silence, "I knew that's what this is all about. Look, Juan, you have been through this so many times before. You always bounce back. Yes, Isabel is a wonderful woman, but so were all the others. And there will be many more. Just enjoy what you have and when the time comes, move on to the next adventure."

"You just don't get it, do you? They aren't "adventures" as you put it. They are women with hearts and minds, with hopes and dreams. They're loving creatures of beauty, both inner and outer. None of you have love in your hearts like I do. You've snuffed it out 500 years ago. I don't know whether that's a blessing or a curse. If it's a curse, I've been suffering from it for far too long. It's time to stop this suffering." His loud, angry voice fell to a near whisper.

Antón pleaded. "It's not a curse, Juan. What's a curse is growing old, slowly losing your ability to function, first as a man, then even as a human. You speak of dreams and plans, but all that exists is the ultimate end of the black abyss of death. What comes after that? Nothing. There is no heaven, no hell. We are extinguished. Plans go unfulfilled. The dying man looks back on his life with some smiles, but mostly frowns from lost opportunities, the might-have-beens and the could-have-beens. Is that what you want?"

He continued with a more logical tone of voice: "And love. What is it? It's nothing more than passion, which, because of our European Church-centered culture and our pseudo-morality, we expect it to last to our dying breath. After the passion dies, what's left but the self-delusion of an empty 'love' with a person we must spend the rest of our life with?"

"Ah, spoken like a philosopher or one of those nineteenth century German thinkers, like Nietzsche. Wait a minute. That was Nietzsche who wrote that. Well, Antón, clearly neither you nor he understand what love is. Nice try, but that line of logic fails with me. I'm sure our ever-faithful Padre would have a different explanation, which would equally fail for the same reason. Those who have never experienced love are in no position to have an opinion about it.

"Love can start from passion, or the passion could just be a temporary lust. Love can start from friendship or for many other reasons. Love can start from passion but then evolves over time as hormone levels drop across a wide spectrum to a deep caring for each other in decrepit old age.

"Look, you know you're my dearest friends and I love you both. But I am not like you, any of you. I am not a simple sailor, as you call yourselves. I never was. Life was always far more complex to me than to the rest of you. Now I'm lost at sea and none of you can help me. I'm on my own. The time has come for the banquet. Go! Leave me."

"Juan, please! You must come with us. Get a hold of yourself. You're our Capitán, our leader, our heart and mind. We need you!" Antón's pleading changed to begging.

Ponce de León silently stared at the fire while his two friends stood and watched. Finally, he answered with a weak and distant voice. "Go. I'll join you later."

All they could do was look at each other in shock, shrug their shoulders, and leave. They found everyone else already seated at the dining table, silently staring at them with questioning eyes. Antón told them that their Capitán was busy with something and would join them shortly. Dinner and wine would not be served until then. This brought low murmuring from around the table.

An hour later, Ponce de León appeared with the haggard face of a man struggling with despair. He gave everyone a weak smile and ordered the wine poured. He raised his glass to everyone and toasted to their good fortune and health. Sitting back down, he motioned for the banquet to start without his customary speech.

Dinner passed as normal as it could with such a great black cloud hanging over them. Dessert came and, one by one, each went down to the Fountain for their drink of reinvigoration. Ponce de León ate little and drank nothing. Antón, the last one to reappear from below, took his place beside Ponce de León. He gripped his struggling friend's forearm and said as sweetly as he could muster: "It's your turn, my dear friend."

Instead, Ponce de León rose and spoke clearly and calmly. He summarized the main points of the discussion he had with Antón and the Padre in the study. He elaborated:

"My dearest friends, you're my family. You probably know that I've been suffering for a long time. I should have reached out for help and advice. But we're proud ancient men from a proud ancient land. Even more, I am your strong leader who has safely and calmly led you through all manner of crisis. For many centuries, I've often not felt so strong inside. I entered my own crisis many years ago and have struggled to pull through, even now as I speak.

"Some of you might have noticed and said nothing, thinking I'll get over it. I knew things weren't right, yet I said nothing. But now I will tell you. My struggle has been dealing with the deaths of the loves who were so important to my life. I am locked in a cycle of falling in love and then slowly watching them die before me. It breaks my heart every time.

"You all know Isabel. She is the next in this cycle of love and death. She wants a normal husband and family with children. As much as I want to, if I continue as normal, I cannot give her these things. So, quite simply, my crisis is to carry on drinking from the Fountain of Youth or to stop and live a normal life."

He fell silent, gathering his thoughts. His friends sat silently, transfixed by the enormity of the words they just heard.

He continued. "It's clear to me I cannot continue like this. I must decide to not partake of our grand ritual and rejoin the ranks of normal men, finding happiness that only they can know. Or I must finally cast aside all doubts and continue to enjoy the wonderful gift of everlasting youth calmly and peacefully forever more.

"I must make that choice tonight. If I choose the first, I must leave you and create a new circle of normal mortal friends and family, sharing in the joys and sorrows of a life that will end one day. If I choose the second, I will banish from my head any more doubts and look upon every new woman as a temporary gift who will leave me one day. I will continue to love, but with reservations. Or perhaps I'll do like you do and call a temporary woman to comfort me as I feel the need. That would be the simplest of all.

"As I mentioned earlier how we are different, none of you have faced the same dilemma as I have. I consider our gift either a blessing or a curse. You clearly believe it's a blessing. As you know, I tend to always overthink everything. My mind doesn't give me inner peace like yours do. Nothing is simple with me. So, I must decide now. What will it be?"

He stood in silence, looking at each of the frightened faces staring back at him, afraid that they may finally lose the great man that has been the center of their lives, their benefactor, for five centuries. Ponce de León seemed almost as if he was expecting an answer to his plight from them. Even Antón and the Padre were speechless.

"Before I answer that, let me describe a dream I had last night. Sometimes answers in personal crisis come to us through dreams. Antón was there with me." Ponce de León described the details of his experience from the night before.

"The spirits of the pond and moon spoke to me silently. They gave my feverish mind a peace. They didn't give me an obvious answer to my dilemma. But they did open a door for me to consider entering or not. They inspired me to make a decision that I still struggled with all day. But I have stopped struggling. I will struggle no more."

Ponce de León closed his eyes in silence. Everyone was on the edge of their chairs, spellbound, waiting for his decision. Antón whispered, "What is it, Juan? For the love of the gods, what's your decision?"

Opening his eyes, Ponce de León spoke in a loud sonorous voice: "Well dear mates, I have lived a wonderful long life. But some time ago, living for the sake of living has lost any meaning for me. Love is the only thing that gives me any meaning at all. I want to be surrounded by the warm love of my family: my wife and my children.

"I finally understood this a few months ago when I visited my family crypt. I was moved to tears by the empty rock space, ready for Isabel one day. But the space next to hers will be for me. I must leave the company of immortals and return to mortal life. I must leave you now. Jorge will drive me home. Farewell, my friends. You will always hold a special place in my heart as long as it continues to beat."

Ponce de León smiled as a great weight had lifted from his heart and peace replaced the angst. He emptied his wine glass in one gulp, turned it over, and placed it on the table upside down. Without looking back, he turned and walked out. Everyone stared at the empty chair at the end of the table. Time had finally come that day, and they were devastated.

The End

FINAL THOUGHTS

Juan and Isabel thank you very much for reading their story and they trust you enjoyed it. This is the result of many years of research and hard work. They ask you, dear reader, to please leave a thoughtful and considerate review on Amazon. These are especially important to the author. The link is below:

https://www.amazon.com/review/create-review?asin=173526069X

ABOUT THE AUTHOR

Born in Philadelphia, Thomas Murray is foremost a storyteller and has been writing all his life. He is the author of The Eye of the Beholder, Red Is a Color, The Adventures of Nuno and Figo, The Amazing Tale of Gwennie, and Only After Dark. He currently lives in Portugal.

Having lived overseas for over twenty-five years on five continents and traveled to eighty-nine countries, he has trained his mind to be sensitive to the wide range of nuances and world views that make up the personalities of everyone he meets. Greatly appreciating global cultures, he includes many details about the places and characters to make readers feel they are part of the story.

When he is not writing, he is travelling and learning foreign languages, currently Portuguese.

You can learn more about Thomas and his writing at www.thomasmurraywriter.com/

Please like his Facebook page: www.facebook.com/thmurraywriter

You can contact the writer at Bastet Publishing: info@bastet.ink

Also by the Same Author

The Eye of the Beholder, Bastet Publishing, 2020 (first in the Gwendolyn series)

A young art forger on the run …

Gwendolyn, a likable rogue with attitude, is secretly a successful fine-art forger rubbing shoulders with society's elite and shady art dealers. When she switches her painting with the original in a private home and escapes, she is confident with another successful heist. Until the next day when the owners are found murdered.

Framed for murder, she must travel to dangerous exotic lands to find the real murderers and clear her name. But as she delves deeper into the dangerous underworld of art forgery and betrayal, she realizes that she may be in over her head.

As the stakes get higher and her enemies close in, Gwendolyn must use all her cunning and skill to survive. Will she be able to untangle the web of lies and clear her name? Or will she become the next victim in a deadly game of cat and mouse?

https://www.amazon.es/dp/1735260606

Red Is a Color, Bastet Publishing, 2024 (second in the Gwendolyn series)

Is it a crime to be a redhead?

Gwendolyn, our favorite art forger and seductress extraordinaire, returns for another hair-raising adventure. Set in the sensuous backdrop of Portugal, Gwendolyn's latest project starts off as just another painting to forge and another wealthy eccentric to con. But as she delves deeper into the lifestyle of her unsuspecting mark, she begins to uncover more questions than answers.

How did he acquire a previously unknown Renaissance masterpiece by Botticelli? Why does he spend every evening worshipfully gazing at his personal goddess of love? Who is his tempestuous friend with an evil obsession with redheads? Who are the fanatical cultists trailing her every move?

The shadows of reality and myth blur, threatening to swallow her up in a deadly abyss... Will she survive this latest escapade with her life, much less her sanity intact?

www.amazon.com/dp/B0D64LM15C

The Adventures of Nuno and Figo: An Illustrated Journey of Two Unlikely Friends, Bastet Publishing, 2020 (first in the Gwennie series)

One clever rat, one tramp steamship, one hungry lynx …

Experience an adventure unlike any other. Follow Nuno, a clever Iberian Lynx, as he embarks on a treacherous journey to Southern California in search of a new life. Along the way, he meets Figo, a streetwise ship rat, who introduces him to the different cultures, music, and cuisines of the ports they visit.

Together, they face perils lurking around every corner as they form an unlikely friendship. Will it endure the journey, or will the dangers of California prove too difficult to survive? With beautiful illustrations by Madalena Bastos, this is a book you won't want to miss. The author will donate 10% of net proceeds to one or several organizations whose mission is to save the wonderful Iberian Lynx.

https://www.amazon.es/dp/1735260622

The Amazing Tale of Gwennie: Homeless to Palace, Bastet Publishing, 2022 (second and last in the Gwennie series)

From homeless cat to palace queen…

How did Gwennie journey from being a forlorn homeless cat in southern California to being the spoiled queen of a palace in Portugal? As the daughter of Nuno, an Iberian Lynx, and Terpsie, a Maine Coon cat, this (mostly) true story continues as the second in the series that started with The Adventures of Nuno and Figo: The Incredible Journey of Two Unlikely Friends (Illustrated).

Gwennie travels to even more exotic places than her famous father. Follow her journey as she incredibly ends up in Portugal, the same country as her father's homeland, a half a world away.

https://www.amazon.es/dp/B0BCS7NNBX

Only After Dark: One Man's Descent into Obsession and Madness, Bastet Publishing, 2021

Prepare to be enthralled by a dark and beguiling world as an American author of horror discovers an alluring and mysterious existence beyond his own in the post-Revolution Portugal of the late 1970s. Running from his past, he moves into an abandoned crumbling palace, eager to make progress on his next bestselling novel. A chance encounter with an unnamed, yet shockingly sensual woman pulls aside the veil of the world to reveal an alluring existence defined by unnatural delights and mind-twisting hedonism.

As his mysterious lover draws him further into her realm of shadows and ultimate pleasure, how much is he willing to sacrifice to keep her? And will there be anything left of his sanity when his would-be goddess is through with him? A tale told in the vein of Lovecraft and Edgar Allen Poe, this book will have you on the edge of your seat and wanting more.

https://www.amazon.es/dp/1735260673

www.ingramcontent.com/pod-product-compliance
Lightning Source LLC
Chambersburg PA
CBHW020739250626
47155CB00003B/829